praise for CLOSED HEARTS

"This is really a great followup to *Open Minds*. It's exciting, it advances the plot, it's heartbreaking, it perfectly sets up the next book, and it pushes Kira into the position of heroine once again...whether she wants to be, or not. There are some truly heart-wrenching scenes in this book and plenty of exciting ones as well. Again, Susan Kaye Quinn knocks my socks off in so many ways, she leaves me breathless. The end of the book was PERFECTION. Frankly, I can't wait until the next one!"

— **Rhiannon Frater**, author of *As The World Dies*

chapter ONE

No one called me Kira anymore.

"Lucy, dear." Mr. Trullite worked hard to think of me as his granddaughter *Lucy*, and lying wasn't easy for a mindreader. "Would it be possible for you to check on the protesters at the gate? I'd like to know if we'll have any trouble." His voice was halting and thick, but it carried in the luxurious quiet of the limousine to the driver up front. Speaking out loud shattered the illusion that I was a mindreader like everyone else, but the driver had seen enough to know I wasn't a mindreader *or* Mr. Trullite's granddaughter. He still didn't suspect who I really was.

Which was a good thing.

"I'm in range now, sir. I'll check to see if there's any change from when we left." Mr. Trullite's mansion was nearly a quarter mile away along the crazy-rich North Shore, well outside the range of most mindjackers. But that wouldn't be a problem for me.

I mentally reached for the minds of the protesters camped

outside the wrought-iron gate and easily pushed into the soft Jell-O of their minds. They were all mindreaders, waving their banners to protest the export of Trullite Electronics jobs to Canada. Each had their own mind-scent, and the flavors clashed in the back of my throat: wild berry from a radical teen girl; wood shavings from an older factory worker; and a musky smell from the leader. A new protester stood separate from the rest, probably because they couldn't tolerate his scrambled thoughts. Dipping into his mind was like riding the Tilt-A-Whirl at Six Flags, and his mind-scent burned with the peppermint taste of someone driven mad by the change into a mindreader at adolescence. In the city, there were lots of demens that roamed the streets instead of being locked up in a demens ward, but it was unusual to find one here in the suburbs of Chicago New Metro.

Just what I needed. No sense in alarming the boss, though.

"The protesters are still there, Mr. Trullite. No jackers, though." I could easily mindjack the demens guy if I had to—it wouldn't be difficult so much as unpleasant—but a mindjacker would be a lot worse. It had been a while since I'd tangled with another jacker, and I was out of practice. I hoped to stay that way.

I smoothed my hands down my tailored dress pants, and the seats adjusted to give me a mechanical hug as I sat taller. The fabric of the seats was like silk, if silk warmed to your touch and rippled like water when you moved. The not-quite-realness of the fabric matched the fake stone lantern by the limo door and the holographic koi pond below our feet. The scent of rainwater wafted through the spacious interior, too fresh to be the water exhaust from the hydro engine.

Mr. Trullite sipped tea from a delicate white cup trimmed in gold, then set it down on the bamboo tray between us. "What about the gentlemen joining us today?" He meant the trio of high-powered executives in the limo behind us, along with my dad and two of Mr. Trullite's bodyguards. They were coming to the estate to negotiate a big business deal. "Are you sure there are no lurking mindjackers? This merger is important, and I want to make sure we're not unduly influenced on either side."

"I'm sure, Mr. Trullite," I said. "Besides, my—I mean Mr. O'Reilly—would have already alerted us if there was a problem." My dad had changed his name too. He couldn't be Officer Patrick Moore of Naval Intelligence anymore, not with a famous mindjacker for a daughter. I skimmed the minds of the executives again, just to give Mr. Trullite a heads-up. "Although the skinny guy in the seat next to him is planning on robbing you blind in the..." I plucked the term from his mind. "...securities package transfer exchange."

"Yes, I know." His thoughts drifted to the delicate mental dance he would perform to secure the merger deal.

I could easily jack the executives to do whatever Mr. Trullite wanted, but he had never asked me to influence a business deal. When he hired my dad and me, he made it clear he wanted mindguard security, not jackworkers to mind control his business partners. And when the jacker clan attacked our home in Gurnee, Mr. Trullite offered to create our own personal witness-protection program, with a move to Libertyville and new identities for my family—it was Mr. Trullite's idea for the granddaughter cover story. He seemed like a guardian angel sent to protect us from the fallout of telling the world that mind-jackers existed.

As we closed in on the compound, the driver focused his thoughts on the mindware interface to switch the limo off autopath. We slowed down, waiting for the gate to open. The protesters surged forward and pounded the hood and darkened windows. The demens guy's scraggly face smashed against the flexiglass next to Mr. Trullite, who flinched and leaned away. I reflexively jacked into the demens guy's head, but the gibberish and rage swirling through his thoughts made me gag. I quickly knocked him out, and the man's eyes rolled back as he slimed down the window, leaving a trail of saliva from his gaping mouth. I heard him thump the ground, even through the limousine's shock-absorbent paneling.

I bit my lip, wishing I had jacked him to walk away instead, but it got the job done. Mr. Trullite straightened his high-collared shirt, and the limo whispered forward so smoothly it didn't even ripple the surface of his half-filled teacup. I scrambled to jack the other protesters to pull the demens guy out of the limo's path.

Once inside the compound, I took a position flanking Mr. Trullite while he waited on the granite entranceway steps to welcome his guests to the mansion. The second limo pulled up, its bullet-diffusive armor shimmering purple in the late afternoon sun. The bodyguards climbed out first, muscles bulging under their custom navy jackets. They radiated hostile thoughts in my direction, as usual. They didn't like having mindguards among them, certainly not a girl who was barely seventeen and looked about as terrifying as a kitten.

I unnerved them.

The executives in shiny *nove*-fiber suits came next, their hard-soled shoes scraping the cobbled driveway as they jockeyed each other with fast-paced thoughts about supply-chain management. My dad followed in his trim black jacket, subtly angling himself between me and the bodyguards. I could easily jack the goons myself—I was more of a threat to them than the other way around—but my dad was extra protective these days.

The executives joined Mr. Trullite on the steps of the mansion, a twenty-thousand-square-foot behemoth with north and south wings, plus a west wing tucked behind the thick marble columns of the entrance. I mentally brushed over the usual assortment of cooks, maids and executive staff inside. A gardener I didn't recognize worked the English garden in back near the pool, attending pansies that were already wilting in the early summer heat. My featherlight touch on his mind barrier popped up his name. *David.* As I pressed into his mind to find more, the gardener surprised me by reacting to my mental touch.

What the...? How had I missed that he was a jacker? Were my skills getting *that* rusty? Maybe he was just a linker—a weak jacker who could only link thoughts, not control minds. Sometimes their mind barriers were really soft, like a reader's.

5

Then the gardener shoved me out of his head and mentally hunted for me, something no linker could do. I was outside the reach of most normal jackers, so his search netted him nothing but the staff inside the mansion. I could easily reach him, but he couldn't reach me.

That was when he panicked and ran.

If he wasn't a linker, maybe he was only a rook—a jacker who passed for a mindreader, usually so they could keep a normal job. But Mr. Trullite was paying me to find hidden jackers, no matter what their situation, even if they were relatively harmless rooks. I left Mr. Trullite's side and sprinted down the south wing of the mansion, skirting the landscaping that heaped onto the tightly trimmed lawn. I needed to get closer. If I'd caught the gardener by surprise, rather than the other way around, I might have been able to knock him out. Now that he was on full alert, I could barely stay in his head, much less stop him from running off. Maybe my skills really had gotten weaker. Back in the camp, when I was mentally wrestling with jackers all the time, I had gotten stronger the more I used my abilities. But the last time I'd wrestled with another jacker was when that angry clan found me, and that was months ago.

I pushed as hard as I could into the gardener's mind, going deeper and distracting him into stumbling. He landed knee-down in the grass. Fear stung his mind as an image flashed through his thoughts: a man in a dark, skin-hugging mask. A contractor from Jackertown. The kind that set up deals between mindreaders with lots of cash and jackers willing to do anything for it.

I sucked in a breath. David wasn't a rook. He was a jackworker.

This was not good.

Picking up my pace, I linked a thought to my dad's mind. *Dad—*

His thoughts rushed a million miles an hour. *What are you doing? What's going on!* I should have linked in earlier, before I took off running. With my Impenetrable Mind, my dad couldn't link his thoughts into my head, so communication was always a little one-sided.

The gardener who works in back. He's on the run. South lawn. I didn't have to say he was a jacker. That was the only threat that would make either of us break a sweat.

Let me handle this! My dad's thoughts burned through my head. *I don't want you chasing after some strange jacker. He could be anyone.*

I slowed to let my dad catch up. *Yeah, well, Mr. Anyone is getting away.* I clung to David's mind, but the farther he got, the more I struggled to keep him from shoving me out. He staggered out of the gardens and tore across the lawn. *And he's from Jackertown.*

My dad let loose a mental curse, the kind he never let my mom hear, and sprinted past. I caught up to him at the end of the south wing, ready to put on some speed. David was a hundred yards away, out of Dad's range, and halfway across the expanse of lawn that pushed back the raw Illinois forest surrounding the estate. I'd still be able to track him in there, and maybe the

7

thick underbrush would slow him down. Then again, maybe the masked contractor that hired him to jack Mr. Trullite would be waiting in the woods with a gun. I pulled out of David's mind so I could sweep the forest to the full extent of my ability. No one was there, but Mr. Trullite's estate was huge, extending beyond my quarter-mile reach. At least there was no one close by, and we'd have a heads-up before anyone could shoot us, even if they could get a line of sight through the trees.

Still, not really a situation I wanted to get into.

I quickly checked back on Mr. Trullite. He had ushered his spooked guests inside, assuring them that his granddaughter "Lucy" was a mindjacker—which thoroughly shocked them. Waves of fear pulsed through their minds and distracted them while Mr. Trullite tried not to think of my real name. He was more concerned about keeping my identity secret than his own safety.

I focused back on the jackworker, more determined than ever to stop him.

Near the edge of the neatly manicured lawn, David was about to disappear into the thickets. As I reached for his mind, my dad stopped cold, drew a gun out of a holster inside his jacket, and fired. Nearly a hundred yards away, the jacker went facedown in the grass. My breath caught, and I stumbled to a stop. *Did my dad just kill him?* Then I realized the gun barrel was too wide for a regular gun, and his shot had made a pop-whoosh sound.

I unlocked my legs and jogged up next to my dad. "Where'd you learn to be such a marksman with a dart gun?" My lungs fought for air between my words. I wanted to ask, *And when did you start carrying a weapon?*

"Weapons training." His face darkened, the way it did when I asked questions about his past, and he marched toward the fallen body of the jackworker. I pushed into David's mind to make sure he was only unconscious, felled by the fast-acting sedative from the dart. The same sedative that the government had used in gas form to subdue jackers in the concentration camp. The orange anesthetic of the sedative overwhelmed David's mind-scent and stung the back of my tongue, bringing back memories I didn't want to revisit. I spent the walk out to his body trying to keep my mom's cheese-sandwich lunch from coming back up.

My dad flipped the body over so we could see his face. "Do you know him?"

"No." He was only a year or two older than me. Were the contractors in Jackertown using kids for jackwork now?

My dad's clear blue eyes met mine. "Did he get a good look at you? Did he recognize you when you were in his head?"

His words made my stomach twist even more than the orange-flavored sedative. "I'm not sure."

We had never discussed what would happen if we actually found a hidden jacker during our mindguard duties. Only the government was equipped to keep jackers contained for any length of time. And I'd rather cut off my own arm than hand another jacker over to them.

The security goons crunched the dry grass as they trotted up.

They would be defenseless against this guy once he woke up. *You're not going to give him to these bozos, are you?*

No. We're letting him go.

I hiked up my eyebrows.

We'll erase him first, my dad elaborated. *Then take him up to Wisconsin.*

I cringed. If we erased his memories and dumped him in Wisconsin, the Jackertown contractor might not find him, or be able to take his lost money out in blood. On the other hand, if we let the jackworker keep his memories, the contractor might piece together who I was and my cover would be blown. And that wouldn't be safe for any of us, including Mr. Trullite. No, erasing him was the best option.

My dad knelt in the grass as he plunged into David's sedative-filled mind. The smooth features of the jackworker's face twitched. He was just a kid, too young for this kind of business.

But he should have known better than to do jackwork in the first place.

chapter TWO

I twisted to look through the rear window of the limo. My dad was staring after me, feet planted wide. *Go straight home*, had been his explicit instructions.

The protesters at the gate shook their fists as the limo approached. I jacked them to look away, and their fists fell slack at their sides. The demens guy was still passed out, so I reluctantly reached into his head to wake him up.

As the limo glided past the protesters, I drummed my fingers on the bamboo tray next to me. I couldn't imagine my dad letting me work security for Mr. Trullite anymore, not when there was a chance I had been found out. Even with the jackworker's memories erased, the contractor would know something had gone wrong. Next time, he would send a stronger jacker or come investigate himself.

I just hoped I wouldn't get my dad fired. Mr. Trullite made it clear from the beginning that we were a package deal—he wanted *me*, the girl who stared down FBI agents to rescue a bunch of changeling jacker kids. Any other mindguard work my dad could get would be more danger for less money. Most jackworkers carried guns, not garden tools.

When my dad quit his job with the Navy (because of me), it left a stone weighing in my stomach. A lot of jackers rooked as readers so they could keep working, but my dad's jacker skills from his years in the Navy didn't translate well to the mind-reading world—except in security. Even my Mom, who *was* a mindreader, couldn't get work because she might give us away. She had stayed home all those years, keeping my dad's jacker secret, and now that it was out in the open (because of me), she still had to lie (also because of me).

Things were so messed up.

I leaned forward to rub my temples and the limo seat shifted with me. If my dad lost his job with Mr. Trullite, we'd end up in the slums or Jackertown, along with the other out-of-work mindjackers. That was no place for my mom. Or Xander, the changeling I'd rescued and who lived with us now. Or me, for that matter—the jackers that attacked us in Gurnee weren't the only ones unhappy that I had forced them out of hiding.

Our rental house was small, but at least it met the range codes and my mom didn't have to hear the neighbors' thoughts in her dreams. It was up to my dad and me to keep our family safely in the suburbs and away from jackers, which was why I didn't tell him that I had no intention of going straight home. I would stop off at our house to change clothes, but I was scheduled for a shift at the Dutch Apple diner, which my dad didn't know about and I wasn't telling him.

My shift wasn't until later, but coming in early would earn me a few extra unos. If my dad lost his job, we would need every uno to hold us over. Plus I had been secretly saving money, in case my brother Seamus lost his West Point scholarship. As a mindreader, life was mesh for him at school—I wanted it to stay that way.

The limo eased to a stop in front of our rental complex in Libertyville, a battalion of skinny four-story houses covered in weathered gray-blue paint and lined up like soldiers in a mile-long parade. They each had the minimum thirty feet of separation, but my dad's garage shared a wall with the neighbor's, and the sound traveled pretty well, even if the mindwaves didn't. At least we were near the street and had a lawn, instead of being buried deep inside the housing rat maze.

The driver waited while I dashed inside to swap my dress pants for a t-shirt and shorts. I managed to sneak past my mom so she couldn't waylay me with questions about why I was home so early, but thirteen-year-old Xander stopped me on the way out. He was wearing one of my brother Seamus's shirts, which was two sizes too big, and his hair stuck up in the back.

I linked into his head, so Mom wouldn't hear us. *What's up, kiddo?*

Where are you going?

Xander was mesh about the need to keep certain things secret, so I usually told him the truth. *Rooking as a waitress at the diner.*

13

Can I come? he asked. *I'll rook as a customer!* My dad didn't like us leaving the house, but sometimes Xander and I snuck out at night, just so we wouldn't go demens being cooped up all the time. We could easily rook as readers—it was the possibility of stumbling on a jacker that had my dad worried. I had changed my looks, but Xander still had the same fresh changeling face that cycled twenty-four seven on the tru-casts for weeks. My dad would freak if he found out about the Dutch Apple, but it would be worse if I took Xander.

Not this time, sport. Be mesh and cover for me, okay? If Mom asks, say I went for a run.

Xander's face fell, but he let me skitter out of the house without any more protest.

The limo driver dropped me off behind the diner, next to the dumpsters and the hydro recharge station. I scurried past the back office, where Mrs. Weissmann was bent over a scribepad, her wild wisps of gray hair pulled back off her face. She was madly entering the latest receipts for her tiny business, watching every uno. I whizzed through the kitchen door and automatically reached out to link into every mind in the kitchen and the dining room beyond. A wave of awareness passed through their minds, nothing strong enough to draw their attention, just enough for me to pass as a reader.

The perfect rook. For a couple hours, I could pretend I wasn't the girl who jackers hated and readers feared.

The customers' mind-scents blended with the smell of burgers and onions steaming up from the short-order cook's station.

I stepped past his assistant chopping vegetables under a forest of dangling silver pots and dodged another assistant as he cycled through the mindware interfaces on the flash ovens. I grabbed a short apron from the employee closet at the far end of the kitchen and tapped the nameplate until it brought up *Lucy*. Maintaining the lie here was important, and not just for me. Mrs. Weissmann had her own peculiar ideas about jackers: she knew I was rooking, and she still let me work for her. But her customers would flee if they knew a jacker waitressed at the Dutch Apple.

I checked the mirror on the employee closet door and smoothed a hand over my gelled flat hair, dyed black now with nano-color and trimmed short. The sleek hairstyle and the synth-tattoo that snaked up my throat and cheek pegged me for an asynchroner—a rebel who thought it was somehow mesh to listen to music without a melody. Asynchroners could rail against the tyranny of synchronous thought all they liked, but I knew that being "out of sync" with the world was anything but mesh. However, the twisted black vine and blue thorns on my cheek made for excellent camouflage. Too bad it was starting to fade.

Tracey, the waitress on shift, stopped behind me. *Early, aren't you?* Her mind-scent was as sugary-sweet as her cherry-red lipstick, and her hands were full with the two plates of hamburgers and chips she had just picked up from the cook. My shift didn't start until six, but it was Friday, which meant better tips, and I didn't want her to think I was trying to steal hers.

Got off early from my other job. I glanced at the plates. *I'll finish up these orders, but you can keep the tips.*

She handed over the plates with a bright smile. *Table two.
You can take the tips, hon. I know you need them. And you can
have table five—they haven't placed their order yet.*

Thanks. I grinned all the way to table two and delivered the
plates, but the couple barely noticed me slide the hamburgers
onto their red-and-white-checkered table. A tru-cast had drawn
the mental attention of everyone in the diner, dimming the mental chatter as everyone gazed at the screen suspended on the far
wall. A tru-caster stood outside the gleaming capitol building in
Springfield, her lips unmoving but her thought waves captured
by the boom-mic and translated into words scrolling along the
bottom of the screen.

*A vote by legislators in Springfield today has made Illinois
the first state to recognize the presence of mindjackers among
the populace.* The willowy reporter brushed back the hair that had
blown across her face. *Politicians in several states are likewise
considering legal classification for people exhibiting these mutant
powers, a move seen by many as a step to pressure Washington
into action against the growing threat they pose. Senator Vellus
promises to introduce such legislation soon in the U.S. Senate.*

A picture of Senator Vellus, Illinois's most outspoken anti-
jacker politician, flashed on the screen, and I gritted my teeth
against the murmur of approval that swept through the minds of
the diner's occupants, including Tracey. If she knew who I really
was, she certainly wouldn't be sharing tips with me. Whispers of
fear, loathing and outright hatred wafted through the diner like
a bad smell.

The tru-cast camera panned to a group of protesters carrying placards and pumping their fists in the air. They were synchronizing their thoughts, trying to amplify the volume, a favorite technique used to disrupt businesses that the anti-jacker groups suspected were employing jackers. It made for great tru-casting, if you liked helping them augment their hateful message by casting it around the country. Their chant must have reached the boom-mic, because fragments scrolled along the bottom of the screen.

Lock them... stop... do it now...

The tru-caster's thoughts cut in. *It would appear that the vote today has much support throughout the community of citizens who have traveled to the capitol to express their concerns.*

Concerned citizens. *Right.* Maria, the tru-cast reporter who helped me expose the government experiments on jacker changelings, would never have pretended this kind of hate was news.

Mrs. Weissmann strolled into the dining room, obviously alerted by the change in mental volume, even from the back office.

Wass is los? She scanned the diner with her hands on her hips, shorter than me but with twice the presence. Thoughts weren't really a language, just waves of energy that beamed from people's heads, but Mrs. Weissmann's thoughts always came out flavored Pennsylvania Dutch, like her apple pies. *Do I serve such schleck that you must watch this trash?*

People shifted in their seats, unease spreading through the diner on murmured thoughts. No one wanted her feistiness directed at them. They all liked the pie enough to want to keep coming back.

Mrs. Weissmann threw up her hands and stalked toward the screen. *These narrow-minded imbeciles do not know their bottoms from a hole in the ground. They are the ones that should be locked up!* With a sharp mental command *make the screen off!* the tru-cast went black. Mental conversations bubbled up again, but were subdued.

I had to fight back a smile, but it died when two couples in the far corner got up to leave. They were afraid that Mrs. Weissmann was a jacker sympathizer. Their fear left a bitter taste in my mouth even after they scurried out the door.

Mrs. Weissmann walked between the chrome-and-red tables, distracting her patrons with discussions of pie and trying to mute their fears. The world was running more and more scared from jackers every day, and Mrs. Weissmann was already paying a price for her tolerance. The last thing I wanted was for anyone to find out that she had a jacker working for her. It would kill her business, and I didn't want any more ruined lives on my hands.

I'd had enough of that already.

To my relief, Mrs. Weissmann worked her magic, and the mental chatter slowly turned friendly in her wake. A trio of teenage boys with fashionably sweeping hair teased her about the excess of chili sauce she put in the omelets.

If you don't like it, you take your business elsewhere! The boys' mental laughter warmed the tables around them.

I forced my shoulders to relax and shuffled to table five. The couple's discussion centered on how Mrs. Weissmann should be careful with her thoughts. When I reached their table, I forced myself to link a neutral question to them.

Can I take your order?

They ignored me. *Doesn't she know she could be targeted?*

All it would take is someone thinking that she was a sympathizer—

Yes, yes, and then what? She's not so young and spritely anymore. The couple's thoughts slid fast and furious over each other.

I think she lives alone. Does she live alone? The man ran his hand through his short-cropped silver hair and the woman shifted in her vinyl-covered seat, twisting her gnarled hands. *Do you think she knows any jackers? Maybe she doesn't.*

How would I know?

But if she does, the jackers could turn on her—they might even come to the diner! I've heard jackers kidnap readers, and whole families end up as slaves. You know they can jack into your pet's mind and turn them against you—

I leaned across them to scoop up the tip left by the previous customers and to interrupt their thoughts. The rumors that flew through readers' minds about jackers kept getting wilder and wilder: it was like the world had gone demens, all ten billion souls feeding off the paranoia of each other.

I tucked the tip in my pocket, making a mental note to give it to Tracey before her shift was done. *Can I take your order, please?*

The couple simultaneously gave me their orders. Eight months ago, sorting the barrage of their thoughts would have made my head hurt. Now, I quickly scribed their meals on my pad and cast it to the kitchen without thinking. I tucked the pad in the pocket of my apron and scurried to get their drinks.

They resumed their argument as soon as I turned my back.

I had filled two glasses with ice and started to pour their tea when the front door dinged, announcing a new customer. I glanced up, hoping they might take a table in my half of the diner, but I froze when I saw who it was.

Raf.

Familiar dark curls and trim soccer physique. My smile was automatic, and my heart missed a beat, the way it did every time I saw him, but between that skipped beat and the next, I saw who was behind him.

His parents!

Raf blocked the doorway, his hands reaching for the door-frame, and his dark brown eyes went wide. His parents bumped into him from behind, and Raf's broad shoulders hopefully prevented them from seeing me.

What was he doing here? And why had he brought his parents? He knew I worked at the Dutch Apple! Raf peeled his gaze away from me and turned back to his mom, apologizing to the diminutive Mama Santos for nearly knocking her off her three-inch heels. He was buying me a second of time. I set down the cold glasses of tea, now slippery with condensation, and fled for the kitchen.

I just prayed I could get out before Raf's parents gave me away as a jacker.

chapter **THREE**

wove through the kitchen of the Dutch Apple, dodging the short-order cook and linking a thought to Tracey. *Tables are all yours. Order's up on table five.* Mrs. Weissmann had returned to her office, working on her recordkeeping. *Taking a break, Mrs. Weissmann,* I linked as I rushed past.

A break! Of course. Why do you bother to come? But her thoughts held no malice.

I linked back to check on Raf and his parents, to see if my cover had been blown. Raf was humming one of his awful synchrony band songs, "It's Not Like You," to mask his worried thoughts that he had given me away.

Don't stand in the doorway! his father thought.

What is wrong with you, Raf? Mama Santos thought. *Stop that humming! It's not polite.*

I shoved open the back door of the diner and fled for the relative safety of the parking lot. I kept going along the back of the building, across the crumbled pavement, and didn't stop until I was next to a dumpster that reeked of yesterday's rotting vegetables—out of Raf's mindreading range, and more importantly, his parents'. Of course I could still hear their thoughts.

There's plenty of room here! Mama Santos thought. *And you were worried it might be full.*

Lucky for us, Raf thought. *I know you wanted to try the pie.* With me out of the room, it was easier for Raf to pretend that I had never been there, which made the tension in my body step down. Mama Santos and Raf's dad busied themselves with picking out a table.

Convinced that I'd escaped unnoticed, I pulled back from their minds. I wanted to ask Raf what he was thinking, showing up in the middle of the Dutch Apple and especially bringing his parents! He knew I had a shift tonight. It was risky for me, risky for Mrs. Weissmann. Even risky for him if his parents found out he was still seeing me. I could have linked that thought to his head, but then his careful attempts not to think about me would have been scuttled.

The official story was that Raf and I weren't seeing each other anymore, after my family changed names and left Gurnee. Which made his parents happy—they were convinced that I had been jacking him all along, because otherwise why would he want a girl like me? When I was a non-mindreading zero, they didn't mind, but now that I was a mindjacker, they wanted Raf to have nothing to do with me. It didn't help that I had been wearing Mama Santos's frilly red blouse when I had rescued the jacker changelings on a national tru-cast.

Even my family didn't know about me and Raf. Well, I had told Xander, because I needed him to cover for me when I snuck out of the house to meet Raf, which didn't happen often, only every other week or so, between my work and his soccer practice. Mostly, we spent our time sending furtive scrits, but if he wanted to see me, we could have arranged it. He certainly didn't need to risk coming to the Dutch Apple.

Raf and his parents would probably stay for a while. Maybe I should hail an autocab and go home. As I tried to figure out what to do next, the back door opened, and Raf stepped into the afternoon sun, shading his eyes. I hesitated to link any thoughts into his head—he was still in thought range of the rest of the diner.

When he saw me, he beamed the irresistible grin that I loved, but I waited while he sprinted across the pavement with soft soccer footfalls. When I was sure he was out of range of the diner, but before he reached me, I linked a thought to him.

Have you lost your mind?

He slowed as he came up alongside the dumpster with me, his smile bright white against the light olive of his skin, just starting to darken with all the time he spent in the summer sun.

Hello to you too.

I crossed my arms and checked that the back door had swung shut. When I was sure our spoken words wouldn't drift in to cause any more problems, I said, "What are you doing here?"

He held out his hands. "My parents heard about the Dutch Apple and got this demens idea to come early for dinner, to beat the rush. I knew you had a shift tonight, but I couldn't remember when, and I couldn't think about it too hard or they'd totally pick that up. It was either come with them, or let them go without me, and I figured this would be safer." He gestured to my shorts pocket. "They were nearby, so I couldn't exactly scrit you to ask."

I slipped my hand into my pocket to check that I had my phone. Raf and I kept our scrits to when his parents weren't nearby to catch a stray thought wave. If they found out I was working at the Dutch Apple, they would tell everyone that a jacker waitressed at the diner, and I would have to quit. Mrs. Weissmann's business would be hurt, and my dad would go ballistic.

"What did you tell them just now?" I asked. "They have to be wondering why you're sneaking out the back of the diner."

"I told them I saw a cute waitress I wanted to ask on a date."

"What?" I leaned away.

"That way they'll be sure not to follow me out," Raf said patiently. "They would never guess it was you, or I wouldn't be telling them, right?" He dipped his head to peer at me through the dark lashes framing his soft brown eyes. "You know I would never blow your cover."

I gave a small nod. Raf was second only behind my dad in the over-protective department.

Raf smiled, shifted closer, and slipped his arm around my waist. "Although I can't complain about having you alone for a change, *Lucy*." He tapped my name badge with his free hand, his light touches paging through the names of the other wait staff.

"Sandra, Karen, Elizabeth. If you have to be someone else for a while, I think it should be Elizabeth."

"Next time I change my identity, I'll let you pick the name."

His arm tightened around my waist and he dropped his voice. "Someday you won't have to be anyone but yourself."

Raf was convinced that eventually the world would settle down. I hoped like crazy he was right. I wanted to believe that one day the world would forget about Kira Moore, face of the jackers, and we wouldn't have to hide anymore.

"It'll take time," Raf said, "but even my parents will change their minds about you. Someday they'll see you the way I do."

"How's that?" I pushed back the dark curls that had fallen in his eyes.

"A really cute girl who has really *awful* taste in music."

I smiled as his soft Portuguese accent drew out the word *awful*. "Maybe someday you'll decide to listen to music that's worthwhile."

He tucked my hand against his chest, trapping it as he wrapped both arms around me. Then he whispered in my ear. "Link with me, Kira."

My name on his lips, whispered close like that, melted me. I linked gently into his mind, and his lips found mine. Linking thoughts while kissing was the closest we would ever come to the synced hearts and minds, completely shared and open, that mindreaders felt when they touched. At least Raf's mind was open. I tried to be honest, here in his embrace, his lips pressed to mine. I let my mind roam, floating along with the eddies and curls of his feelings. The scent of his mind hinted at fresh linen that had been warmed by the sunshine of his thoughts. There was no trace of worry or concern.

This is how we should be. Always, thought Raf. *No hiding.*

I won't hide anything from you. But even that wasn't true, as I kept my darker thoughts quarantined in my own mind: thoughts about the risk he took in seeing me; about how I should have stopped seeing him after we moved; how I shouldn't make Raf learn to lie for me, like my mom had lied for years for my dad. Yet when Raf kissed me like this, with his heart wide open, it was impossible for me to stay away.

If the world knew this part of you, he thought, *they would never be afraid.*

I pulled out of Raf's mind, guilt getting the better part of me. He made a small sound of disappointment as soon as my mind's presence disappeared from his. When we did have a chance to be alone, he couldn't get enough of me linking in and sharing thoughts with him.

"More kissing, less talking," he whispered against my lips, knowing I had pulled back so we could talk out loud.

I tucked my head down and played with the rough Blue Devils patch on his shirt. "We're lucky your parents didn't see me. It was risky for you to come." *Risky for you to be with me.* But I couldn't bring myself to say that out loud. He held me loosely now, giving up for the moment on kissing. Being patient. The way he always was with me, for reasons I didn't understand, even having linked thoughts and gently explored his mind. I knew that he loved me. I just didn't understand why.

"I'm getting better at focusing my thoughts," Raf said. "And humming. All things considered, I thought it went rather well." Raf was proud of his deception, which I guess he should be, given how hard it was for mindreaders to lie, Raf in particular.

It still made me cringe. "You should have let them go and tried to scrit me before they got here. I probably could have left in time."

"Maybe. But if you hadn't gotten the scrit, it would have been worse. Besides, if I hadn't come along, I wouldn't have had a chance to kiss you by the smelly dumpster."

"Yeah, well you're right about that," I said. "I would at least have picked somewhere more romantic."

"Like where?" Raf snuggled me closer.

"Like..." Kissing or even hand-holding was such an intimate sharing of thoughts and feelings that mindreaders usually did their touching in private, out of range so that other minds wouldn't be privy to the comingling of their thoughts. "Maybe we could take a drive to the forest preserve?"

"Oh yes. I'm sure your father would let me borrow the hydro car for a spin."

"Or maybe we could take an autocab."

"Now you're thinking," he said. "A long autopath, circling through Chicago New Metro. I'd take you up north of the city. I think they have beaches on Lake Michigan up there."

"Beaches are mesh."

"Speaking of romantic things with your extremely mesh boyfriend..." Raf released me for a moment to dig something out of his pants leg pocket. He held up a transparent film with red lines scrawled across it. It took me a moment to realize the lines were folded into two Celtic knots that curled around each other into the shape of a heart.

"A tattoo?"

He frowned. "Is it not romantic enough?" He held the film up to the sky, peering at it. "It only lasts a few months, you know, in case you decide to trade up for a boyfriend who's got more game in the romance department."

I took his cheeks in my hands. "You are the most romantic guy on the planet, Raf. There are ballads being sung right now about your romantic powers."

He smiled under my palms. "You know it's true."

"So," I said, taking the tattoo by the edge of the film. "Where should I put it?"

He dug in his pocket again and came out with another film. "Actually, I have a matching set." He held up my left wrist, placed one of the films on the skin right below it, and looked up at me. "Ready?"

I nodded, and Raf blew a long, hot breath to activate it, then clamped down to press it into my skin. It burned as the acid from the synth-ink etched into my flesh, but the pressure made it easier to bear. I did the same for him, trying to make sure I gripped his wrist hard enough for the tattoo to take.

He grinned at me while we waited the thirty seconds for

the transfer to complete, then we peeled them off. I sucked in a breath when the fresh air met the acid and the stinging grew sharper. Raf lifted my hand to gently kiss my wrist, then leaned in close to kiss me on the lips. I linked into his mind again, for a proper thank you.

A solid marble presence was suspended there. *A jacker was in Raf's head!*

Before I could react, Raf slumped into me, all two hundred pounds of soccer physique weighing me down as he fell. A growling scream surged up through me, but was muffled by Raf's shirt in my face. I plunged deeper into his mind, shoving out the jacker that was there. Raf was alive, but he was knocked out. I struggled to keep him upright, but Raf's dead weight pulled me down to the ground with him.

"He should'a listened to you, little Kira," rumbled a voice nearby. I flung out toward the jacker, reaching for his mind as a tug of awareness made me think *I know that voice.*

I jacked deep into the firm gel of the jacker's head and his name instantly popped up. *Molloy.* Ruthless jacker Clan leader that I had betrayed and left behind in an Arizona prison camp. He was supposed to be locked up with FBI Agent Kestrel, but instead he was here, at the Dutch Apple, knocking out Raf.

I struggled with Raf's body while I wrestled with Molloy in his mind. Heavy footsteps scraped the rough pavement next to me. I had to keep Molloy from executing whatever plans he had for me until I could get Raf safely away. I tunneled deeper in Molloy's mind, searching for the places where I could inhibit his heart rate, make him stumble, anything, but he was too strong for me. He shoved me around, parrying every thrust I made.

I linked a threat to him, hoping to slow him down. *I swear, if you hurt him, I'll...*

Something struck the side of my face, hard, flinging any thoughts right out of my head. I didn't feel the pain for a full half second, then a blinding throb ripped across my face. My breath stopped with the force of it. I slumped on top of Raf and tried to get my bearings.

"I thought you might be some trouble, little Kira," Molloy said, his giant face a gray blur near mine. "Which is why I brought this."

An electric shock arced across my back and my entire body froze into a statue that clutched at Raf's shirt. With a slithering itch, the shock rushed my brain, which sizzled and sparked like there was an electrical storm raging in my head. Then it shorted out and blackness descended on me, even though my eyes were wide open. The last thing I saw was Raf's limp hand on the ground. In spite of all my efforts to hide, in spite of all my attempts to be someone else, it had come to this.

The people I loved would pay the price for everything I had done.

chapter FOUR

I awoke to the feel of a finger brushing my cheek. It left a trail of pain in its wake, even though the touch was feather soft. I flinched, then I realized someone was *touching* me. Some praver that liked to touch girls when they were unconscious. I lashed out and my mind plunged deep into his. My entire body seized up, and my mind reflexively jerked away, like a hand dropping a red-hot plate. Only then did my brain register the sensations gripping my body. Icy pain. Bottomless grief. A deep dread, like all the brightness had been sucked out of the world.

I drew in a shaky breath and tried to process what was happening, but the feelings faded, like a strange momentary hallucination.

"I didn't tell you to beat her up," said a quiet male voice close to me. I struggled to open my eyes and found the source of the voice inspecting my face. He was young, only a year or two older than me, and his face had a soft, warm quality that made me want to like him, even though I couldn't think of one rational reason why I would like a praver who touched me in my sleep.

"She put up a fight." Molloy's enormous bulk blocked the light above us. I was laid out on a lumpy couch with a line of white columns on either side. The columns were connected by metal racks that stretched up to form a narrow canyon. My blurred vision could barely make out a highway of lights floating far above us. The place smelled of old plastic and machine grease. The boy leaned close, perched on his chair, elbows on his knees, fingers laced.

"Your methods are barbaric." His words were for Molloy, but his eyes roamed my face, like I was a rare specimen Molloy had captured and he was checking me for damage. I tried to move my lips, but my face was still numb from Molloy's shock device.

The boy saw me struggle and bent closer, speaking so softly it was almost a whisper. "I'm sorry to bring you here this way. How are you feeling?"

His almost transparent blue eyes were intensely curious, as though he thought my feelings held the answer to the universe's greatest mystery. I thought he might try to jack in to get the answer to his question, but there wasn't any pressure on my mind. What had happened when I tried to jack him before? My mind groped for an answer, but it was like a bad dream where all you remember is that you don't want to remember it. I wondered if he was a jacker at all.

The boy nodded, as if I had answered his question, which I hadn't.

My lips unstuck enough that I could lick them, dry and coated with a fine grit. Then I remembered: "Raf!" It came out as a croak and I tried to sit up, reaching out to search Molloy's mind for what he had done with Raf. Molloy easily swatted me away. I had no mental strength whatsoever. The boy steadied me as I swayed on the couch, but I shrank from his touch.

"We're not going to hurt you, keeper."

Right. Which was why I was sprawled on his couch with an electric hangover. And why was he calling me *keeper*?

"Wha..." My tongue was a useless lump in my mouth. I swallowed and tried again. "What did you do with Raf?"

The boy frowned and turned to Molloy, who tilted his head down the skeletal row of shelving. "She means the reader."

I craned my head so that I could see Raf, but I was stiff and achy, and my vision was so blurred I could barely see past the end of the couch.

"Why did you bring the pet?" the boy asked Molloy. "We don't need him."

"Insurance." Molloy folded his beefy arms, his red hair wild and flowing down to his shoulders. "I'll not be trusting her again, Julian, and you won't either, not if you know what's good for you. Believe me on this."

I rubbed my eyes and tried to think. They hadn't killed me yet, and it sounded like Raf was alive too. *Insurance.* The word sent a shiver through me. I didn't know what this boy Julian wanted or what Molloy's plans were, but I was sure none of it would be good. I squinted, trying to see more in the dim light.

We were in some kind of warehouse or factory. The closest rack held a mattress and crumpled blankets, like someone had slept there but not made the bed. My couch and the chair Julian sat in comprised a sort of living room. A few more makeshift bed racks stretched down the row, then rectangular shapes the size of doors dangled from a crossbeam between the columns. At the end the row opened into a larger area where several fuzzy figures moved about. Molloy said Raf was down there. That was probably also the way out.

Julian studied me again, stroking the scruff on his cheek with his long fingers. His dark hair was mussed, like he had used his fingers for a comb, and he was either deeply tanned or possibly Latino.

"Trust is something earned, is it not, keeper?" His voice rumbled smooth, almost hypnotic. Or maybe it was the electrical storm still fuzzing my head.

"Why do you keep calling me that? And what do you want with us?"

"I'm calling you what you are, Kira." His smile glowed in the low light. "I've admired you for a while. Your performance with the changelings was very impressive. And letting the world know of our little secret..." He templed his fingers and tapped his lips with them, as if choosing his words carefully, then he leaned forward and dropped his voice. "Well, I can't thank you enough for that."

I moved away from him, pressing my back into the musty fabric of the couch. Why was he grateful for me outing jackers?

Most jackers seemed to think I had ruined their lives with that piece of honesty.

He leaned back, giving me space again. "But what are you, precisely? Mr. Molloy tells me you are a keeper, which I can see for myself is true. Which is very fortunate for us." He pursed his lips. "Perhaps not so much for you."

I didn't know what this hypnotic jacker wanted with me, but I needed to find Raf and get us out of here. Considering I was barely able to sit up without feeling woozy, that meant going along with whatever his game was... for the moment. Until I figured a way out of this mess.

"What is a keeper?" I asked. "And why does it matter to you what I am?"

"You are the one who started everything, and yet you don't seem to understand." He eyed my name badge, which still said *Elizabeth*. "Maybe you're confused about who you are."

I sat up straighter. "I know who I am just fine. Thanks for your concern."

He sat back in his chair, amusement playing on his face. "A keeper is a jacker who can keep their thoughts. Their mind barrier is virtually impenetrable, at least to normal jackers. And in your case, even to me. Which is very interesting." Again he tapped his fingers to his lips. "As much as I'd love to know why that is, we don't have time for that. But it does make you just what we need."

"And what is that?" I hoped to cut to the chase. If this Julian person wanted something from me, maybe I could bargain our way out of this. Or at least get Raf out of the equation and then go from there.

"I have a job that you might be interested in."

"I'm not a jackworker."

"No, of course not," Julian said. "I wouldn't expect someone like you to be jacking for something as simple as money. I knew you would be interested in much more than that, keeper, which is why I brought you here."

"*You* brought me here?" I flicked a look to Molloy.

"Well, I'll admit that it was Mr. Molloy's idea," said Julian. "Although I was entirely for it, once he confirmed the rumor about your keeper abilities. Finding you was a bit of a problem, with you rooking in the suburbs, but there aren't many father-daughter mindguard teams in Chicago New Metro. Getting our jackworker into Mr. Trullite's compound to conduct a little surveillance, to make sure it was you, was the easy part."

My eyes went wide. *The gardener.*

"To bring you here," Julian continued, "I needed someone who knew how vital you were to our plans. Someone who could ensure you would consider what we had to say." Julian glanced at Molloy. "I'm sorry Mr. Molloy took my instructions a little too literally."

Molloy grinned like he enjoyed the process of bringing me in. "That driver was quite the helpful lad with information on your whereabouts." A chill ran up my back. Molloy had jacked the driver, and he already had Raf. That meant Molloy knew everything: where my family lived, where my dad worked. I had no doubt that Molloy would kill them all if I didn't do what he—or this Julian person—wanted.

My hands bunched the loose fabric of the couch next to me. "What is this jackwork you want me to do?" I asked Julian.

But it was Molloy that answered. "It seems that Agent Kestrel has a particular interest in you, lassie. And we aim to feed you to him."

My head snapped back to Molloy. "What?"

He smirked, obviously enjoying my shock. When jacker Agent Kestrel had dropped off the grid, I was furious that he had gotten away with everything: sending innocent jackers to the camp, experimenting on changelings as young as twelve. He had slunk underground, and worse, he had taken the camp prisoners with him, including the changelings I had been forced to leave behind. The only good part was that he had Molloy too. Only here he stood, threatening to hand me over. That Kestrel would want me back was no surprise: he wanted my DNA for his research, plus I'd put three darts in him and sent him into hiding. That Molloy would be the one to hand me over was a possibility I hadn't even considered.

It would have been better if Molloy had simply killed me in the parking lot.

"Why?" I asked Julian, my voice weak. "Why would you turn anyone over to Kestrel?" An icy trickle made my stomach seize up.

Julian stabbed Molloy with an unappreciative look. "I'd never turn another jacker over to Kestrel." His voice gentled when he turned back to me. "And I wouldn't ask anything of you, keeper, that I wasn't willing to do myself. I'll be going with you. Together, maybe we can stop that monster and free the jackers he's holding prisoner in that torture chamber of his."

"Wait, what?" The chill drained out of my stomach when I realized that Molloy had been joking. Or perhaps exaggerating. Or maybe not, with the smirk that still lit his face. "You're *asking* me to turn myself in to Kestrel?"

The tiny smile was back on Julian's face. "The last thing Kestrel will expect is to have *you* come looking for *him*, no? We can talk more about the details later. First, I need to know what you can do."

First, I needed to get out of there, and fast. I didn't need to know any more about Julian's plans. If it involved me going within a mile of Kestrel, they could count me out. Whatever revenge Kestrel had planned for me was sure to be unpleasant, not to mention deadly.

But I needed to keep Julian talking until I could figure a way out of this.

"You already know what I can do," I said. "I have a hard head. A keeper, or whatever you called it."

"Yes, but Mr. Molloy tells me you can view at long distances like Ava, as well." He gestured to the distant figures. My vision was coming back into focus, and I could see one of the figures breaking away from the group and striding past the door-shaped panels that dangled between the columns. Ancient industrial machinery snaked along a far wall, its metal frames dotted with large wheels and circular blades. I guessed that we were in an abandoned factory, maybe one of the ones left behind when the city depopulated under the range ordinances a hundred years ago. The building around us was cavernous, and we were dead center, at least a hundred feet from the edges.

Just far enough to be out of normal jacker range.

I made a mental note to check out what lay beyond the walls as soon as I got some reach back. A petite girl with long blond hair glided down the row. Her features were delicate, and her wide blue eyes made her look like a child, but she was probably in her mid-twenties. She came to rest next to Julian, her fine-fingered hand alighting on his shoulder.

"Kira, meet Ava," Julian said. "Ava can reach minds much farther away than a normal jacker. She's a mage, like the rest of us. With the exception of my burly, ill-mannered friend, Mr. Molloy. You don't have any hidden talents you've forgotten to share with me, do you, Mr. Molloy?"

"I have a talent for smacking jackers who are a little too full of themselves," replied Molloy dryly, but he made no move against Julian.

Julian just laughed. Why was Molloy—Clan leader and general thug with no compunction about killing readers and jackers alike—willing to take ribbing from Julian, a boy with delicate manners and a smooth voice? Something didn't fit. What kind of jacker *was* Julian?

"What's a mage?" I asked. "Sounds like a magician."

"Well, *you're* a mage," Julian said. "Haven't you figured that out by now?"

"I'm just a jacker." Prior experience told me that keeping my abilities to myself was usually best.

"You're much more than that, keeper." He was eyeing me again, as if assessing me for some kind of test. "Mages are jackers who have extra abilities, beyond the normal jacking, like Ava here." He rested his hand on her hip in a friendly way. I wondered if they were lovers, but it didn't seem so. Julian had an ease about him, like he was comfortable with everyone. "She can reach for miles, reading minds in every direction, including up." He seemed to find her ability delightful. "Didn't you view an airplane coming in for a landing at O'Hare yesterday?"

"That was simple." Ava's voice was as airy as the rest of her. "Not that the passengers were thinking anything interesting."

"I can't reach that far," I said. Knowing that Ava could reach farther than me made me feel more... *normal*. "I can only reach a few thousand feet, not even half a mile." The words slipped out before I knew what I was doing. I cursed myself inwardly and resolved to keep a closer eye on Julian. He was slippery. Then I realized that my theory about being special, about being Kestrel's genetic key for his research, might not be true after all. I thought I was unique in having extra jacking abilities, but if there were others like me, with even stranger abilities—

"She can do more than that, Julian," Molloy said. "She can jack at those distances too. And she can fight off the gas as well."

I bit my lip. Molloy already knew some of my abilities from our time together in the camp, but that didn't mean I needed to share any more.

"Interesting." Julian dropped his hand from Ava's hip and leaned forward. "I haven't heard of anyone able to fight off the gas. I wonder if that's part of being a keeper. Tell me, how does it work?"

"Magic."

A smile flashed across his face, like this was a game. "It certainly seems that way, doesn't it? That's okay, keeper, you can have that secret for now. As for jacking at long distances... that *is* impressive. So you have at least two abilities, three if you count jacking and viewing as separate ones. Tell me, is it true what the rumors say? That you can jack even the most hardened mind? That no one is impenetrable to the Impenetrable Mind?"

"Yes, and I can shoot lasers from my eyeballs as well."

Julian laughed outright, then nodded to Ava. She drifted back down the row, and I squinted after her, trying to see the figures that milled by the tables at the far end. One of them started to twirl around and around, doing pirouettes. He drifted into a spot of light, and I saw it was Raf. The pravers at the far end of the building were forcing him to dance like a marionette.

I heaved myself up from the couch, startling Julian who tipped his chair backward, and I reached toward Raf with my mind. My mental strength was coming back, but I could barely brush into his mind, much less wrestle with the jacker whose presence was burrowed deep inside, making him perform this grotesque dance. Worse, my body still hadn't recovered, and I didn't get two feet from the couch before stumbling to my knees, grinding them on the rough carpet.

"Make them stop!" I cried, hoping against hope that Julian might actually do it.

Julian was on his feet now, leveling a cold stare at the far end of the room, and when I looked back, Raf was on the floor, motionless.

No! "What did you do?" I forced my arms and legs to obey me and lunged toward Julian, who caught my weakened arms in his hands with ease. I fought against his hold, then jacked into his mind, but my entire body convulsed as I forced my mind into his. Horror filled me, a screaming terror that erupted out of my mouth. My mind recoiled from his, and my body rebelled as well, as if it knew it should run for its life. Julian held me fast, and I sagged, all fight fleeing from me.

"Let him go." I was surprised how much it sounded like a sob.

Julian softened his hold on me, but didn't let go. Which was probably a good thing, because my legs were failing me and his grip was all that was holding me up. "Keeper, your pet is fine." His voice was warm and gentle. "The other mages won't play with him again, I promise. He's just... resting for now."

I couldn't catch my breath, but I managed to twist out of Julian's grasp and stumble to the couch, bracing myself as I fell onto it. Raf still lay unmoving on the floor, and I reached to him with my mind. He was asleep, like Julian said. Sprawled on the concrete floor with one knee in the air, but asleep, with no jacker presence in his mind. I gave a shuddering sigh of relief.

"Whatever it is you want from me," I said, trying to calm my ragged breath, "you're not getting it if you hurt Raf. I swear I'll make you pay for anything you do to him."

Julian picked up the tipped-over chair and sat with a wide smile on his face. "Now, that's the spirit! I knew the girl who stared down the FBI would have some fight in her." His face grew more serious. "It was never my intention to have your... um," he said, glancing at Raf's inert body, "friend involved in this. I only asked Mr. Molloy to bring you here so we could ask for your help."

"You have a funny way of sending an invitation."

"Well, I knew you might be hesitant to consider our proposal," Julian said. "But if you hear me out, see what we're planning, I'm sure you will want to be involved."

"I doubt that."

"I wouldn't have needed your help at all if my sister hadn't gone missing," Julian said. "Anna's a keeper like you, but she was snatched a few days ago. There have been a lot of disappearances from Jackertown in the last month. I believe that Kestrel is behind them, rounding up new victims. Mr. Molloy here has precisely the information we need to find him."

I narrowed my eyes at Molloy. "You know what rock Kestrel is hiding under?"

"I managed to escape the new facility where he's experimenting on jackers," Molloy said. "No thanks to you, lassie." His voice could cut glass.

"Are the changelings still there?" I couldn't help wanting to know. That was the one thing that Molloy and I had in common—our horror at children being locked up with the most dangerous jackers on the planet, not to mention that Kestrel's experiments left them with damaged brains.

43

"Aye," Molloy said with a sigh. "And my brother as well. Kestrel had him all these years, all this time..." He choked up. "I couldn't bring him with me in the escape." For a fractional second, I felt sorry for Molloy. Then I erased that thought from my mind. Molloy didn't deserve my sympathy.

"Which is why," Julian said, "Mr. Molloy will be helping us get back in, where we can free the jackers being held by Kestrel. This is your chance, keeper." Julian leaned close, his hands laced together. "To put right a wrong that has been going on too long. One you know very well, I believe."

Julian's words tugged at me. It still haunted me, not being able to save the changelings Kestrel had sent to that hellhole in the desert. Maybe if I helped Molloy, I could earn my way out of him wanting to kill me and the members of my family, including Raf. And Julian was right—what Kestrel was doing was hideously wrong and should be stopped. I had tried to do just that, and failed. I managed to rescue a few changelings, but only by exposing the hidden mindjackers of the world and painting a target on my back. My family had been paying the price for that ever since.

No, protecting my family and Raf had to take top priority. Besides, I knew better than to trust Molloy. And Julian was a strange entity—something I had never encountered before. The urge to run from him still sang through my body. For the moment I would play along. But the second we had a chance to run, I was taking Raf and leaving.

"Okay," I said. "I'm in."

chapter FIVE

Molloy's shock device slowly wore off, and my mental strength returned, along with full use of my limbs and eyesight, but I bought time by playing it up like I was still incapacitated. I would need all my strength to get us out of the mages' lair, and even more to get Raf safely away. Now that Molloy knew where we lived, my family would have to move again. Farther this time. But first I had to get me and Raf out of here.

I hadn't reached beyond the walls of the converted door factory, but I figured we must be in Jackertown, on the edge of downtown Chicago and probably the worst place on the planet for me. The jackers here were the ones that had been hardest hit by going public. My disguise wouldn't keep them from recognizing me as the girl responsible for the mess their lives had become. Especially if my Impenetrable Mind made them extra curious.

If it was a bad place for me, it was even worse for a reader like Raf.

Julian sat across from me at a beat-up wooden table. We had moved from the bunk area clustered in the middle of the factory to the common area where they kept Raf. He was sleeping on a nearby couch that looked as broken-down as the hundred-year-old machinery. I made them pick him up off the floor, although Julian seemed baffled about why I cared. Ava fluttered nearby in their makeshift kitchen. The cabinets must not have been mindware-enabled, because she was opening them by hand. They were old, doors dented and scarred with time and a thousand uses. The shiny flash oven appeared newly installed, but the rest of the cabinets, tables, and chairs seemed to be left over from a lunchroom for the original factory workers.

The mages apparently lived here, beds clustered in the middle and outside jacking range of the city beyond the walls. There were a dozen bunks, but I counted only four mages: Ava, Julian, and two men who lingered by the bunks, talking to Molloy. I wasn't sure if Molloy counted as a mage or not. The group of tables where Julian and I sat was far enough from the bunks that it was out of their jacking range. Not for me, of course, but probably at the limits of what the others could do.

A door beckoned from a nearby corner of the factory. I had no idea if it was locked, but red-tinged light seeped underneath it from outside. It was getting late. I tried to keep my eyes from wandering in the direction of the door. Darkness might help, but then again, the idea of being in Jackertown after dark made me shudder.

I pretended the shudder was a full-blown shiver and pulled the scratchy blanket Julian had given me tighter around my shoulders. He inspected me again, his eyes taking a long time to cover the space between my hands clutching the blanket and my face.

"Are you feeling better?" he asked. Ava placed a cup of tea in front of me and drifted back to the kitchen.

"A little," I lied. I was an expert liar. I just hoped that it would hold until I could find a way out.

Julian crossed his arms, crinkling the shiny *nove*-fiber shirt that fit him a little too well, like it was custom-made. Between the shirt and his tailored pants, he looked out of place, like he had accidentally wandered into the dingy factory from a corporate boardroom.

"The effects of the butterfly should be wearing off by now."

"Butterfly?" I asked. "Is that what Molloy zapped me with?"

He nodded. "It's one of the new anti-jacker technologies the government has been hard at work developing since we became, well, more of a threat." He held his hand palm up, like I was Exhibit A of the threat jackers posed.

"Then how did Molloy get hold of it?"

Julian pulled a delicate metallic device that looked like an insect from his pants pocket and placed it on the table. It had netted wings and a central body with pointed metallic feet. "Mr. Molloy tells me he used it in his escape from Agent Kestrel's facility. It's like a taser, but it appears to have much more severe effects on jackers. I haven't had time to have it reverse

47

engineered, but my guess is that it's specially tuned to the electrical frequencies of jacker minds." Julian was a study in opposites: he looked like someone from my high school, but he talked like a philosophy professor that would happily spend the day musing about the fascinating implications of jacker mind frequencies. His mind was something entirely different.

The tiny metallic butterfly tempted me from the table. A weapon other than my mind would be very handy in getting past Julian. I tore my gaze from it, hoping I hadn't given away my thoughts.

Julian's brow wrinkled. "It shouldn't be taking you this long to recover. I can't imagine that keepers are any more affected by the butterfly. If anything, it should be the opposite."

I shrugged and looked for a way to change the subject so Julian wouldn't get too suspicious. Raf's deep artificial sleep on the couch was also going to be a problem.

"It's giving me the creeps to see Raf like that," I said. "If we're going to work on this Kestrel thing together, I want him awake."

"If he's awake," Julian said, "he'll know far more than I'd like for any reader to know about where we live. He can't know anything about our plans. It's much better for him to sleep until we're through."

Better for Julian, maybe, but not so much for my escape plans. For that, I needed Raf awake and ready to run. "I'll wipe his mind. He won't remember a thing about this place or any of you."

Julian cocked his head. "You are so attached to him, yet will-ing to wipe his memories? Does he not mind? It's fascinating that you hold such a person, someone you can so readily control, so close. I have to say, keeper, I didn't think you were the type of person who enjoyed that kind of power."

I gripped my blanket a little tighter. "Just wake him up."

Julian waved a hand in Raf's direction. "Do it yourself," he challenged me. I made a great show of focusing on Raf. I could easily have lifted his heart rate and summoned him from that deep sleep, but I faked frustration instead.

"I can't! Your butterfly has wiped me out!"

Julian sighed and waved Ava over to wake up Raf. I don't know why Julian didn't do the jacking himself, but my body flooded with relief to see Raf rub his eyes and struggle to sit up. I hesitated to link into his head, not wanting Ava to sense my mental strength, and I put an artificial stumble in my walk. The couch was overly soft, and I sank way too deep into it, but I man-aged to wrap my blanket around Raf's shoulders.

The look on Raf's face betrayed his panic. He couldn't read Ava's or Julian's thoughts and surely knew right away that they were jackers. He shrugged aside the blanket and wrapped a protective arm around me, glaring at Julian and Ava as if they were circling tigers ready to pounce.

Ava smiled but averted her eyes, the automatic embarrassed reaction of readers and jackers alike to blatant in-the-open touching.

Julian's face had gone blank. "Now I see how it is."

My heart sank as I realized the tactical advantage I had just lost. My earlier actions had given away that I cared for Raf, but as long as Raf was asleep, Julian could imagine I used him for my own selfish purposes. An awake Raf radiating his love for me? Unless Julian thought I was truly a monster, he had to see right through my claim that I would wipe Raf's memories. I linked into Raf's mind, hoping Ava had fled and ready to shove Julian out, but was surprised to find them not there.

Less of a surprise was that Raf was freaking out. *Are you okay, Kira? What's going on? Who are these people? How did we get here?* His fresh-linen mind-scent was laced with the sour bite of fear.

It's okay, I linked to him. *I have a plan. Just stay calm.*

Unfortunately, that's when Raf noticed the bruise on my cheek. He gingerly touched my face and I struggled not to wince. *What have they done to you?* The look he threw at Julian would have killed him on the spot if Raf was a jacker. Julian caught his stare and held it with a dangerous glare of his own. Raf's thoughts burned in my head. *Did he hurt you, Kira? I swear, if he hurt you...*

I could feel the heat of Julian's eyes on us, and I had to stop Raf's train of thought, but the idea of jacking him made my heart twist. I needed a monumental-sized distraction that would stop them both at once.

I shoved my fingers through the soft curls at the back of Raf's neck and pulled him into a fierce kiss. It short-circuited his thoughts as fast as if I had jacked them clean. While he scrambled to figure out what I was doing, I brushed Ava's mind. She had turned her back on us, just as I had hoped. I didn't dare reach for Julian, afraid any contact with his mind would bring on another horror show. I heard a huff from the table, as well as a creak from his chair and the quiet padding of his footsteps across the industrial carpeting.

I kept kissing Raf until I was sure Julian wasn't coming back.

When I pulled away, Raf's thoughts were substantially less freaked and the sour scent in his mind had faded. *Well, this isn't the most romantic setting I can think of, but it is an improvement over the dumpster.*

I couldn't help but smile; then I stole a glance at the table. Julian had left the butterfly there. I restrained my urge to leap up and grab it. I needed to be smart about this, but we needed to act fast.

I left the blanket with Raf, placing it forcefully into his hands. "You probably need this more than I do." *Be ready.* I stayed linked into his mind, but I didn't want to tell him my plans, in case Ava linked in. I shuffled to the table and picked up the metallic butterfly while Ava's back was turned, tucking it into my palm and covering it with the mug of tea.

I pretended to take a sip. "This is really great," I said to her. "Helps with the shakes."

She threw me a smile over her shoulder, still hovering by the sink. "Julian tried to get Molloy to leave the butterfly behind, you know. I've felt what those butterflies are like, and they're no fun. A jacker should never use one of those on a fellow jacker."

She sounded like she was quoting Julian. I wondered again if they were lovers. Or maybe *she* simply loved *him*. I didn't have time to waste worrying about it.

I put on a smile, feeling only the slightest twinge of guilt that I was planning on using the tiny butterfly on her. I tried to be casual as I closed the space between us.

"Thanks," I said. "Molloy's not exactly the type to listen to anyone else."

She cast a glance at Raf. He was folding the blanket, masking his thoughts by humming. Which wouldn't have kept Ava out, but she wasn't trying to link in.

When I reached her, she leaned close and dropped her voice. "He *is* very cute," she said. "I can understand why you might want to keep him."

I mustered another fake smile and hoped she couldn't hear the pounding of my heart. "Yeah, well he's kind of shaken up," I said. "Could you make a cup of tea for him too?"

"Sure."

As soon as she turned away, I whipped the butterfly out and slammed it against her back, pushing the sharp metallic feet of the device through her long blond hair, her shirt, and probably her skin. She didn't make a sound as she froze up. I tried to ignore the wide-eyed look of horror on her face and grabbed her arms so that she wouldn't fall. Raf was off the couch in a flash and caught her before she hit the floor. He swept her up in the blanket and quickly hauled her to the couch.

We have to run. I grabbed Raf by the hand and towed him toward the outside door, but he quickly outpaced me. I didn't dare reach back to see if we had been noticed, but there was no way they could miss us sprinting across the factory floor. Raf tried to yank the door open, but of course it was locked. What was I thinking?

Raf searched the door, but instead of a passkey sensor it had a numeric key pad. The sheet-metal door seemed like it had been rusting for the last hundred years, along with the machinery. Raf kicked the door with his strong soccer legs. It rattled and shook, but it didn't give. The boom echoed off a hundred hard surfaces around the factory. If they hadn't noticed we'd run before, they certainly would now. I turned my back to him, bracing for their mental reach. They would try to jack Raf first, and I needed to keep them away from his head for us to have any chance of escape.

Raf stopped kicking and rustled behind me. Molloy, Julian, and the other two mages were running toward us, but we were still outside their reach. I plunged into Molloy's mind and wrestled with him, as well as the other two. Their names automatically popped up but I ignored them, searching for ways to slow them down. I couldn't stop all three of them, and I didn't even bother with Julian, afraid the recoil might slow me down.

A loud cracking sound made me jump. Raf had pried open the door! He tossed aside the rusty metallic rod, grabbed my hand, and hauled me through the open doorway. I stumbled after him into the damp summer night's breeze.

I ran but Raf was faster, and my breath heaved as I tried to keep up with him. The massive building of the mages' hideout was crammed next to a string of boarded-up businesses. Twilight pushed through the distant skyscrapers of downtown to the nearby low-rise buildings of Jackertown. Plasma lights spotlighted old-style brownstones and tiny merchant shops across the street. People scattered around the sidewalks, pushing through the doors of businesses and standing in groups under the lights. I reached out, skimming minds.

They were all jackers.

Everyone was on high alert, reacting immediately to my soft brush of their mind barriers, and awareness of us swept through their thoughts like a roll of thunder. I quickly pulled back. Protecting Raf in this city of jackers was going to be like shepherding a baby sheep through a gauntlet of wolves. I linked into Raf's head, ready to shove out anyone that might try to jack him. At the same time, I continuously swept ahead and behind us, trying to keep anyone from even getting close.

Raf veered down an alleyway, and I did my best to keep up with him. I dodged a spill that oozed from a tipped-over barrel and held my breath past the dumpsters overflowing trash onto an abandoned armchair. I reached back to check on our pursuers, careful to brush only Molloy, who I knew wouldn't be able to detect my mental touch at this distance. He was cursing and scanning the street. At least we were out of their line of sight, around the corner before they spotted us, and now we were out of range too.

I waved to Raf to get him to slow down. We wouldn't stand out so badly in the darkening Jackertown streets if we weren't running for our lives. I caught up to him and by the time we exited the alley into yet another street filled with broken businesses and boarded windows, we were walking briskly but not at an unduly suspicious pace.

A couple of boys, no older than fourteen, lingered outside a convenience store. When they saw us, they scurried inside. Unfortunately, we caught the attention of a trio of men standing next to an ancient electric recharge station out front. One smacked his partner on the shoulder and gestured toward us with his chin.

Toward Raf, actually. The reader who had wandered into their wolf den.

The force of their minds slammed into me, then dipped into Raf's head, but I was able to shove them out. They quickly retreated. Testing me, maybe, but they already knew too much just from that. I grabbed Raf's jersey sleeve to pull him into the shadowed doorway of a furniture store, clearly abandoned when the jackers took over. Raf tried the door, but it was locked.

Should I knock it down? he thought.

I don't think we can hide. The store was too small to get us out of jacking range. Half the street was staring at us, with the other half busy with their own business, haggling amongst themselves. I kept mindguarding Raf, sweeping for more jackers trying to reach us, but no one was. The trio of jackers was having an animated, silent conversation, probably about us, but brushing their minds to find out exactly what they were thinking would only bring the confrontation quicker. Running wasn't a great option either. I didn't even know how big Jackertown was.

We need to find transportation, I linked to Raf. More urgently, we needed to move out of range of the trio. I edged out of the doorway, with Raf close behind. We crossed the street and walked away from the men as fast as we could without actually running.

Can we hail an autocab? he asked.

In my panic, I hadn't even thought of using my phone. I grinned and fished it out of my pocket. I quickly jacked into the mindware interface and pulled up a taxi-paging service. There were no autocabs for miles. I nudged the closest one, but the holographic display flashed red and disappeared: Service Not Available.

I frowned. *Looks like even the autocabs avoid Jackertown.* Regular bus service, and indeed any kind of traffic at all, gave Jackertown a wide berth. It was almost like a little island, hanging on the edge of downtown, which wasn't the friendliest of places to begin with. Especially at night after all the regular downtown workers fled for the relative sanity of the Chicago New Metro suburbs.

I can call my dad, Raf thought. *He can come pick us up.*

My shoulders hunched up. If Raf's dad knew I had gotten him dragged to Jackertown, I'd never see Raf again. They would probably move back to Portugal, where Raf's parents had been born. I put a hand on his arm to keep him from pulling the phone all the way out of his pocket. *Your parents are readers. It's not a good idea to bring them here. Let me try calling my dad.*

We had moved out of range of the trio of men, but now they were stalking toward us, keeping pace. I kept up my sweeps around Raf's mind and picked up our speed, passing a string of boarded windows that were plastered with dozens of photofilms. "MISSING" was stamped in red across the faces. I guessed Julian was telling the truth about the missing jackers, but that wasn't my problem.

I flipped through my phone list and nudged my dad's number, but it went straight to message. My throat closed up. Had Molloy caught up with him as well? I hesitated only a moment before pulling up Mr. Trullite's number. The one he had given me for emergencies. The one my dad didn't know I had.

It picked up right away. "Lucy?" There was a rumble of concern. Or possibly annoyance. I seriously hoped I wasn't about to get my dad fired. "Are you okay, dear?"

"Um, Mr. Trullite, look, I'm really sorry to be calling you like this," I said. "I wouldn't, except I can't get hold of my dad and I... I really need to get hold of my dad. Is he still with you?"

"I'm in the middle of that meeting we discussed earlier." Definitely annoyance now. "Perhaps you could wait until we are through to speak to Mr. O'Reilly."

"Mr. Trullite, I'm in Jackertown."

There was silence on the other end.

"I see."

57

"I really need my dad to come get me." Fear hitched a ride on my voice. "Could you please just tell him to call me?"

"Of course, dear," he said. "I'll send a driver right away."

"Oh! No, wait, don't do that—"

The phone went dead.

I stared at it.

What did he say? Raf was nervously checking behind us. The trio of jackers had formed a triangle, with the older ones slightly behind, guarding their rear flank.

He hung up on me. I'm not sure. I think he might be sending a car. I urged Raf to cross the street again, but half a dozen girls were camped on that side, and their stares weren't any friendlier. I tugged Raf into the middle of the empty street. It seemed like a hundred eyes and minds were tracking us from behind the boarded-up storefronts. I kept up my vigilant scanning, mind-guarding Raf. I felt a surge or two against my head and struggled to swat them away from Raf, but it was only a fraction of the people watching us. If any of them got serious about jacking Raf, I doubted I could hold them off for long. I tried not to let all of my fear show by breaking into a flat run.

My phone vibrated my hand, startling me. I flicked it with my mind to turn it on.

"Kira?" It was my dad's voice.

"Dad!" I held the phone close, whispering. "I need you to come get us! We're in Jackertown, at..." I squinted at the street sign, faintly glowing with biopaint. "The corner of 23rd and Laramie."

"Us?"

"Me and Raf—"

My dad's curse cut me off. "You and *Raf*?" he said. "I thought you weren't seeing him any more—"

"Dad!" I said. "I'll explain later, okay? Molloy found us and—"

"What?" My dad's voice turned rough. "Are you okay?"

"I'm fine." I decided now was not the time to mention the bruise. Or the butterfly. "But we need to get out of here before Molloy and the others find us." I glanced back at the men, who had paused, probably listening to my conversation. I dropped my voice to a whisper again. "We're heading east—"

"Jackertown isn't safe for you, Kira," my dad cut in. "You don't need me to tell you why. And Raf—"

"I know!"

"Mr. Trullite gave me a car to come get you." His voice sounded strained, and the hydro engine hummed in the background. He must be hauling through the suburban streets if the car was making noise I could hear over the phone. "I'll be there as soon as I can."

Raf pointed behind us. The men leered, drawing closer. "I gotta go, Dad. Just call me when you get close."

I hung up the phone and abandoned any pretense, grabbing Raf's hand and turning to sprint down the street, only to find another two jackers standing dead in the middle, blocking our way. One was a woman, tall and bony, the other a man with a face that had taken a few punches. He could probably arm wrestle Molloy and win. Raf and I stumbled to a stop, trapped between the men behind us and these two in front. I glanced back. The men were holding their position.

I realized too late that they had been herding us.

The woman's mind slammed into mine with enough force that I swayed back, then she dived deep into Raf's head. It took me a half second to recover and I was able to shove her out of Raf's head, but I wasn't strong enough to wrestle her back into her own mind.

She suddenly pulled back. "Now there's something I haven't seen before, Henry," the woman said.

"What's that?" Her partner's sneer made his face even uglier.

"A keeper running trade in Jackertown," she said. "With your pretty face and that closed head of yours, I'd imagine you could fetch a fine rate all by yourself."

I had no idea what she meant.

She kept talking. "So why would a keeper be running trade in Jackertown, Henry?"

Henry looked me up and down, taking in my waitress apron with the Dutch Apple logo. "Don't know, boss. Maybe she's bringing us some pie."

"Bet they don't suspect you at all in that Dorothy from *The Wizard of Oz* getup." They both smiled wide, and I had a feeling they were mentally laughing at my expense, but jacking into their heads to listen in seemed like a very bad idea.

"So." She flicked a look to Raf. "How much for your trade?"

I didn't know what she meant by trade, but the way she was eyeing Raf, I didn't think it was because he was cute. More like how much she thought she could get for him on the open market.

Tell her you're just here for business, Raf thought.

What? I resisted turning toward him. "I'm, um, here for business," I said to the woman. *How do you know anything about this?* I linked to Raf.

I have a world-famous mindjacker for a girlfriend, he thought. *A guy's got to be prepared.*

I was working full time to keep the shock off my face, but the woman looked surprised enough for both of us. She took a closer look at Raf. He gave her a cool stare in return. My heart was giving my ribcage a beating.

"Your patron looks awfully young to be hiring out jackwork," she said. "And he doesn't look rich enough to afford it either. Although he already has a keeper for a mindguard. That can't have come too cheap. Maybe you'd like to change your mind about trading, keeper? I'm sure I can get a good price for him."

"She's not going to trade away her unos supplier," Raf said in a confident voice. "We're looking for someone who wants an easy jackwork job."

I had maybe two and a half unos in my pocket, leftover tips from the diner. I tried to affect the same outwardly cool expression Raf was now wearing, while my mouth was running dry. *What are you doing?*

Trying to talk our way out of this. Raf pictured a pocket-sized mini-taser in his mind. *Just in case it doesn't work.*

What? You're armed? I was starting to wonder who this Raf was and what he did with my boyfriend.

The woman appraised him again. "What kind of services are you looking for, sweetie? My crew could probably handle your needs, if the price is right. We're not wetjacks, but you look too sweet for that." She smiled at Raf in a way that made my fists clench. "Do you want us to jack someone into going to the prom with you?"

Raf's jaw worked but his voice was calm. "I have a trust fund that I'm coming into when I'm eighteen, but I'm tired of waiting."

She curled a smile. "Maybe we'll ransom you instead, sweet thing. I'm sure your mommy will pay handsomely to have her darling boy back."

"My father's wife is spending my trust fund on her jewelry collection, something I'm hoping you might be able to fix." Raf slipped his hands into his pockets, looking casual, but his thoughts showed that he had gripped the taser. If Raf tried the taser on them, there was no way I'd be able to keep the woman and her crew out of his head.

I had to think a way out of this, and fast.

The woman tsk-tsked Raf, like he was a foolish boy. "Not very smart, coming here, sweet thing," she said. "Your mindguard should have told you that."

"I warned him," I said. "I offered to contract for him, but he wanted to meet the jackworker for himself." They outnumbered me five to one, and they'd have Raf in an instant if they wanted to take him, so I needed to keep them talking. "You know these trustfunders. No sense in their heads. Since you don't want our business, we'll just be on our way."

I grabbed Raf's arm and edged us out from the squeeze between the woman and her crew.

"No need to hurry," said a rough voice. One of the men had crept up on us.

"I've never met a keeper before, Norma, have you?" Henry said. "They're what you call 'rare' I think. Like one of those mage types, right? How much do you think we can get for one of those?"

"A fair amount, I'd say," she said. "And the boy might fetch a nice ransom, if he's a trustfunder like she says. Because I'm sure a keeper would never lie."

That got a laugh all around.

"Look, we don't want any trouble..." I said.

"It's no trouble at all," said the man with a battered face.

Raf's fists were clenched at his side, the taser tucked inside. *Kira, if they take me, you run and find your dad.*

I'm not leaving you here!

Suddenly a small hand reached out to grab mine. I jerked my hand back and turned to see one of the two boys who had disappeared before. The other had hold of Raf, tugging him away from the jackers menacing us. I quickly brushed the soft Jell-O of their minds. They were barely changelings and I could easily jack them, but their thoughts showed they wanted to help us find a place to hide. Raf was giving them a suspicious look, but he couldn't read their minds like I could. Strangely, Norma and her crew were letting the changelings pull us away. I shuffled backward, unwilling to turn my back on the crew.

The burly man jutted his chin out. "Another time, keeper." Raf and I and the changeling boys turned and ran full tilt down the sidewalk, hugging the abandoned shops. We didn't stop until we turned down another alleyway teeming with trash.

"Thank you." My voice was raspy from the run and the left-over tension. How on earth were these two able to extricate us from Norma and her crew? "We need a place to stay, just for an hour."

The boys edged closer, and they reminded me of changelings from the jacker camp. Hair disheveled, jeans tattered at the knees and well-worn, like they had one pair and they'd been wearing them for a long time. They must have been thrown out by their parents. They would only be in Jackertown if they had nowhere else to go.

The younger one, all of twelve years old, crept closer. "We can't read you," he said softly. "Are you really a keeper?" There was awe in his voice. I was glad he hadn't figured out I was Kira Moore, face of the outted jackers.

"Yeah," I said. "I'm a keeper, and my friend and I are new here. And thanks. For back there." I fished in my apron pocket for the bit of tips I had inadvertently taken from the diner. "It's all I have, but I can pay you more when my dad gets here."

The older one, who was maybe fourteen, said, "We don't need your money," but the younger one dashed his small hand out to scoop the change from my hand. I added on a smile.

The older one frowned, but said, "Come on. We know some-one who will let you stay."

Raf and I followed the boys out the far end of the alley. The next street was mostly brownstones that hadn't been rehabbed to bring them up to range codes, all short and squat and packed too close together. The boys scurried up a set of stairs to a door with curls of peeling paint. They didn't knock. It was opened by an elderly woman who ushered them inside. Raf and I quickly followed without saying a word.

The woman was shorter than me, her slender frame wrapped in a flowered housecoat and layered with a knit cardigan that looked handmade. She folded her bony arms, feet planted wide, and appraised us for a moment. "You look like you need a place to stay. The street isn't any place to be at night, not in Jackertown." She nodded to Raf. "Especially not for little lost lambs." He looked put out by her description.

"Thanks for taking us in," I said, before Raf could ruffle our guardian angel. "We just need a place to stay for an hour or so."

She swept a gnarled hand out, inviting us into a wallpapered sitting room off the entryway. It had lace hanging from the windows, the lamp shades, and even the shelves. A look from her sent the boys scurrying off through a doorway at the end of the room. In spite of Raf's amazing performance before, his face was pale and it twisted my insides. I didn't care that our grandma-savior was standing right there. I buried my face in his chest and gently linked into his mind.

Raf, I'm so sorry. His arms enveloped me, warm and strong, and I quivered against him.

It's okay, he thought. *Everything's going to be fine. Your*

65

dad will be here soon. Raf's thoughts were tinged with the sour taste of worry, mostly about how he couldn't protect me on the street. I loved him for that thought, but the idea of *him* worrying about protecting *me* was upside down.

I'm so sorry, I linked the thought again. *You shouldn't be wrapped up in my mess.*

Raf lifted my hand from where I clung to his jersey and leaned down to kiss my wrist, the two tangled pieces of the heart tattoo disappearing under his lips. *I'm just mad my one chance to have you alone was interrupted.* He kissed my forehead, lightly lingering there. *Wherever you are, that's where I belong.*

Raf was completely wrong. Where we were was absolutely no place for him.

Twitters sounded from the other side of the room. I didn't detect any other mindjackers in his mind, so our thoughts were private, but we were giving quite a show with the touching, which wasn't very mesh. The grandma's smile wrinkled up her face, and the boys spied on us from the doorway. She waved them off and they disappeared in a burst of giggles.

I disengaged from Raf, pulling out of his mind before he could tell me any more intimate thoughts that might make my cheeks burn even more than they were already.

"I'm glad you found your way here," the woman said, waving at two overstuffed chairs stamped with flowers. "Make yourselves at home."

"Thank you," I said, but we stayed standing. "We won't impose on you long. I called my dad. He's going to come get us soon."

66

"Your dad, Kira?" she said. "He must be worried with you here in the city."

My jaw dropped. "You... know me." The hairs rose up on the back of my neck.

She swept a finger along her cheek, mimicking the synth-tattoo I had along mine. "It's not much of a disguise, dear."

A nervous laugh bubbled up. "Well, I didn't plan to come here, where people might recognize me."

She nodded. "Yet I'm sure you have quite the stories to tell. Why don't you have a seat while we wait?"

Raf and I slowly sat in the chairs, which were stiff like they were rarely used and smelled faintly of lilacs. The changelings peeked in again from the kitchen doorway.

I inclined my head toward them. "Do you take care of all the orphans here?"

She sent a quick sideways look to the boys and they slipped back through the swinging door. "I look out for all kinds of people who have lost their way." She perched on a chair opposite us, her light body barely making a dent in it. "You must tell me, dear: how did you break out of that desert camp, just you and no one else?"

Her question made me squirm. "It's complicated."

"Yes, I'm sure," she said. "You must know that the change-lings all talk about you. I'm sure the truth is more amazing than the stories they've made up."

I didn't know what stories she was talking about, and I wasn't sure where she was going with this, but it was straying into things I didn't like talking about. Especially with Raf nearby and unable to keep things a secret with his reader mind. As I was working up a good answer, there was a click at the front door.

I frowned. There was no way my dad could have gotten here so quickly, even if he had managed to find us by tracking my phone. I was on my feet and reaching out when Julian came around the corner.

"There you are," he said, looking at me. Then he turned to the woman. "Thank you so much for keeping her for us, Myrtle."

I gaped at him and whirled on Myrtle, trying to jack into her mind, but she pushed me flat back into mine with such an intense pressure that it made me drop to my knees. Raf went limp in the chair next to me.

"Oh, I wouldn't do that, if I were you," said Julian. "Myrtle is the strongest jacker I've ever met. And I've met quite a few."

chapter SIX

Just as I was sure my skull would crack, the pressure from Myrtle cut off.

Her slippered feet shuffled back, and I blinked away the stars that were zipping in front of my eyes. An older jacker, mid-twenties, stood to Julian's side, calm but ready. I vaguely recognized him from the mages' lair. His hair looked like he cut it himself in the mirror, and his jeans were not quite ragged enough for holes. His stringy fingers tapped a rhythm on his folded arms, but his face was impassive, as if he was awaiting Julian's orders to either strangle me or escort me out the door, and he didn't much care which one it was.

Julian's lips pressed into a straight line. I gripped the upholstered chair and struggled to my feet. Raf had slid from his seat and lay like a doll slumped on the ground. I quickly linked into his mind, but he was only passed out. I held still, in case any sudden moves would bring Myrtle down on my head again.

"Hinckley," Julian said. "Could you take care of the keeper's friend?"

My back stiffened as Hinckley strode over to Raf, but he simply hooked his thin but muscular arms under Raf's and hoisted him back into the chair. He propped Raf so he wouldn't fall out again, even as his head lolled.

"She has a phone," Myrtle said. "Said her father was coming to get her." My heart climbed up in my throat.

"You called your father to come get you?" Julian's voice was incredulous, as if that was the stupidest thing I could possibly have done. At the moment, I was thinking he was right. My dad would be walking into a trap.

Julian curled a fist and eyed the door. "Well, that will only make this mess even bigger. I suppose that means we can't stay here." He pressed his fist into the wing of Raf's chair. "I might need your assistance, Myrtle."

"I should say so."

Raf jumped up from the chair, startling me so badly I nearly fell back into mine. But he wasn't awake at all. The overwhelming presence of Myrtle filled his mind. Hinckley jogged to the door to open it before Myrtle puppet-walked Raf through. I hurried close behind Raf, resisting the urge to grab his hand. Julian and Hinckley followed so close I could hear Julian breathing through his teeth.

More jackers filled the street since we'd gone inside. Gathered in bunches on the steps of their brownstones, they looked like the jacker gangs in the camp, minus the arm bands.

Both of Hinckley's hands fluttered, playing an invisible piano in the air and turning away the stares of the street as his gaze swept forward and back. How could he control so many jackers at once? A long time ago, I had managed to knock out an entire warehouse of jackers, one after another, but that was only because I caught them off guard. Controlling a host of readers at once was reasonable for any jacker, but turning the heads of this many hyper-alert jackers?

Even people forward of Hinckley's head-turning trick retreated up their steps and inside as we neared. Julian walked with his chin up, not obviously controlling anyone. Were they fleeing before Hinckley could reach them? Or was it Julian's presence that made them retreat to the safety of their houses?

We moved as a pack past an alleyway, as well as another shop papered with jacker faces stamped "MISSING." After rounding the corner, it became clear we were going back to the mages' headquarters. I couldn't think of anything else to do but go with them. Raf and I wouldn't last on the streets, and I couldn't take any risks with Myrtle. She was so strong, she might accidentally kill Raf without even thinking about it.

We passed the street where we had left Norma and her gang, but there was no sign of them. It was nearly dark, the bluish plasma of the streetlights replacing the reddish glow of the sunset. When we reached the crumbling brick entrance of the mages' headquarters, a dark-skinned boy a couple of years older than Julian knelt in the doorway, welding a metal patch to the frame. His mini laser welder threw sparks on the sidewalk and singed the air with a sharp smell. Shiny black goggles cupped his eyes.

"Sasha." Julian raised his voice to be heard over the sparking of the laser. "How is the door coming along?"

Sasha flicked off the laser and set it down. He stood, lifting the goggles and perching them on his forehead, trapping his curly black hair underneath.

Instead of answering Julian, he said, "So, you found her." He turned his dark brown eyes to me. They were almost black, like a bottomless pit that couldn't reflect light. "That's too bad. I was hoping you might have gotten lost."

"Sasha." Julian's voice was filled with patience. "The door?"

Sasha tugged off his welding gloves. "It will hold for now," he said. "I can rig up a passring sensor and get a new door frame in the morning. Assuming Kira doesn't decide to break down our door again." He said my name like it was something bitter, then stepped back to let us pass, tracking me with a cold stare. Julian ushered us into the dim light inside, trading the damp summer air for the stale machine-grease smell of the converted factory. Sasha scooped up his welder and clanged the metal door shut, followed by a click that signaled we weren't going anywhere.

Raf walked with stiff legs to the kitchen table and carefully sat in a rickety chair, staring vacantly at the carpeted floor. Myrtle took up a station next to him. My heart was ripping into pieces at the blank look on his face, so I turned my back to the table. Hinckley sat on the edge of the broken-down couch, where Ava was roughly bundled in a thick blanket. Sasha knelt by her, smoothing her hair and sending me a look that sent a shiver through me.

"Ava's not going to be happy with you when she wakes up," Julian said. He leaned against the kitchen counter, retrieving an apple from a basket and taking a noisy bite. I didn't like Julian before, but the loathing I had for him was reaching new heights.

"Let Raf go." I didn't care that desperation crumpled my voice. "I'll do whatever you want, just don't hurt him."

"Hurt him?" Julian stopped mid-chew. "I don't think you quite understand the situation you're in here." He gestured with the apple. "This is Jackertown. There're quite a few jackers who don't realize how important you are—to us, to jackers everywhere—and who would be happy to see you dead for your trouble."

I had no idea what Julian meant about my *importance*, but I understood quite well that plenty of jackers wanted me dead. Sasha seemed like he would be happy to do the honors.

"I have some influence here," continued Julian. Hinckley gave a snort from his perch on the couch. "Which is why I was able to get you to Myrtle's safe house. And back again. But him," Julian said and pointed at Raf, "he's as good as dead out there. That, or a ruthless crew that doesn't have much in the Morals Department will use him for a pawn. I had thought you would understand that and not go dragging a reader through the streets."

Julian's patronizing tone lit a fire in me. Maybe he had gotten us off the street, but we were hardly safe. "You're the one that dragged us here in the first place!"

73

"I had no intention of bringing him here!" Julian pushed away from the counter and threw the apple in a small trash can, knocking it over. "I thought..." He seemed at a loss for words for the first time since I'd woken up on the couch. He swiped a hand across his mouth and glared at my fists curled up by my side. "I don't understand what you see in that mindreader, but for whatever reason, you seem to care about him. I never intended for him to be here, but now that he is, it's better that he stay safely asleep."

With those words, Raf's body caved facedown onto the dingy table. Myrtle took a seat next to him, and Molloy drifted from the back to land by Raf's side, his meaty arms folded as he loomed above him. My fingernails were digging trenches in my palms.

Julian crossed his arms again and leaned back against the kitchen counter. "Sasha, the keeper will sleep on the couch tonight. Can you take Ava to her bunk and keep an eye on her?" Sasha gave me one last glare, then gathered the blanket tighter around Ava and easily scooped her off the couch, carrying her toward the cluster of bunks.

Julian lingered a look after the two of them. "As much as you seem to be protective of your mindreading friend," he said, "my sister is currently in the hands of that monster Kestrel, so you can perhaps understand my urgency to not wait around while issuing invitations. I'd rather not have to chase you all over Jackertown either. I can understand that you don't want to go near Kestrel again, but I thought... I thought we would have more common cause than we apparently do."

He paused to wipe his hands on his neatly pressed pants. "In the morning, you can return to rooking in the suburbs and pretending you're merely a waitress in a diner, serving closed-minded readers their pie." The distaste in his voice seemed to emanate from him.

Did I hear him right? "You're not going to force me to help you?"

"It was never my intention to force you into anything, keeper." He massaged his temple with two fingers and stared at the floor. "But I'm not going to send one of my mages to shepherd you and your pet reader through Jackertown at night." He nodded to the slumped-over figure of Raf. "He'll be safer here. In the morning, Mr. Molloy can escort you both back to the suburbs."

"Now wait just a minute," said Molloy, his voice low. "What about the plan? I don't care much for the lass, but she's a key part of it. You can't just let her..." Molloy drifted off, looking confused but innocent, like a small child. As if he had lost his train of thought and couldn't find it again. "Then again, maybe there's no rush. There must be a way we can figure a plan that will work without the lass. Can't put my finger on it, though."

My eyebrows hiked up. I glanced at Julian, but he didn't acknowledge Molloy, merely tapped his fingers to his lips. I jacked into Molloy's mind and he didn't even notice me at first, he was so swirled around in his own confused thoughts. Finally, he realized I was there and pushed me back out.

Hinckley hopped off the couch and stepped up to Molloy. "Do you want me to take him, boss?"

"Take me where?" Molloy asked. "I'm fine right where I am, mate."

"No, I've got him." Julian waved Hinckley off in an absent-minded way.

Hinckley glanced in my direction. "So, what's the plan?" he asked Julian.

"We'll make new plans in the morning," Julian said. "You can turn in if you'd like." Hinckley shrugged, snagged an apple from the kitchen, then strode to the back of the factory.

"Yes, plans in the morning sounds right enough," Molloy said. "Meanwhile, I've got a raging hunger. What have you got for food here, Julian?"

I stepped out of Molloy's path as he ambled to the kitchen in search of a snack. What kind of jacker *was* Julian? He seemed to get others to do his jacking for him, and when I pushed into his mind, it was a horror show—something I never wanted to do again. Yet he was doing *something* to Molloy.

Julian strolled over to Myrtle, who was softly tapping her fingers on the table next to Raf. "Thank you for your assistance, Myrtle. I'll contact you on the short comm in the morning, when we have an idea of our next step."

Myrtle flicked a look to me. "I think I'll stay a while," she said. "Maybe have some tea." She got up to join Molloy, who was rummaging through cabinets in the kitchen.

"What did you do to Molloy?" I asked Julian in a hushed voice.

Julian followed my gaze. "I didn't think you cared much

for Mr. Molloy. He's not injured in any way, just... calmer. His instincts are quieted so that his strongest urge right now is to get a snack." Julian tilted his head to tap the base of his skull where it met his spine. "This part of the brain controls instinctual responses. Fight or flight. Survival mechanisms." The corner of his mouth tipped up. "Mating instinct."

I narrowed my eyes at him.

"It's the oldest part of the brain, evolutionarily speaking," he said, slipping into his professor voice. "Reptiles have it. We don't use it to think or feel. It controls how we react, without us ever having to think about it at all."

"So, you jacked into that part of Molloy's brain?" The idea sent a shiver down my back. When I jacked into other people's minds, I could feel the different parts: the thinking parts, the memory zones, the emotional centers. The part that controls respiration and heart rate. But they were fluid, not necessarily all in the same spot from person to person or one jack to the next. I found them by feel more than anything else.

"I don't quite jack in." He regarded me. "When you jack someone's mind, you feel something, yes?"

"Like plunging my hand into a bowl of goo."

"Goo?" A tiny smile appeared and then left. "You feel something because you are interfacing your mind field with theirs. There's a natural resistance between the two fields. An interference, you might say."

"A mind barrier."

"Indeed." The smile came back, but my shoulders hunched

up. I didn't want to discuss the finer points of jacking. Julian said he would let us go in the morning, but I didn't trust him any more than I could jack him, which was to say not at all.

"So what are you saying?" Impatience crept into my voice. "That it doesn't feel that way to you?"

"No, it doesn't," he said. "It feels like dipping into an endless bath of dread. Or an infinite sea of joy." He spread his hands wide. "Or a myriad of flavors in between. Everything in the reptilian part of our brains is a wash of energy on a spectrum from positive to negative."

I looked at him like he was demens. He shrugged one shoulder. "I've never met another handler, so I'm not sure if it's the same with everyone."

"Handler?"

"That's just what I call it," he said. "When I slipped into Molloy's reptilian brain, it was inflamed with a protective instinct, to save his brother from Kestrel. The protective instinct is very strong. It's the kind that makes you run into a burning house to save a child, even though it puts your own life in danger. Mr. Molloy thinks you're the key to our plan to break into Kestrel's facility, but his methods of persuasion are more extreme than I'm willing to entertain. So I flipped his protective instinct to its opposite."

I had a flash of fear and understood why those jackers on the street fled into their houses when they saw him coming. How could you fight someone that messed with your instincts?

"What's the opposite instinct?"

"Peace," Julian said. "It's the opposite of almost any negative instinctual response. It's not unlike the love he no doubt feels for his brother, but I don't traffic in emotional manipulation."

"Right." I laid the sarcasm on heavy. "Because that would be beneath you."

He laughed in a lighthearted way, which rubbed raw against the nerves strung tight throughout my body. "No. Because I don't know how. I don't jack like you do, keeper, or like most other jackers."

"No, you just play around with people's instincts for survival."

"Yes, precisely."

Suddenly I wondered if he could control me. If so, why didn't he just jack, or *handle*, me into doing whatever he wanted in this crazy attempt on Kestrel? Then I realized Julian must have already tried.

"Wait. You were planning on *handling* me into turning myself in to Kestrel, weren't you?"

His lips pinched in. "No, I wasn't. Even if I wanted to, it doesn't work that way, not for something so complicated." He examined me again. "Although I was surprised to find that I couldn't access the primal parts of your brain, keeper. Even Anna wasn't able to keep me out, not that I ever would handle her. No, I thought... I thought that you would be different. That you would be more interested in the opportunity I had to offer." He drew a long look along my Dutch Apple apron. "Obviously I was wrong about that."

My heart twisted at his insinuation that I didn't care about freeing the changelings. But I didn't need to explain myself to someone who was effectively holding me and Raf hostage. "So you'll let us go?"

"In the morning," he said roughly, looking away from me.

"What about Raf?" I said. "If you're going to make him sleep, at least move him to the couch. I don't think I'll be sleeping much, anyway."

Julian was about to speak when banging at the front door made us all jump, even him. Then he calmly called to Myrtle in the kitchen. "Would you answer the door, please, Myrtle?"

She pulled her cardigan a little tighter and focused on the door. I felt a little sorry for whoever was on the other side, having been on the receiving end of a mental push from Myrtle.

She turned back to Julian. "It's a contractor. He's looking for the keeper. Has business for her."

"Let him in," Julian told her. He shook his head at me. "Well, it didn't take long for word about you to get around. Don't worry. I'll send a message that you're not available for business. I don't need every contractor in town looking to make a few spare unos."

Myrtle's slipper shoes made swishing sounds on the concrete floor. She punched in a code at the keypad and pulled open the door. A man in a jacket with the hood thrown back stood on the other side. He was wearing a Second Skin face mask, the kind that hugged the features of his face, only this one was all black and covered his eyes and mouth as well. He could surely see through the thin film, but not an inch of skin showed. He bent his head and the mask moved with his lips as he spoke words I couldn't hear. Myrtle swept her hand out, inviting him in. His stride was firm as he stepped across the threshold. He surveyed the room, pausing at Raf, still passed out at the table.

Then he found me, and his eyeless face stayed trained as he came to a stop just short of the carpeted patch of the kitchen. The way he was staring at me unnerved me, so I reached out to surge into his mind, like the jackers on the street had done, to get him to back off. When his name popped up automatically, I had to clamp my mouth shut to keep myself from blurting it out.

Dad.

chapter SEVEN

In the middle of the mages' lair, sheathed in a black contractor mask, stood my dad. I linked fast into his mind. *Dad! What are you doing?*

Stay calm. I'm getting you out of here. His thoughts roamed the room, taking in all the players: Myrtle behind him, Julian standing near me, Molloy settling in by Raf at the table and biting into an oversized sandwich.

"Either you're a very stupid contractor," Julian said, "who thinks strolling into a mage cell is an easy way to hire out jackwork, or you're reckless and looking to prove something to your crew. I hope for your sake that you're merely stupid."

"I have jackwork for the keeper," my dad said. I held absolutely still. "What's her price?"

"She's not doing business," Julian said. "She's a guest under the protection of my crew."

"Name your price." My dad's hand flexed, like he was itching to do something besides talk. "My patron has plenty of money."

His brow twitched as he took in Molloy's noisy eating.

"I told you, she's not doing business." Julian stepped so that he blocked the line of sight between me and my dad. "You'll simply have to explain to your patron why she's not available. Or perhaps you could persuade him out of his desire to use mindjackers for his dirty business. I suggest you go now before my patience runs out and my friend here," he inclined his head to Myrtle, "decides to dump you in the street with your memory wiped."

I peered around Julian in time to see my dad twist toward Myrtle, his hand in his jacket. Myrtle crumpled to the floor. I gasped, but before Julian could react, my dad had his dart gun trained on Julian's head.

"I'm only here for the girl and the reader." His voice froze all the air in my lungs.

"I see." The tendons in Julian's neck flexed. "I take it you're not actually a contractor." He turned his head to the side and said, "So, this is your father, then? You're turning into a lot more trouble than I expected, keeper."

My dad lowered his gun, his hand slack at his side. He had the same confused look that Molloy had earlier. I linked into my dad's mind, but there was no hard marble, nothing I could jack or get hold of, no presence of Julian that I could push out of my dad's mind. Just a swirl of jumbled thoughts wondering why he had felt it was so important to come get me.

"Stop it!" I cried, taking a step toward Julian. "Leave him alone!" He twisted around to face me and threw up his hands, taking a half step back. Until that moment I hadn't realized I had balled up my fists in front of me, like I was about to pummel him.

His jaw worked, like he was chewing on the words he wanted to say, but he kept them inside. He lowered his hands and straightened. "Your father just shot my strongest jacker. And pointed a gun in my face. Are you planning to hit me, or can we stop now?"

I wanted to hit him more than ever, but my dad's mind was in Julian's grip and hitting Julian wouldn't help things.

I forced my hands to lower and unclench. "He was only trying to bring me home." Tears stung my eyes. Now my dad was embroiled in my mess, which just seemed to get more horrible by the minute.

"Obviously." Julian took a breath and rubbed his face. "For the time being, your father's lost that great urgent need he was feeling to take you home. You certainly manage to complicate things, you know that?"

My dad holstered his gun and grabbed the bottom edge of the mask, pulling it up and off, leaving his hair mussed. He stuffed the mask into his pocket and stared at the floor as he puzzled through the conflict in his head. He was trying to figure out why he was pointing a gun at Julian when an *all is well* feeling filled his mind.

I blinked back the tears. "Look, my dad is here now. You can let us go. You don't need to send any of your mages with us. I'm sure my dad has a way out of town."

"Oh yes. Absolutely." Julian's dark chuckle hollowed out my stomach. "You truly don't understand anything about Jackertown, do you? From your hideout as a rook in the suburbs."

His insult felt like a cage that was growing smaller and smaller.

"You know, he's right, Kira," my dad said casually, as if he were talking about the Cubs' chances this year. He rolled up on the balls of his feet and bounced slightly. "Traveling through Jackertown at night is pretty dangerous. There're lots of people out there that would probably kill you first and check your pockets second. Might be better if we stayed here. Yes, definitely better." He nodded to himself.

Julian ignored my dad and flung his hand out toward the town beyond the cracked brick walls. "I just paraded you past half of Jackertown, letting everyone know you are under our protection. If I let a contractor come in here and whisk you away, I'll have no end of trouble from the gangs that are waiting for a sign of weakness. There's a balance of power here that's very delicate, and I'm not going to upset all of that simply because your father came in here, guns blazing."

"You said you would let us go!" The tears were close to falling.

"In the morning!" His face pinched in and he took a deep breath. "I wasn't the one who called him here in the first place, keeper. That was your mistake."

Molloy startled me by speaking. "You're the one who's making a mistake, Julian." Molloy's confused face had regained focus. When did that happen? Julian was controlling my dad now, so maybe he couldn't control Molloy at the same time? "We need her to get inside Kestrel's horror shop. The plan only works with her."

"We'll find another way!" Julian's words bit the air, but he quickly calmed. "Mr. Molloy, would you be so kind as to take our reader guest to a spare bunk?"

Molloy's face mottled a color almost as red as his hair, but he didn't argue. Instead, he lifted Raf out of his chair as easily as Sasha had picked up Ava and threw him over his shoulder. My throat closed up, watching Molloy carry Raf away. When he reached the racks, he dropped Raf onto a vacant bed. His body lay curled on his side.

Would Julian really let us leave in the morning? He seemed to hold all the cards, and the feeling of being trapped was cutting off my air. I sucked in a couple of quick breaths. To have any hope of getting my dad and Raf home safe I needed to stay calm and not give Julian any reason to keep us here. Or make him any angrier than he already was.

I turned away so I wouldn't have to look at Raf's unmoving form. My dad meandered to the kitchen and poked through the cabinets one by one. Julian sank into the chair where Raf had just been, the heels of his hands pressed to his eyes. The chair creaked when I eased into the seat next to him, and I gripped the rough edges of it to keep my hands from shaking.

Julian had Myrtle, whose jacking strength was unlike anything I'd ever felt, plus Molloy, Ava, and Hinckley's puppeteering hands. I didn't know what Sasha could do, but he was one of Julian's mages. He had to have some special skills.

"Why do you need my help so badly?" I asked.

Julian dropped his hands from his face and spread them on the battered table. "We need a keeper to get close to Kestrel without him knowing what we're planning. Anna would have been the perfect person, but she went missing—"

"Wait," I said. "I thought you were breaking in to get your sister out. If you were planning on breaking into Kestrel's facility before that—"

"Anna's disappearance," Julian said, cutting me off, "brought a certain urgency to our plans. But we've intended for some time to finish the job you left undone, back in the camp. To liberate the rest of our brothers and sisters who are being tormented under Kestrel's needles."

I blinked. This wasn't only about rescuing his sister, which I could understand. I'd done the same thing for Laney, and she wasn't even my sister. He wasn't just after the changelings either. Julian wanted more—to *liberate* his brother and sister jackers. He was some kind of jacker revolutionary.

He took my silence for something else. "Are you now reconsidering my proposal?"

"No." Rescuing changelings was one thing. Liberating all the dangerous jackers that Kestrel had locked up wasn't worth risking my life, or anything else. I'd left people like Molloy behind in the camp for a reason.

The flash oven beeped as my dad put in a teapot. He watched as the light went on and it heated the water, as if he didn't have a care in the world. Even the tiny lines in the corners of his eyes had disappeared in Julian's artificial peace.

I clasped my hands on the table and watched them turn white at the knuckles. All the risks that I had taken were catching up to me at once. It wasn't fair for my father to fall into the mages' net, but I could see how that would have happened regardless. There was no scenario I could imagine where my dad wouldn't have come looking for me. Guilt and happiness for that fact wrestled around in my chest, causing my ribs to ache as if they were actually battling in there.

But Raf... if I had stopped seeing him when we moved, like I should have, he wouldn't be here, trapped in the mages' lair. Guilt for that stabbed my heart like a red-hot poker.

The flash oven dinged its completion and my dad dipped a teabag in the pot.

Up and down. Up and down.

I jumped up from my chair and snatched the steaming teapot from him.

"What's the matter, Kira?" my dad said. "I thought you liked tea. Maybe your friend would like some?"

"I'll do it." The hot ceramic of the teapot scorched my hand, but I grasped it tighter and grabbed a chipped cup from the cabinet, then stalked over to Julian and slammed the cup and pot down in front of him. My dad drifted over and gently placed a second cup in front of me. I shuddered and slowly sank into the seat again. I stared as Julian poured the tea into my cup.

"If you're not taking the couch," Julian said to me, "maybe your father could make Myrtle more comfortable."

"That's a good idea," my dad said. "Sorry about the dart. Not sure what came over me, shooting a little old lady like that. Least I can do is get her off the cold cement floor. That can't be good for someone her age." He hurried over to Myrtle, whose frail body was a heap of cardigan and flowered fabric on the floor.

Julian was examining my face again, like he was fascinated by it.

"What?" I asked. Was he looking for a way into my reptilian brain too?

"It's so interesting," he said. "Your brain, I mean."

I squirmed in my seat. "Well, your sister's a keeper, right? It's not that strange."

"She's not like you," Julian said. "I mean, she *is* a keeper—no one can jack through her mind barrier either. My father called her Diamond, because her head was so hard. No one could reach her, except me. But you..." He waved his hand in front of my face. "There's nothing there. It's almost like you don't exist. You're a ghost." His lips curled up, like he thought he was terribly funny.

"How do you know so much about all this?"

Julian leaned back and draped an arm over his chair. "My mother and father were both jackers. They raised me and my sister to understand precisely what we were and what we would one day become."

"Really?" No wonder Julian was so strange. Once upon a time, I had wished my dad had prepared me for being a jacker, or at least warned me that it could happen. Maybe things would have been different. Or maybe I would have turned out like Julian. "Were your parents mages like you and your sister?"

"No," he said. "They were scientists. I spent the better part of my childhood watching them do research, studying Cerebrus images of brain waves and deciphering what it meant to be a jacker. They understood what we are."

"Er, what is that, exactly?" I asked. "Besides mutants?"

"We're the next step in the evolution of mankind."

Oh boy. It was worse than I thought. Julian was a jacker revolutionary with a little crazy sprinkled on top.

"Sure," I said. "Okay. Wait, you said your parents *were* scientists. What are they now?"

"Now they are dead."

"Oh." I bit my lip, not sure what to say.

"My sister and I were sixteen when they died. Car crash." He traced the rough grain of the table with his finger. "Even jackers have accidents, I suppose."

"Wait, your sister and you were *both* sixteen?"

"We're twins." His brow crinkled. "Maybe that's the reason I can access her mind, but not yours. We have a connection—even now, I know that she's alive. I can't tell you how I know, but whatever Kestrel has done to her, he hasn't killed her yet."

I fought down the tiniest bit of sympathy welling up for Julian. "Yeah, Kestrel doesn't kill them. Not right away, at least."

Julian leaned forward, templing his hands again. "When you

rescued those changelings before," he said, "what sorts of things was he doing to them?"

"I didn't see much," I said. "They were injecting them with serums. I think Kestrel was targeting certain parts of their brains, or at least that was the result. There were... dead spots, where their brains didn't function anymore."

"It takes time, though, right? It could take a while for these injections to take effect? Anna's only been gone for a week." His shoulders drooped, like the weight of time was pulling them down. "Maybe he hasn't started with her yet."

I nodded, not sure what to say. I flat-out hated Julian for bringing me here and endangering Raf and my dad, but he hadn't hurt them, and he saved us from the pravers who wanted to sell Raf to the highest bidder. Maybe he would actually let us go in the morning. I felt genuinely bad for his sister, or any jacker in Kestrel's clutches. I understood wanting to get her out. If it weren't ridiculously dangerous, I could even see helping them.

I shook that thought out of my head and wondered if Julian had slipped into my mind after all. "You know this is demens, right?" I said. "Breaking into Kestrel's facility, trying to rescue people?"

"The plan will work just fine, little Kira," Molloy's voice rumbled behind me. He must have finally returned from dropping off Raf. "It will go right as rain, if we use you as the bait Kestrel can't resist. Only this time, you will go alone, so you don't have a chance to leave a fellow jacker bleeding in the desert."

I turned from him, refusing to acknowledge his accusation, but my mind couldn't help flying back to that time in the desert with Simon. I wasn't the one who killed him, I reminded myself. The guards did that with their high-powered rifles and their camp in the desert. Ultimately, it was Kestrel's fault for sending us there in the first place.

Molloy chuckled. "The worst that would happen would be you going into Kestrel's facility and not coming back out. Wouldn't break my heart none."

"Wow. Great plan." I hooked a thumb back at Molloy without looking at him. "Is that all you've got? The Red Giant's idea of irony?"

Julian dismissed my concern with a wave. "Don't listen to Mr. Molloy. Although you *were* the key to making sure that Kestrel wouldn't escape. You were going to be our Trojan Horse, an impenetrable fortress of the mind that would only open when you surprised him with your intent to destroy him. He wouldn't know what hit him."

I couldn't help it. I liked the sound of that.

"Now we'll simply have to find a different way to assure that Kestrel is—" A metallic screech cut him off and rent the air. The door to the factory flew off its hinges and skidded across the concrete floor. Figures in black vests and pants and gas masks lurked right outside the doorway, like a flood of SWAT team members being held back by an invisible dam. Before I could do anything but drop my mouth open, three pops burst the air and canisters trailing orangish gas sailed toward us. Julian grabbed my hand and hauled me out of my seat, half-dragging me across the carpet. The canisters crashed into the kitchen cabinets and the couch, spinning and spraying misty spirals that looped the air.

"Wait!" I reached back for my dad, linking into his mind just as a metallic butterfly buzzed the air and pierced his hooded jacket. A freezing jolt of mindjacker-tuned electricity pulsed through his mind. My body seized for a split second before my mind recoiled from his. He slumped to the floor, a statue lying inert in the gas that curled around him.

"Dad!"

I reached for the black figures beyond the door, but an unyielding barrier stopped me right at the doorway. The black figures weren't held back by it, they were *hiding* behind it—protected from my reach by a barrier that felt like granite but was completely invisible.

Julian jerked my hand. "It's too late!" He dragged me toward the back of the factory, and I stumbled, banging my leg into a metal shelf as I struggled to catch my footing.

"We need to get Raf!" I cast toward the racks of beds, but Julian yanked my arm, pulling me against him, and we both nearly tumbled to the floor. A butterfly whizzed through the empty space where I had just been.

"This way." He grasped my hand so hard it hurt, weaving us through white columns and using racks and equipment to keep the assault team from targeting us. My mind was a crazed jumble. *My dad... Raf... I can't leave them...*

A whiff of orange spice reached me, the first hint of the gas. The attackers remained behind their invisible shield, waiting. Another butterfly buzzed past my face, embedding its pointed feet into the paneling next to me and sending blue sparks skittering across the metallic surface. I sobbed as Julian hauled me toward a doorway in the crumbling brick wall. Even if I could pump the gas out of my brain to go back for Raf and my dad, the butterflies would get me.

I had no choice but to leave them behind.

chapter **EIGHT**

The street was in chaos.

Julian crushed my hand as we hovered at the edge of the alleyway. Gas canisters slammed against buildings and spun down the street, spraying an orange cloud that skulked after the fleeing jackers. People leaped up stair steps and slammed doors against the gas, sprinting for the shadowed alleys and away from the streetlights beaming spots on the sidewalks. A police van the size of a tank rolled down the street and screamed an alarm. A huddle of black-garbed, gas-masked figures with POLICE stamped on their chests led the van, their crossbow-like rifles pointed in an outward-facing half circle. One marched in the middle, no weapon, just a gas mask and a ramrod-straight step. I reached out, thinking I might be able to stop their leader, only to find he was a jacker. His head whipped to face us, and every weapon in the circle pivoted to release a flurry of butterflies. Julian's arm swept me flat against the chilled wall of the alley and the whirring butterflies narrowly missed us.

Julian dropped his arm and sagged against the gritty concrete wall. At first I thought one of the butterflies got him, but then he rubbed his eyes. The gas was affecting him, and I could feel it seeping into my own brain, although adrenaline hyped my heart and kept much of the effect at bay.

For the moment.

"We need to get inside!" I shouted over the ebb and flow of the alarm. I might be able to fight the gas in my own head, but there was no way I could jack into Julian's to control the effect of the gas on him. He wouldn't last long on the street, and I wasn't sure I would either, with these new anti-jacker weapons.

We shuffled down the trash-strewn alley, away from the approaching garrison, but the SWAT team at the opposite end was still assaulting the mages' headquarters, hiding behind their shield. I reached out but I had never had to jack *around* anything before, and now wasn't the time to figure the shield out. I might get a taser shock for my trouble.

Julian found a slim center alleyway that cut between the streets, with brownstones on one side and the rear entrances to businesses on the other. The blare of the police siren stepped down a notch as we dashed into the darkened canyon between the buildings, lit only by the spots of light spilling from the windows above. Our footsteps echoed off the dumpsters and weathered brick walls, and Julian kept stumbling over the broken pavement hidden in the shadows. He needed to get out of the gas soon or the police would find him passed out next to a trash bin.

My heart shredded with every step we took away from my dad and Raf.

We reached a street that was clear, sprinted across it, and darted down another alley. Julian threaded us between businesses, finding tiny, jagged passageways that bypassed the streets. Jackertown was a maze of brick and concrete buildings held together by a web of side alleys jumbled with decades of debris. We dodged couches with ripped cushions, rusty cans of paint hazardously stacked, and abandoned bicycles missing tires and seats. The labyrinth was dotted with teetering fortresses of trash, as if the demens had carved cubbyholes into the city. Their homes were built from overturned benches fortified by crates and stuffed with blankets, as well as the occasional discarded boost canister of hydrogen for cars that had long since fled the city. Now the demens had left as well, run out by the jackers moving in.

Finally, Julian stopped at the side of a three-story brownstone and smashed a red button on the concrete wall. A metal fire-escape ladder unfurled from the top floor, and Julian fumbled to grab hold of the rungs and scale it. I held the ladder to keep it from whipping around and followed him up. After only one story, I felt the effects of the gas lessen. Julian climbed onto a narrow, wrought-iron balcony on the third floor and pounded the glass door that beamed light from inside. A young boy came running and mentally activated it to slide open, and I recognized him as the older changeling who had "rescued" Raf and me from the streets.

Once inside with the windows and doors closed, there was almost no trace of the gas. Julian quickly became alert, and the boy and I trailed after him as he took the stairs two at a time down to the main floor. Two changelings—the younger boy from before and a girl—stood in the wallpapered sitting room, haunting the edges near the windows. We must have made it back to Myrtle's, only I hadn't recognized it from the back. The faint smell of lilacs had been replaced by a trace of orange from the gas. The rail-thin girl, who was probably less than twelve, pulled back the lace-covered curtains to peek out.

"Don't, Olivia!" Julian said. Olivia jumped as if she had been shocked. He gentled his tone. "We don't want to give them any reason to come looking in here."

"Are they coming for you, Julian?" she asked.

"Maybe." He gave her a smile. "But they haven't caught me yet."

She beamed a row of perfect white teeth. Julian turned to the older boy who let us in and placed a hand on his shoulder. "Joshua, what about the other cells? Have they checked in?"

Joshua shoved his hands into his weathered jeans. "Just Sherman and Ming."

"That's all?" Julian stumbled to one of Myrtle's over-upholstered chairs. "They got Myrtle for sure, and Ava," he mumbled. "Sasha wouldn't leave, so probably him, too. Maybe Hinckley got out." He looked up at Joshua, whose face had drawn down at the mention of Myrtle. "The police—did they come here first, or do you think they were targeting us?"

By "us" I was pretty sure he meant the mages.

"They came rolling through the street a little while ago." Joshua jabbed a thumb toward the covered window. "The police weren't shooting, but most people ran inside anyway. The gas canisters just started flying a minute ago."

Julian ran a hand along his face. "So they *were* targeting us." His eyes narrowed at me. "Or maybe they were looking for you."

I took a step back. "How would they even know I was here?"

Julian pushed up from his chair and came at me quickly, forcing me back against the stair railing and nearly making me trip over the steps. If the intensity of his glare alone would let him slip into my mind, I would have already lost my instincts and started making tea. I stood on the bottom step and held my ground, almost eye to eye with him now. After all, he had dragged me into this mess. Whatever came out of it certainly wasn't my fault.

His unnerving blue eyes stared into mine. "Maybe your father wasn't so stupid after all."

I drew back from his accusation. Could my dad have brought the police raining down on Jackertown? I knew Mr. Trullite was a powerful man, but could he command a police raid? Just for me, his sometime mindguard?

"My dad *isn't* stupid," I said. "He was only trying to get me out of here. He knew the danger of me being in Jackertown—more than you, apparently."

Julian released me from his stare, rubbing the scruff on his cheeks like he couldn't decide what to think of me. The alarm outside cut off, leaving an eerie silence behind, as if the air was hollow. Empty of life. Olivia pulled back the curtain again, unable to resist. The sliver of street outside was deserted.

Julian joined her at the window in the sitting room, peering outside. "Maybe this isn't targeted to the mages." He let the curtain fall back, then held his chin with his hand. "Maybe this is simply the government cracking down on jackers doing trade and business out of Jackertown. Trying to intimidate us, show us that we're not invulnerable." His gaze fell on Joshua. "I need to know who's missing."

Joshua gently elbowed the younger boy next to him. "Dimitri and I can get on the short comms. Make contact with the other cells, see what they know."

Julian nodded. I shifted away from the stairs, out of the path of the boys pattering by. Olivia chased after them. Julian focused on the wall screen at the far end of the room, near the kitchen door. I edged into the sitting room to see animated ninjas somersaulting over each other on the screen. Julian paged through the sim-casts and brought up a local tru-cast program. He must have some linking ability, if he could control the mindware interface of the screen. Could he link, but not jack? Figuring out Julian took a back seat as the tru-cast reporter on the screen started to interview Senator Vellus.

It must have been a previous interview, because it was daytime. They were standing in front of a gray concrete building that looked like cubes on top of cubes, stacked in a squarish and severe manner. The most frightening part, of course, was the barbed razor wire that topped the wall surrounding it, just in case someone thought of climbing over.

Words from their captured thought waves scrolled across the bottom of the screen.

Senator Vellus, can you tell us about the features of your newly finished jacker Detention Center? She held a palm up to the structures behind them. *I'm sure it would be reassuring to people everywhere, especially the neighbors of the Center, to know that it is truly secure.*

Well, I would love to tell you all about the innovative technology we've implemented at the Detention Center. Senator Vellus's smile was a bright light against the gray backdrop. *But that would undermine our security systems. Let me assure you, this facility is secure, and its location was carefully chosen within the city limits, well away from any populated areas.*

By "populated" you mean the regular mindreading population, isn't that right, Senator?

Exactly. Senator Vellus nodded. *The Detention Center is buffered by a large abandoned section of the city that doesn't meet range codes and is generally only populated by individuals suffering from Teledementia.*

And it's not far from the no-readers land known as Jackertown, the reporter added.

That is true. The Senator's face became grave. *The legislators and I revere our Constitutional laws and cherish the protections it provides. But the mindreading population needs to be protected from these mindjacking individuals, much like we strive to keep ordinary citizens safe from Teledementia patients by housing them in demens wards when they are deemed violent. Which is why the Illinois Legislature decided just this morning to create a new rights classification for mindjackers. It's not their fault that they have a tendency toward violence. It's quite literally in their DNA to control people's minds and it's natural for them use that power. The new Vellus Detention Center will provide a safe place to house these individuals when they commit crimes.*

Senator, how will the police handle arresting mindjacking criminals in the first place? asked the reporter. *Isn't it true that mindjackers can erase your memory, make you forget that a crime even occurred?*

Yes, which is what makes it so difficult to prove when someone has been jacked, thought Vellus, *much less arrest the mindjacker. This is why we have begun arming the police in the city with the latest anti-jacker technology. There are also special judicial chambers inside the Detention Center that will keep mindjackers under control during trial proceedings. The Detention Center also provides—*

Julian let out a growl and the screen went blank at his mental command.

"DNA." He was grinding his fist into the palm of his hand, like he wanted to use it on Vellus's face. "I knew it would come to that sooner or later." He took a breath and let it out slow, dropping his hands. "I think sooner is here. Vellus has found a place to keep us. Now, it's only a matter of rounding up jackers and locking us up."

"He can't put people in there just for being jackers! It's only for people who have committed crimes, right?"

Julian slowly turned to face me. "What crimes? The crime of using your jacking abilities? Of being who you are? Didn't you hear him? It's in our DNA to be violent, to commit crimes which are very difficult to prove even happened. Once you're in Vellus's Detention Center, I'm sure they will invent some unprovable act that you've committed, just to make sure you stay 'housed.'"

I cringed. Of course the government had no problem doing exactly that when they created the desert camp where they kept thousands of jackers prisoner without even the charade of a trial. But that was secret. People didn't know about it. How could anyone stand for this to happen in broad daylight, down the street?

Julian saw the wavering on my face. "Yes, that's where it's headed, keeper. Don't forget it. We have to fight it now, before it gets worse. Before people think that jackers are a subspecies, because we're not. It may take a generation or two, like it did with readers, but eventually everyone will be a jacker. It's the next evolution from mindreading and they can't fight it. Until we become the dominant force, we can't let them put us on the gas and keep us rotting away in prisons. If we let that become acceptable, it will be only a matter of time before someone like Kestrel becomes a hero, rather than having to hide under a rock. Eliminating us will be the next logical step."

That thought pulsed a chill through me, followed by another realization. "Wait, what are they going to do with the jackers they rounded up today?" My breath caught. My dad was almost certainly captured when I left him behind. Would they take him to the Detention Center? Or would he have a one-way ticket to Kestrel's secret facility?

"What do you think?" Julian's voice was low and dangerous. "Vellus has no plans to let them go, regardless of whatever crimes they may or may not have committed. He's proving the necessity of his detention center by filling it with jackers."

"But my dad—"

"Is just another jacker to them."

"But... what about Raf? He's not even a jacker!"

"Who knows what the gas does to readers?" He swept his hand out to the streets outside Myrtle's brownstone. "This isn't a sim-cast, keeper. I very much doubt Vellus cares who gets caught in his sweep. Your pet is simply collateral damage to them."

The room started to tilt. *Raf... in a jail... filled with jackers.* My knees went soft and I had to brace myself on the smooth wallpapered wall of the sitting room. "We have to get them out." The words leaked out of me on a wisp of breath.

Julian cocked his head. "Ah, so *now* you're starting to think like a mage? Well done! Glad to finally have you with us." His voice lost the sarcasm and got serious. "Yes, we need to get them out. I'd prefer to get everyone out, but we at least need to get out Sasha and Myrtle, and Hinckley too, if our mission with Kestrel is going to succeed."

Kestrel? He was the last thing on my mind. "What about my dad and Raf? We have to get them out too!"

"So you're with me, then?" He arched an eyebrow. "You're not planning on running back to the suburbs to serve pie?"

I ignored his jibe and pushed off the wall to stand up straight. "I guess that depends." I took two strides to bring me close enough to glare up into his face. "Do you have a better plan for getting them out of the Detention Center than you had for breaking into Kestrel's facility?"

Instead of answering, he dropped his voice and edged even closer. "You're part of this, keeper. Help us fight this, and jackers here will understand who you are. That you're meant to lead them." His voice was nearly a whisper now. "You belong here. Tell me you see that now."

I stepped back again. "The last place I belong is here!" There was no way I was meant to lead jackers anywhere. I pictured my dad and Raf, gassed and on their way to the Vellus Detention Center. "All I want is to get my dad and Raf back. That's it. You'll have to fight your revolution on your own."

Julian's face fell, then he gave me that examining look again. I wished he would stop doing that. It felt like he was trying to creep into my reptilian brain.

Finally, he nodded. "Of course. You must protect your family first."

"I'm glad we got that straight."

Joshua, Dimitri, and Olivia clattered down the stairs behind us, breathless with their news. "We checked with all the cells!" Olivia rushed out.

Dimitri jumped in, his face lit up. "Hinckley made it to Jackson's cell!"

"Any other mages check in?" Julian asked.

"No one's seen Myrtle," Joshua said, his voice tight. "Or Sasha or Ava. And there's no answer from Yee or Mary."

"Mary? Hers wasn't even an acknowledged mage cell yet." Julian frowned. "Maybe they weren't targeting the mages after all and it was just a general crackdown. How many are missing altogether?"

"We don't know." Joshua stared at his shoes, ragged black canvas sneakers that looked like he'd outgrown them months ago. "Everybody's kind of... upset. They're not really sure who's missing, but everyone says the police have left."

"It's okay, Josh." Julian gave him a grim smile. "You did a fine job." He stepped past me to the front door and peered through the chiseled glass portal. "It looks like the mist has dissipated. People are returning to the streets."

Olivia crept up next to him and peeked out. "What are you going to tell them, Julian?"

Julian's smile warmed as he looked down at her. "That everything's going to be all right." He turned the knob and stepped through the doorway. The changelings followed close on his heels, as if they weren't flooding out into the dangerous streets of Jackertown at night.

Outside, it looked like the aftermath of a war. Jacker bodies littered the sidewalks and steps, their arms twisted at crooked angles, probably felled by butterflies as they ran. Other jackers were attending to them. Or possibly picking their pockets.

A few jackers left the sidewalks to wander into the street. They didn't gather in clusters like before. They weren't wary-eyed crews, just disjointed stragglers creeping out from wherever they had found cover. The scent of the gas lingered, creating a halo around the plasma lamps that cast everything in an eerie blue light. The skyscrapers of downtown glittered in the distance, a remote island of normalcy against the cold reality of the police raid that had rolled through the street.

Julian stood at the edge of Myrtle's landing, Joshua at his right and Dimitri and Olivia perched on the steps below him. He surveyed the wreckage in the street, towering over it, then raised both hands as if he were embracing it.

"Friends." Julian's voice bounced off the storefronts across the street, carrying over the stunned silence of the street. "Senator Vellus has decided we need a new home. He's built a complex just for us, complete with gas and barbed wire." A murmur rippled through the air. More jackers flowed from their hiding places behind doors and up fire escapes, filling the street with shambling bodies and loose groupings as crews found one another.

"He's already taken some of us there." The crowd stilled, listening. There were a few curses, but mostly silence as that information sank in. Was Julian using his ability to affect them? His words alone felt like a stone on my chest.

"They have their gas and their tasers and their shields, but they don't have *us*," he said. "They can't own our hearts and minds, unless we let them. *We* are the more powerful ones here, friends. *We* are what humanity will someday become. The Senator Velluses of the world cannot stop us any more than they can stop a bullet once it is fired."

Every face was focused on him.

"I promise you, this act of violence is only the beginning. But not the kind Senator Vellus imagines. It is *our* beginning. The beginning of a future where we don't hide who we are, or cower in the dark, or run from gas and butterflies. A future where you will have the lives you deserve."

Was it only the power of his words that lit their faces with hope? Or was he slipping into their minds to stir their instincts? I couldn't be sure, but Julian's words vibrated through me as I hovered in the doorway.

"A few have fallen today, but we cannot let them pick us off one at a time, like sheep. We cannot afford to be divided by crews or clans any longer. If we come together, if we work together, the readers and their police will have no chance against us."

There were murmurs of agreement. Anger pulsed like a live thing through the air. I took a half step back and gripped the peeling wood of the doorframe. I couldn't decide if the crowd's response was alarming or exciting. My body hummed from the energy of the group outside, but Julian's words also set my nerves on edge.

"Go back to your crews," Julian said. "Report your missing to one of the mage cells. No matter where you come from, we are all one crew today. I promise you..." He paused. "I promise you, we will get our loved ones back."

Someone gave a cheer that was echoed by several others. Julian raised a hand to the crowd, then turned back to me. An audible chatter swelled up from the jackers milling in the street behind him.

Julian's face was lit with the same hope and fire and anger of the crowd.

"That's a lot of promises," I said from the doorway. Julian's idea that someday jackers could have normal lives, not having to hide or be afraid, made me want to cheer, just like the crowd. But the thought of all those jackers working together also terrified me. They weren't all as altruistic as Julian, or even most of them. Fear already ran rampant through mindreaders' heads, and that was with most jackers still rooking as readers so we could have normal lives. How much worse would it be if jackers banded together, pumped up by Julian's revolutionary talk? How much easier would that make it for people like Vellus to lock us up?

I backed up, making room for Julian to step into the entryway. The changelings gathered around him, drawn like magnets, and I let the door slowly close on the scene outside.

"What can we do?" Olivia asked.

"We want to help!" Dimitri said. They were falling all over themselves to sign up for whatever revolution he had planned.

"What should we do, Julian?" Joshua asked. I shook my

head slowly and hoped Julian wasn't planning on including the changelings in whatever scheme he was cooking up. He caught my disapproving look and gave me a wry smile, then turned back to the changelings.

"I need you to be my contractors," he said, conspiratorially, as if this were all a game. "Can you find your masks and run between the cells? Gather up pictures of the missing jackers and bring them back so we'll know who needs to be released from the Detention Center."

All three sprinted up the stairs, no doubt to get their "contractor" costumes.

"Are we only rescuing people on the approved list?" I asked, a little surprised by how sarcastic I sounded.

Julian's face lost its humor. "I'm not leaving anyone in there, if I can help it."

I took a deep breath, not sure how we would get anyone out. But I had no doubt that Julian meant what he said, and that included getting my dad and Raf out. "So what's your plan?"

He leaned against the hallway doorframe. "I thought you had the plan."

"What?" I pointed at the closed front door. "All that, and you've got no plan?"

"I wouldn't say that." He smirked. "Vellus's new Detention Center likely has all the latest anti-jacker technology built into it, and it's probably even harder to break into than it is to break out of. But I'm sure there's a weakness. We just have to find it."

I had a whole lot less confidence we could find a way into the Detention Center, much less out. I edged into the sitting room and mentally flipped the tru-cast on again, making it rewind to the program where the tru-caster was interviewing Senator Vellus. Ignoring the scrolling words at the bottom, Julian and I stepped closer to examine the structure of the building itself.

"Look there." I froze the shot while it panned the Center. "It looks like a guard station." In front of the twelve-foot-high concrete wall sat a smaller concrete box with a guard. It was stationed next to heavy metallic doors that looked like they could sustain a blast from a ton of explosives.

"He must be behind an anti-jacker field," Julian said. "Otherwise any jacker could stroll in. Vellus isn't stupid. He wouldn't leave so obvious a flaw in a detention center carrying his name."

"You mean an anti-jacker field like what they hid behind back at the factory?" I asked. "Fantastic. That will make things easy."

Julian ignored my sarcasm. "I've seen a shield like that before, but only on a building. It repulses a jacker's mental reach, so it must be tuned to jackers the way the butterflies are. Maybe it operates on a frequency that interferes with our mind-field. They would need something like that at the Detention Center to prevent us from jacking the guards to get in, even if all the jackers inside were under sedation. It's unlikely we will be able to simply walk in."

"Do you know of a way to defeat the shield?"

"Not from the outside," said Julian. "The shield is relatively new technology. I've got some people working on the concept, but we haven't captured one to reverse engineer it. The shield probably requires a major power source, and I thought it had to be physically attached to a structure to anchor the field, but it had to be portable to bring it into Jackertown and set it up outside our door."

I didn't know where Julian got all his fancy technology, but apparently he had "people" working on it. Since the world discovered we existed—since I told the world we existed—the government and private industry both had been spending billions in research to develop anti-jacker technology. The government was ahead, probably because they already knew jackers existed.

"The shield technology can't be too portable," I said. "Otherwise, the rifle squad that shot butterflies at us would have been shielded."

He nodded. "To my knowledge, they haven't developed any personal anti-jacker technology yet. But it's coming."

Julian was right about that. It was only a matter of time before personal protection fields were developed. Readers were clamoring for it. Whoever invented one would make a zillion unos, since everyone would want one.

"So we can't get through the shield," I said.

"Short of bombing the front gate? No." He stroked his cheek. "Although that has merit in showmanship. Still, I'd rather not start a full-scale war at the moment. Not while my sister is wasting away in Kestrel's lair."

"It makes sense that they would expect jackers to break in,"

I said. "But what about a reader who was jacked to sneak in and turn off the power to the shield from the inside?"

"Anyone we jack won't make it past the gate without the jack being cut off."

"What if they were jacked with a longer-term command?" I asked. "The jack might hold until they were inside."

"Perhaps," he said. "But once in, their thoughts would be clear to everyone. I doubt they would get far enough to cut the power or disable the shield without the other readers realizing what they were doing. The only way the staff won't hear their true thoughts is if the person walking in is a jacker."

"So we're stuck."

Julian crossed his arms, examining the screen. "With their anti-jacker technology, they probably think they're impervious to a jacker assault. They won't expect readers to work willingly with us. With the proper ID from a respected reader, they shouldn't suspect us. We might be able to get in with that."

"A respected reader?" I asked. "You have one of those handy?" My thoughts flitted to Mr. Trullite, but I wasn't sure if I could call on him again. Or should. Maybe he had ordered the raid in the first place.

"Not at the moment."

A snippet that had scrolled by earlier on the tru-cast jogged my brain. I knew a respected reader, one who I trusted quite literally with my life. I flicked the tru-cast to roll again and the words scrolled along the bottom. *Senator Vellus will be holding a press conference tomorrow morning, where he promises to demonstrate a few of the security measures that will make his detention center the envy of other major cities around the U.S.*

I flicked the mindware to pause the tru-cast midstream.

"That," I said, pointing to the words, "could be our ticket inside."

chapter NINE

I figured Maria would be up late—she was always working a story for the *Chicago Tribune*—but I was surprised she was the breaking tru-cast reporter for the roundup in Jackertown. I knew there was a reason I loved her.

"Are you okay, Kira?" The worry in her voice quickly morphed into anger. "And what the hell are you doing in Jackertown?"

I held the phone slightly away from my ear. The *Mindjackers Among Us* story had propelled Maria to journalistic super-stardom—she would be on a national tru-cast by now if people didn't suspect her of being too friendly with jackers—but I knew she also felt responsible for the fallout my family endured.

I brought the phone back. "I didn't plan on being here." Which made me think I should have made better plans. If we had moved farther away, my dad and I wouldn't have been able to work for Mr. Trullite, but maybe Molloy wouldn't have found us either. Julian leaned against the entryway doorframe, listening to our conversation with high interest.

"I wouldn't bother you, Maria, if I didn't really need your help. My dad and Raf got caught up in the sweep. I think they're on their way to Vellus's new detention center." I cleared my throat to cover the cracking of my voice. "I need to get them out, Maria. Raf won't last five seconds in there."

"Raf's in the Detention Center?" Her voice hiked up. "How can that happen? He's not a—"

"They're not exactly asking questions before they start shooting."

"Which is why this kind of thing is completely illegal!" Her voice dripped acid from the phone, and I heard her fingers drumming the desk. I wondered how many other reporters were working late to be disturbed by our spoken conversation. A wave of fatigue pulled on my eyelids.

The drumming stopped. "Well, I can lead with that in my tru-cast tonight. Make the accusation that a regular mindreader was caught up in the sweep. Vellus might be embarrassed enough to let Raf out, and they can't hold your dad either without charges. This is still a free country!"

Not so much for jackers, I thought, but I didn't want to say that in front of Julian. Might give him ideas about me joining his revolution.

Maria was just getting warmed up. "I would love to prove that Vellus had wrongfully locked up innocent people—"

"Actually, I had a different idea," I broke in, before she got too far.

"What's that?"

"Vellus is holding a press conference tomorrow at the Detention Center. I figured you would be going, and that you might need a couple of assistants."

There was a moment of silence.

"Well," Maria said slowly. "I'm not attending the press conference tomorrow." Another pause. "But I am hosting an exclusive interview with Vellus in the morning here at the Tribune Tower."

"You'll have Vellus in your office?" My voice rose. Could we just jack Vellus to release the prisoners? Julian pushed off the doorframe and strode over to listen in. I held the phone slightly away from my ear so that he could hear Maria's voice.

"Yes," she said slowly. "I can make the case to Vellus that he's made a terrible mistake. Arrested the wrong people." She paused again. "Maybe even give him a list of people who should be released. It will all be live on the tru-cast."

"Maria, you're completely mesh, you know that?"

"I'm only going to try to convince him with the facts and the law," she said. "You're just going to be there as an assistant, to observe. Right?"

"Right." I was sure Maria knew I planned on jacking Vellus, but we had to pretend that I wasn't, so she wouldn't have it on her mind and give us away. "There's just one thing." I peeked at Julian, his face still close. "You're going to need two assistants."

There was a substantially longer pause this time. "Who's the other one?"

"Another jacker." I wasn't quite sure how to describe Julian.

Friend? No. Hostage taker? Well, that wasn't exactly accurate. Charismatic leader of the Jacker Rebellion Movement? "He has some skills that might help me... observe."

Julian nodded in approval of my discretion. Which only made me feel sick inside.

"Come to the Trib Tower tomorrow morning at nine thirty," she said. "I'll have press credentials for both of you."

"Maria, you're the best." I hung up. The changelings had crept back down the stairs in their black "contractor" masks. Olivia and Dimitri were sitting on the bottom steps with Joshua standing next to the railing, all listening to my conversation.

Julian leaned away and beamed. "You certainly have a way of making things happen, keeper."

"Yeah, well, I don't know." I couldn't help a yawn breaking through. "How are we going to jack Vellus without anyone realizing what we're doing?"

"We can make plans in the morning," Julian said. "You look like you need some rest." He waved the changelings from the steps, and Joshua hustled them out the door, off on their mission to gather up pictures of the missing jackers. Julian tipped his head toward the stairs, beckoning me to follow. My legs dragged like fifty-pound weights were attached to my ankles. I yawned again. At the top of the stairs, Julian turned into a bedroom that wafted a scent of lilacs even stronger than the rest of the house. Tightly patterned flowery wallpaper covered every surface, including the ceiling. It peeled at the seams and warped in the middle, like it was a hundred years old. Brownstones like

Myrtle's were too expensive to rehab, so they were abandoned, left to the demens. And now the jackers.

Julian pointed to a four-poster bed heaped with pillows and a puffy pink comforter that matched the dizzying wallpaper. "You can rest here in Myrtle's room. There are clothes in the closet—I don't think your current disguise is the best for impersonating an intrepid young tru-cast reporter."

My Dutch Apple apron was marred with dirt from our run through Jackertown, and a purple bruise stained my shin. Scratches ran along my legs, left bare below my shorts. Julian was probably right about needing new clothes.

He closed the door on his way out. I kicked off my running shoes and sank deep into the silky soft comforter. All the aches drained from my muscles, and my eyelids tugged themselves shut.

~*~

The next morning, Julian watched me while I stuffed a muffin in my mouth. He was stifling a laugh with his hand, but I didn't care. I hadn't eaten since well before my shift with Mr. Trullite, which seemed like a week ago, but was only yesterday around lunchtime. I swept the crumbs off the wooden kitchen table, worn smooth by a thousand uses, and searched for a trash bowl to flush them away. I couldn't find one, so I dumped them in the sink. Olivia peeked in from the sitting room, watching me with wide eyes and making me wince. Here I was, taking their food.

"Have the changelings eaten?" I asked Julian.

Olivia disappeared before he could twist around. "I'm sure they can take care of themselves," he said. "You, on the other hand, apparently need help dressing yourself."

I'd picked the least grandma-like outfit in the closet. My running shoes didn't exactly go with the black stretch pants that only reached halfway down my calves, but whatever. They were reasonably normal compared to the pink ruffle-collared blouse that made me look like a poodle. It wasn't a shining moment, but my regular clothes wouldn't work.

"I didn't have much to choose from," I said. "I swear Myrtle is a midget."

Julian chuckled. The clothes would do. I was more worried about being recognized—especially standing next to Maria—so I had changed my hair color again. Jackertown was short on amenities, and coming up with a decent nano-color had been impossible, so I'd had to settle for a cheap bleach. My hair was now a brilliant shade of blond and the rough treatment had left the short strands sticking straight out. My transformation into a poodle was nearly complete, but it should distract anyone from looking too closely at my face.

Hunger drove me to keep searching the cabinets. "So, won't it be obvious if I jack Vellus? Won't his jacked thoughts echo on the boom mics? Someone's sure to notice that on the tru-cast recordings, even if I jack everyone in the room to ignore it." I found a bag of homemade brownies, inhaled the mouthwatering chocolate scent, hesitated, then put it back on the shelf.

"Which is why you won't be jacking him," Julian said.

"You're handling him instead?" When Julian was in my dad's head, I couldn't tell he was being jacked at all, except that he had instantly lost the desire to whisk me away from Julian's hideout. Having Julian handle Vellus wasn't a bad plan.

"It should be undetectable," Julian said. "Especially if I don't have to handle him too much. Depends how strong his anti-jacker views are. If it's simply political posturing, I can handle him from farther away. But if his campaign to lock us up is coming from a deep-seated fear or hatred, I might have to get closer." He leaned back in his chair. "Hinckley can help us at the Detention Center once the prisoners are released, but I truly wish we had Sasha with us. It's a tragedy to have an opportunity like this and not have him here to help."

"Why? What can he do?" I kept searching the cabinets and hit the mother lode with a pantry shelf filled with cans and boxes.

"Sasha is a scribe." As if that explained anything.

"Which is?" I pulled a box of wheat crackers from the pantry and rejoined Julian at the table.

His face grew serious. "A scribe completely rewrites a person's mind."

"Every jacker knows how to wipe memories," I said around the crackers in my mouth.

"A scribe doesn't wipe memories," he said. "They rewrite the entire brain—memories, stored knowledge, learned behavior. There are a lot of things that we think are intuitive, like how to walk, that are actually learned behaviors tucked in the recesses of our brains."

I thought about my complete inability to park in tight spaces—clearly a learned ability I hadn't quite mastered. "Still, isn't that just a really big memory wipe?" I asked. "I mean, if I had enough time, I could probably wipe all your memories."

He cocked an eyebrow at me, watching me stuff in more crackers.

"Ok, maybe not *your* memories," I said. "What is the deal with your head, anyway? Why the horror show? And won't that be a problem when we're at the Trib Tower?"

"It won't be a problem." He dismissed my question with a wave. I wanted to ask Julian more about how his strange brain worked, but he kept talking. "Sasha's scribing is much more complete than a memory wipe. Everything is gone, right down to key things like personality. It's like reformatting the storage banks of the brain." Even Julian looked chilled by the idea, but it sent shivers right down to my toes. "All you are is what you have learned, from the time you start to crawl until the news you saw last night. A scribe takes that away." He snapped his fingers. "Like that, you're a different person."

The shivers worked their way back up and raised the hairs on the back of my neck so they were sticking out like the rest. "And Sasha does this?"

"Yes." Julian's soft face grew sharp, bringing out edges I hadn't noticed before. "It's a very powerful weapon. One I don't use lightly, but it would be incredibly useful if we could use it on someone like Vellus. And I think Kestrel is especially deserving of it, don't you?"

I couldn't argue with that, although it seemed less cruel to just kill him. If you killed someone, that made you a murderer... unless it was in self-defense. But this scribing thing? What did that make you? If you erased someone's being, what was the right name for that?

I thought of Sasha's dark, empty eyes, and the crackers ran dry in my mouth. I slid the box away and swallowed down the last chalky bits. "Well, it's just going to be me and you in there. If you can handle Vellus into releasing the prisoners, great. But what if he has mindguard security? Or do you think the most famous anti-jacker politician in the country won't use mindguards?"

"No, you're probably right," Julian said. "He'll have mind-guard security, but they won't be able to defend themselves against my handling, and they can't jack into your mind. It will be easy for you to keep them under control once I've reduced their instinct to defend themselves." He captured me with his glacier-blue eyes. "We make quite a team, you know."

I ignored his soft tone. I wasn't part of any "team" with him, except for this one time. "So, our plan is to get in, handle Vellus to release the prisoners, and then leave?"

"With any luck, we'll have everyone out in time for lunch." He smirked, like this was a game he was looking forward to playing, then glanced at the time on the wall screen. "Are you ready?"

I left the crackers sitting on the kitchen table, hoping Olivia might eat them when she showed again.

chapter TEN

Julian managed to hail an autocab with his phone, even
though Raf and I hadn't found one for miles the day before. He seemed to have technology and resources that reached
everywhere. The autocab dropped us downtown at the Trib
Tower, its ornate limestone blocks glinting above us in the early
morning light. The last time I was in Maria's office, I'd had to
leave by hydrocopter off the roof to avoid the protesters beating
on the revolving doors of the lobby. Today there was no one,
only a few businessmen fighting a gusty warm breeze off the
Chicago River.

I could reach the entire Trib Tower building and jack any
reader inside, but I wasn't sure how far Julian could reach.
"Maybe you can handle Vellus from here, out on the street,"
I whispered with my head bent close to Julian. We had to be
careful that no one saw us talking, and I wasn't about to link into
Julian's mind again.

"Unless they're holding the press conference in the lobby,

it's too far for me to handle him from here." Which I guessed meant Julian's range wasn't any farther than a normal jacker's. He went back to checking his phone, sending another scrit to Hinckley, who was stationed outside the Detention Center.

Maybe Julian and I could stay to the back of Maria's office, within range for him, but out of sight so no one would recognize my face. When I was camped out there with the changelings, waiting for their parents to claim them, the cast room seemed to take up the entire floor.

"We can't link into Maria's head to talk, you know," I said. Julian kept his attention on Hinckley's scrits. "It will just give us away if she knows too much of what's going on."

"Agreed." He peeked at me through his lashes. "Maybe we should have secret signals. One wink means jack, two winks means don't jack."

I wrinkled my nose. There was no part of this that was funny.

"Or," he said, "you could simply scrit me your thoughts, if you have an urgent need to share them." He returned his attention to the phone.

"What if Vellus brings a whole squad of mindguards?" When my dad came into the mages' converted factory, Julian seemed distracted into losing his grip on Molloy. Maybe. "Are you sure you can manage that?"

"I can manage it." He didn't look up.

"What about when they realize we're jackers? What are you going to do? Give everyone a sudden urge to fulfill the mating instinct?"

He finally peered up, looking affronted, which would have been funny if I wasn't dead serious. My dad and Raf could be locked up in Vellus's prison, and this was my one chance to get them out.

"If things get out of control, I'm pretty sure I could induce a riot." His shoulders stiffened. "In any event, the mindguards won't know *I'm* a jacker, although I'm sure *you'll* be hard to miss. But it won't matter. I'll handle any panic out of them; you take care of the jacking part. Just keep calm, and it will be fine. How about you earn your keep in this operation by doing some reconnaissance?"

I must have touched a nerve.

I shook my head and reached into the lobby. The guard was simply a mindreader, and we hadn't caught his notice yet. I mentally pushed past the lobby to the cast station, where a crew was prepping for the interview with Vellus. They were all mindreaders intent on getting the lighting set and the cameras ready, so that must be where we would do the interview, instead of Maria's office like I had thought. I flitted across the ten floors up to Maria's office: nothing but readers, mostly reporters working the Saturday tru-cast. No sign of any jackers: mindguards, rooks, or otherwise. On the tenth floor, I searched but couldn't find Maria. I had a small panic moment until I pulled back and scanned the elevators and found her whizzing to the ground floor.

"There are no jackers inside," I said, "but Maria's almost here. We should go in."

Julian pocketed his phone, and we pushed through the revolving doors, automatically linking into the security guard's mind and rooking as mindreading junior reporters. At least, I linked in. I couldn't detect Julian's presence in the guard's mind. I glanced at Julian, but he was focused on the elevators, which had just slid open.

Maria stepped out in her heels and black tailored suit, camera ready and clutching a scribepad. Her bright red shoes clicked across the marbled lobby floor. She passed through the weapons detector, eyes darting over Julian and then settling on me, with a skeptical look for the hair and tattoo. Talking out loud with her was out of the question, so I linked into her mind. Her normal mind-scent hinted of freshly cut apples, but today a sour nervousness was laced through it. There was no trace of Julian.

Hello, Katelyn. She concentrated on my name as her thoughts broadcast to the guard. He didn't look up. She handed me a thin, filmy badge. *Don't lose this.* The words *Katelyn O'Hara PRESS* were stamped across an official *Chicago Tribune* logo. It was an ionic patch that would adhere once pressed, so I smoothed it onto my poodle-like blouse.

Julian gave a slight bow of his head. *It's a pleasure to meet you, Ms. Lopez,* I heard faintly through Maria's thoughts. He must have linked strongly enough, just short of jacking, that I was able to hear his linked thoughts. How could he be in her mind at all without me sensing him? Julian was a puzzle that was hurting my brain.

Glad you could join us, Michael. She didn't have to con-
centrate on his name as much. For all she knew, Julian's name
was Michael. *You come highly recommended from your junior
reporting at the* Morning Star. She smoothed a badge across his
collared shirt that had *Michael Madigan PRESS* stamped over
the logo of the *Morning Star.*

Thank you, Julian thought with a smile. *I'm hoping to get a
promotion soon.*

I resisted rolling my eyes.

Once Vellus arrives, Maria thought, *I'll let him get settled in
before I pound him with questions. Do you have a list of people
who have been detained without due process?*

That must be the angle Maria was going for.

Yes. Julian pulled out his phone. *Our research shows there
are a dozen jackers as well as one reader who were illegally
arrested in the sweep. I can cast it to you, if you'd like.*

Maria tapped her scribepad and accepted the list Julian
cast from his phone. She briefly looked over it, then closed it.
Probably didn't want to linger on the names there. *Rafael Lobos
Santos. Patrick Moore.* My throat was closing up, so I tried not
to think of them too.

I have several pointed questions planned for Vellus, Maria
thought. *I've even arranged for a Truth Magistrate to verify
Vellus's answers. Hopefully that will put pressure on him to
release the prisoners who have been detained unlawfully. I
expect you two to observe, take notes, whatever. You need to
take care of yourselves. Understood?*

She meant that she didn't want to know anything about our plans. It would be no small feat for Maria to grill Vellus without giving us away—or herself as a jacker collaborator—with the live boom mics picking up her thoughts. She didn't need our plans literally on her mind.

I smiled, appreciative of the risk she was taking for us. *Understood.*

She turned on her spiked heel and stalked back toward the weapons detector. Julian and I hurriedly followed. The guard looked up and Maria waved to him.

Just bringing my two young assistants back for the big interview, George, Maria thought.

Sure thing, Ms. Lopez. The guard's face broke into a smile, and he didn't bother to get up to check our credentials. I kept my eyes forward on Maria, hoping George wouldn't recognize me. Maria breezed through the detector, past the elevators, and toward the large glass double doors of the tru-cast station. In curling ink-black letters, the words *Chicago Tribune New Metro Division* were etched into the glass. The doors slid open at Maria's mental command and her heels muted as she stepped onto the soft, sound-absorbent carpeting of the cast station.

The high-ceilinged room was abuzz with screens and scrolling words and images. I had to blink a few times to orient myself. As I linked into all the readers' minds, Maria headed straight for the brightly lit center dais, elevated above the rest of the room and nestled in a semicircle of twenty-foot-high screens. A live street shot of the Vellus Detention Center bustled behind her.

The sun reflected off the sidewalk, and a couple dozen journalists milled around the guard gate, scribbling on their e-slates or getting stock footage with their ear cameras.

In the station room, three workers nudged their spiderlegged tru-cast cameras across the floor, testing shoot angles of the center interview area. Threads of boom mics dangled down from the ceiling. On the opposite side of the room, another three people faced a dozen screens. A thin guy bobbed his head, mentally orchestrating the media streams with his mindware interface. Real-time scrit feedback scrolled in front of him, and he monitored how people were re-casting the news. The two other people—a visual artist and a programmer—were designing segments to weave into Maria's tru-cast interview.

I had no idea casting the news was so complicated.

One of the camera workers indicated we were in his camera path, waving us out of the way. Julian and I shuffled away from the creeping of the cameras and into a shadowed corner of the room. The tru-cast station was smaller than I had hoped: even tucked far from the interview spotlight, we were only forty feet from the action. It was out of mindreading range of the empty interviewee seat, soon to be filled with Vellus, but not by much. Any mindjackers in the room would be well within reach and definitely aware of who I was.

I only hoped Julian could deliver on keeping any mindguards sedate enough for me to jack while he worked on Vellus.

Sitting in an upholstered chair out of the spotlight was an elderly man whose thoughts showed him to be the Truth

Magistrate. He watched a girl flit around Maria, who was perched in the spindly interview chair. The girl held a tiny black square up to Maria's face and clothes and hair, and the lighting subtly adjusted to her mental commands. Maria ignored the girl and focused on her scribepad, running through her prepared questions. Her anger was ramping up to a slow burn in the back of my throat as she cycled through her planned attack. She seemed to be doing it on purpose, pumping up her emotional state, probably to make it easier to ignore the fact that Julian and I were here to jack her interviewee.

Julian nudged me and held up the face of his phone, where he had scrit, *Check out the screen.*

Behind Maria, the screens focused on the gate at the Detention Center. It was a double-door system, with the second door visible when the first was open—both no doubt controlled by the guard, safe inside his bubble of concrete, glass, and the mindjack shield. I hoped that jacking Vellus was going to work, because breaking into the Detention Center looked daunting at best. A nurse in trim scrubs got clearance to go inside, and I pictured the med facility within the walls. My dad and Raf could well be in there. The chill of that thought trickled into my stomach. At the very edge of the screen, Hinckley leaned against the door of a shuttered business across the street, arms crossed.

Waiting.

Hopefully we would have some prisoners coming out soon for him to usher back to Jackertown. I linked into the mindware interface of Julian's phone and nudged a scrit. *I hope you know what you're doing.*

Before he could respond, something caught his eye by the double doors. They whooshed open and a skinny man, mid-twenties in a tailored *nove*-fiber shirt, strode into the cast station, stumbling in his haste to arrive ahead of the troupe behind him. Close behind were three bodyguards who reminded me of Mr. Trullite's over-muscled goons. I brushed their minds and all three were mindreaders. The skinny man scanned the room and focused on the dais, immediately noting that Maria's chair was slightly higher in elevation than the interviewee chair and would have to be adjusted before the Senator would proceed with the interview.

He activated a mindware-enabled earbud phone and scrit an all-clear signal. A moment later, Vellus appeared in the doorway and seized the attention of the room like a magnetic force. His strong stride carried him across the threshold of the double glass doors, his suit flowing perfectly over his trim body. His hair was stuck in the rolling waves that were the latest fashion for powerful men, and his smooth skin made him look young, but the crinkles around his eyes said he was my dad's age. His assistant scurried to the side to give him a clear path to the dais. A thought wave murmured through the room, with the light and design women openly admiring Vellus's strong jaw. I supposed he was a classically good-looking man, but seeing the king of the anti-jacker crusaders in real life made my stomach want to throw up the morning's crackers.

I brushed Vellus's mind, bracing myself for the prospect of dipping into his thoughts. He was out of mindreading range, so I didn't link thoughts to him. That would only make him more aware of our presence, and the thoughts I'd like to link would definitely blow my cover anyway. Vellus's smile was wide as he basked in the admiration of the women, but his mind was vacuous, filled with echoes of the other mindreaders' thoughts. I had never linked into the mind of a politician before, but he was even less substantial than I had supposed they were. Even his mind-scent was nondescript, like it was diluted down to nothingness.

He was intent on Maria, whose thoughts were tightly focused on the atrocities she imagined Vellus had already committed. He was halfway across the room before two more security suits flowed into the room behind him, one large and bulky, the other tall and slim. I brushed their minds and they instantly noticed my touch—both were jackers on high alert. *Mindguards.* My head whipped to the one farthest from me.

There, standing tall in an ill-fitting gray security jacket, was my dad.

chapter ELEVEN

My dad. A mindguard. For Vellus.

The shock of it pulsed through my body, seizing up every muscle. My eyes locked with my dad's across the span of the tru-cast room.

What are you doing here! I linked to him. Instead of answering, he stiffened, his face twisted in wordless pain. A bottomless terror clawed his thoughts, and my mind reflexively recoiled. At the same time, he took a shaky step back, eyes wide. He must have tried jacking into Julian's head, only to get the same horror show that I had experienced the first time.

Julian's hand gripped my elbow, hard. "Keeper." His voice was a whisper of warning. My dad, showing up as Vellus's mindguard—it had to be freaking him out. It was freaking *me* out. If I didn't do something quick, Julian would end up handling my dad again.

I linked back into my dad's head. *Dad, don't try to jack him! It won't do you any good.*

My dad's face was turning red. *What is this jackworker forcing you to do?*

Back at the mages' headquarters, Julian had handled my dad out of rescuing me and Raf. How could I explain that Julian was now helping me rescue Raf? *Julian's not forcing me to do anything! And since when are you doing mindguard duty for Vellus?*

Julian? The acid sting of anger overwhelmed my dad's normal mind-scent. *This jackworker is not your friend, Kira. I don't know what he did to me in Jackertown, but he's dangerous. Whatever hold he has over you, it's not real.*

By this point, the bulked-up mindguard at my dad's side had shoved me away from his mind and slammed me back into mine. The pressure grew, forcing me out of my dad's head, but then it suddenly cut off. Julian must have handled him out of trying to jack me, so I plunged back into the mindguard's now-compliant mind. He was confused as to why he considered a young tru-cast assistant such a threat, when clearly the cast station was secure. I jacked him to forget about me and Julian lurking in the shadows at the edge of the room. Julian shoved his phone in my face. Scrit across the screen were the words, *Your father is going to blow this operation. Get him to stand down.*

I pushed the phone away with the back of my hand and linked back into my dad's head.

Whatever mess you're in, Kira, I'll get you out. My dad's face was turning an even darker shade of red. *I don't know what this jackworker is doing to Vellus's mindguard or what he's planning for Vellus, but you don't need to be a part of it.*

Julian's helping me get Raf out of Vellus's prison!

Raf's not in prison! my dad thought. *This jackworker's lying to you.*

Is Raf with you? I asked, my hope soaring. *Did you escape the raid with him?*

No, I landed in the Detention Center with the rest of the jackers, my dad thought. *But I made sure they weren't holding you and Raf before I left.*

You were in the Detention Center? How did you get out? He still hadn't answered my question about how he ended up on Vellus's mindguard squad, but I was piecing it together. He was swept up in the raid, but had bargained his way out of prison by agreeing to work for Vellus. My stomach churned.

I had to agree to mindguard for Vellus again, my dad thought. *It was the only way to get out so I could find you and Raf!*

Wait, what? Again?

My mind sputtered on that for a moment. Vellus's other mindguard was now idly checking the messages on his phone, while Vellus stepped up on the dais. Maria rose to greet him with a half bow. Vellus's assistant fussed with the interviewee chair so that it was the same height as Maria's. Vellus beamed as Maria struggled to balance her aggressive tru-caster thoughts with being a gracious host. The oversized image of the Detention Center loomed behind her.

Wait, I linked to my dad. *How can you be sure Raf isn't in the Detention Center?*

I'm sure because I refused to work for Vellus unless Kestrel released you and Raf from the prison too, my dad thought. *Kestrel said he didn't have either of you in custody.*

Kestrel was at the prison? My mouth dropped open. *And you believed what he said?* I had to restrain myself from stomping across the room and physically shaking my dad. *He totally could have lied to you!*

I didn't have any other option, he thought. *Kestrel was picking out prisoners to take to another facility. It was either get out then or go with the rest of them.*

I pulled out of my dad's head and tried to control the shaking in my hands. Raf could still be in the prison. Of course Kestrel would lie. And worse, he was taking the prisoners, including the mages and possibly Raf, off to the facility where he was doing his experiments. How much time did we have? I grabbed Julian's phone and jacked into the mindware to scrit a message. *Kestrel's at the Detention Center, picking up prisoners.*

Julian nodded, as though he already knew. He must have been listening in on our entire conversation. I could only imagine what he was thinking, but so far he hadn't resorted to handling my dad. Maria was settling in her chair and getting ready to start the interview. My heart hammered like I had run a mile. I sucked in a ragged breath. Maybe if we all just kept our heads and gave Julian a chance to do his magic with Vellus, this could still work.

I took a breath and linked back into my dad's head. *Dad, Raf could still be in there. We have to let Julian try to get him out.*

My dad ran a shaky hand through his hair and paused a long moment. *Okay,* he thought. *But if the boom mics pick up that he's jacking Vellus, I'm going to have to take him down. Otherwise Vellus will think I'm involved—that you're involved—and he'll have evidence to put us all in prison. Whether your jackworker friend gets caught or not, once this interview is done, you're coming with me. Understood?*

Fine. I was tempted to pull out of his mind again, because he had some nerve ordering me around while he was doing mind-guard duty for Vellus, but we were both distracted by Maria starting the interview.

Thank you for taking time to meet with us, Senator Vellus. She crossed her legs and leaned forward on her chair, which still seemed to tower over Vellus's, but he was so tall that he dwarfed her. *We won't keep you long, as we know you're giving a press conference today at the new detention center named in your honor.*

It's my pleasure to be here, Ms. Lopez. Vellus's thoughts were less vacuous now, focused on Maria. His thought waves had a deep rumbling quality to them, like a bass guitar you feel as much as hear. Every mind in the room swung to his, even the media tracker, who was quickly pulled back to monitoring his data feeds. The boom mics had captured Vellus's thoughts and cast them out, creating a surge of positive feedback on the nets.

Maria didn't seem as affected by Vellus's charisma, still focused like a hawk on her attack questions. *You've mentioned in previous tru-casts that the Center is designed specifically to hold jacker prisoners. Can you tell us about the security measures that make that possible?*

Vellus beamed an unnaturally white smile designed for a sim-cast. *I can't tell you all the top-secret technology, Maria, but I would like your viewers to rest assured that our guards are armed with the latest in anti-jacker technology and the inmates are kept under a mild, safe, but effective sedative to keep them from using their jacker abilities to harm anyone, including each other. The Vellus Detention Center is a state-of-the-art containment center, but it is not inhumane. The purpose of the Vellus Center is to provide for the general safety of all regular citizens, without any undue harm to those afflicted with the jacker strain of DNA.*

When you say anti-jacker technology, are you referring to the shield that surrounds the facility? Maria asked.

As your fellow journalists will soon find out, Vellus waved to the screen behind them, *a mindwave disruptor field does indeed surround the facility, which effectively prevents anyone from jacking into or out of the Center. All doors are remotely controlled, and no one is allowed in or out of the facility without authorization. A breakout is impossible.*

Your authorization, Maria retorted. The intensity of her stare at Vellus kicked up a notch.

He gazed at Maria with soft brown eyes, as if he couldn't sense the edge in her thoughts. *I simply helped secure the funding for the Center because I felt there was a need for such a facility. I was honored that they chose to name the Center after me, but I assure you that the police follow standard procedures for incarcerating prisoners and holding them while they await trial.*

Does your standard police procedure for arresting mind-jackers include random sweeps through Jackertown? Maria's look alone could have impaled Vellus, but his face remained calm. *What guarantee can you give that innocent people, including mindreaders, won't be caught up in such a blatant violation of civil rights?* An image of a dark, curly-haired boy sprung up in her mind, making my heart twist, but Maria had never met Raf, so the image wasn't as strong as her question about civil rights.

Vellus smiled indulgently. *No reader in his right mind would ever go to Jackertown—unless you were demens, and then you're just like a neighbor coming to visit anyway.* He paused a beat. *But I admire your concern for protecting the rights of regular citizens. And it turns out that rescuing a wayward reader, who had been involuntarily taken to the lawless area known as Jackertown, was the reason behind the arrests last night.*

What? My mind spun. The raid was because of a reader? Was it Raf?

Vellus kept going. *Unfortunately, the kidnapping of readers is becoming a more prevalent occurrence every day. Something I hope the Detention Center will prove a preventative measure against, as a warning to mindjackers that there are consequences for their violent acts.*

Maria hesitated. *So you're saying this was a rescue operation?*

Vellus smiled wider. *Exactly. One I'm happy to say was successful.*

Maria frowned, and her thoughts were spinning faster than mine. She clutched her scribepad tighter and shifted in her seat. *My sources say a mindreader was arrested in last night's raid on Jackertown along with a dozen mindjackers. Are you saying that this mindreader had been kidnapped, and that the mindjackers arrested were holding him captive? Can you verify that the rescued mindreader is indeed the one on my list?* She tapped her scribepad and leaned forward to hand it to Vellus.

I assure you that any mindreaders in Jackertown—Vellus's thoughts were interrupted as his eyes landed on the list.

I have a Truth Magistrate standing by, Senator Vellus. Maria perched perilously close to the edge of her chair. *To verify the accuracy of your answers.*

He waved her away like she was a fly buzzing around his head. *That won't be necessary.* Then he turned to peer from the spotlight and looked straight at my dad.

My dad—he was on the list with Raf! My breath froze in my chest.

I assure you that—Vellus stopped again, mid-thought, only this time, I sensed some confusion in his mind. As he studied the list, a mantra pounded his thoughts that these were dangerous jackers, they had to stay locked up, but it fought against an underlying tug of emotion that made him feel bonded to them.

Like they were *his* people, and he needed to get them out. That they shouldn't be locked in a prison, because they had done nothing wrong. A light sheen of sweat broke out on his forehead and reflected the spotlights.

I glanced at Julian, who was deep in concentration, his eyes fixed on Vellus like a laser beam. He must be handling Vellus now, and not a moment too soon. With my dad's name on the list, Vellus must know something was wrong. But would it matter? Could the rational part of his brain fight off Julian's handling? It didn't seem like my dad or Molloy could resist him.

I think, perhaps, there has been some kind of mistake. Vellus blinked and leaned back in his chair, holding the list away from his body as if it were a snake that might bite him.

Are you saying that it was a mistake to have these people arrested? Maria hung off the edge of her chair. Even though Vellus had extended her scribepad back to her, she refused to take it. *That they were improperly caught up in your attempt to rescue the mindreader who was kidnapped?*

Yes... there must have been a mistake. They... His eyes grew wide, as if he couldn't believe the thoughts running through his head. *These people weren't involved in the kidnapping.*

If it was a mistake, Senator, perhaps we could remedy that mistake now, Maria thought. *Have the prisoners released immediately. A gesture of goodwill that would no doubt go far in reassuring the public.*

Perhaps. Yes, reassuring to the public. Vellus's face turned red, which might be seen on the tru-cast as embarrassment, but

I knew exactly what it was. Vellus was trying to fight the impulse
he felt to free the prisoners. Maria flagged her assistant, the girl
who had fluttered around her before, and she sprinted up to
Maria with a slim silver phone.

We have a phone ready for you, Senator, Maria thought. *If
you would like to make that call.*

Vellus ignored her outstretched hand.

That won't be necessary. Vellus's chest was heaving, like
he was having a hard time breathing. He gestured to his skinny
assistant who jerked like he had been tasered and hurried up
to the dais. Vellus thrust the scribepad into his hands, and
he awkwardly caught it so that it wouldn't drop to the floor.
*These people have been mistakenly detained. My assistant
will make the necessary arrangements to have them released
immediately.*

Vellus's assistant sprinted out of camera range, horrified
at the public-relations nightmare his boss had unfurled. He
stabbed madly at his earbud phone and dashed out of the room
to the lobby to place his call, afraid that the boom mics might
pick up his thoughts and broadcast them, snarling the mess
even further.

Vellus's face was returning to a normal color, now that the
assistant had been dispatched to carry out the urgent need to release the prisoners that Julian had apparently placed in Vellus's
reptilian brain.

I believe our interview is concluded, Ms. Lopez, Vellus
thought, but he wasn't looking at her anymore. He slowly rose

from his seat, his soft brown eyes turning sharp, like a wolf coming out of hiding. He threw a dark look at my dad, then scanned the room, skipping over Maria and the camera people, his head slowly swinging toward me and Julian. I glanced around, but there was nowhere to hide. We were out of mindreading range, so that shouldn't throw a red flag, but I covered my far-too-famous face with my hand before he got a good look. Could I jack him to look away? Vellus was still too close to the boom mics—if I jacked him, it would be picked up and recorded. There would be evidence the world's most famous anti-jacker politician had been jacked, and it would be pinned on me. Or worse, my dad or Maria. Vellus stumbled as he stepped down from the dais, and the heat of his stare landed on me. The intensity of it grew, and then recognition lit his face.

Kira Moore, he thought. *Of course. I should have known it would be you.*

My throat tightened. I glanced at Maria, but she was talking on her earbud phone, and didn't seem to hear Vellus's thoughts. I edged closer to Julian, but he was busy with his phone, furiously concentrating on a scrit to Hinckley. Didn't he realize my cover had just been blown? Julian needed to do something quick—handle Vellus again. Were the boom mics still on? Were they picking up Vellus's thoughts and sending them out on the tru-cast?

Vellus glowered at me a moment longer, and I was afraid he would march back up the dais steps and claim I had jacked him. Instead he swung his head back to my dad, leveled a stare at him, and stepped away from the dais. I was relieved to see him put more distance between himself and the boom mics, but I didn't like the way he was looking at my dad.

Patrick, you seem to be a very ineffective mindguard, Vellus thought. *At least where your daughter is concerned.*

My dad took a half step back, his thoughts careening for an explanation of what had happened on the dais that wouldn't involve me going to jail. *Kira is no threat to you, Senator. She's simply an assistant here. An observer.*

Yes, I'm sure that's the case, Vellus thought. *But perhaps we need to review the tru-cast to see if there's anything unusual picked up by the boom mics.*

My dad's shoulders twitched. His thoughts zoomed in on jacking Vellus now, boom mics or no boom mics, but that would only confirm what Vellus suspected—that I had jacked him into releasing the prisoners. We'd both end up on the run. His thoughts swung to exposing Julian, pinning the blame on him, so I would go free. My dad's thoughts must have pulled in Julian's attention, because he was gripping my elbow again. If my dad exposed Julian, things would get bad in a hurry. Julian would end up handling everyone. What did he say? Induce a riot?

Dad, no! I elbowed Julian, hopefully holding him back from doing anything yet.

Vellus was creeping closer to my dad, waiting for his response. Finally, my dad linked an answer to him. *There's no need to check the boom mics, Senator. I'm sure there's nothing to be found there. And it would be unfortunate for the world to learn that you had been mindjacked.*

I glanced around the tru-cast station, but my dad must have linked those thoughts only to Vellus, because no one seemed too alarmed that he had just implied that Vellus had been jacked. Vellus stopped a few feet from my dad, then gave him a snake-like smile. *Yes, you are quite right. That would be unfortunate. I wouldn't want people to lose faith. They need to be assured that mindjacker influence doesn't affect the important decisions made by their elected officials. That's your job, isn't it, Patrick? To make sure that doesn't happen?*

For the moment, sir.

Perhaps you'd like to revoke our previous agreement? Vellus arched his eyebrows. *That could be arranged. For both you and your daughter.*

My dad's gaze didn't waver. *That's not necessary.*

Good. Perhaps you can manage to do your job more effectively when your daughter is not in the room. And I do believe it's time for us to leave. We have a press conference to attend, where I will need to manage the public relations aspect of today's interview. Or do we need to stay here and review the recordings?

No sir.

Vellus strode past my father and out of the tru-cast station, tailed by the three over-muscled mindreader goons. The bulky mindguard turned to follow Vellus, then stopped. *Are you coming, Moore?* He was still under Julian's influence and not overly concerned by Vellus's thoughts. In fact, the whole tru-cast room was carrying on with the post-production of the interview as if nothing had happened.

My dad stared at me from across the cast station. He didn't want to leave me with Julian, but if he tried to bring me along now, Vellus might put us both in the Detention Center—and not as mindguards.

I only agreed to mindguard for the press conference, Kira, he thought. *After that, I'm coming for you.*

My throat closed up as my dad turned to follow in Vellus's wake.

Once the entourage was on their way out of the building, Julian shoved his phone in my face. *How long has your father been working for Vellus?* was scrit across the face.

I grabbed the phone from his hand, holding it at my side, but not looking at it or Julian, just keeping my eyes on the screens behind Maria. Julian's question felt like a punch in the gut. I wanted to say my father would never work for someone like Vellus. That he was a good, decent man who had only tried to jack Julian because he was trying to protect me. I wanted to make up an excuse for the obvious fact that my dad was mindguarding for an anti-jacker politician. Say that Vellus was just another praver who hated jackers but used them for his own purposes when it was convenient. But Julian had heard my father's thoughts explaining that he was working for Vellus in exchange for getting out of prison.

And he heard that one little word. *Again.*

Finally, I jacked into the mindware interface of the phone, scrit a reply, and shoved it back into Julian's hands.

I don't know.

I turned and stalked out of the cast room.

chapter TWELVE

Numbness crept through my body as I tried to process what had happened in the tru-cast room. I ignored Julian's pointed looks as the autocab whispered through the streets toward Jackertown. The city was void of life or cars with only a breeze that tumbled trash down the bleached-white pavement and the occasional demens staggering for a place to rest out of the bright morning sun.

When the autocab rolled up to the mages' headquarters, my legs itched to get out and find out what had happened at the Detention Center. Had Hinckley brought the prisoners back already? I reached for the handle of the autocab door, but Julian leaned across and stopped me by trapping my hand with his.

"I need to know, keeper," Julian said. "Was Vellus truly after a kidnapped mindreader? Or did your father ask him to raid Jackertown for *you*?"

I shrank from him and jerked my hand away from his. Did my dad pull in a favor with Vellus and trade a dozen other mindjackers' freedom for mine? I didn't want to believe it. "Well, if he did, I'm sure he didn't plan on ending up in Vellus's prison."

"So you believe him?"

"What do you mean?" My voice was rough.

"You believe your father when he claims he was only working for Vellus in order to get out of prison?"

"Yes!" I choked on the word. I didn't want to believe that my dad was lying to me. Had been lying all along.

Julian nodded. "It was reassuring, actually, how hard he worked to make sure you knew it was just a temporary arrangement. I have to admit, when I saw your father come into the station, for a moment I thought that maybe you..."

"That I *what*?" I demanded.

"I thought maybe I had you all wrong, keeper," he said. "That you and your father were *both* working for Vellus."

"I would never do that!" The idea of working for Vellus crawled across my skin and made me shudder. How could my dad work for someone who hated us so much?

"I believe you. But you're not at all the person I expected." Julian waved his hand in the air, as if trying to explain the unexplainable. "The girl who rescued a half dozen changelings on a tru-cast? The girl who went on-air in a live interview with a Truth Magistrate to show the world that jackers existed? I thought you would be more..." He seemed to search for just the right word, then his eyes sparkled when he found it. "Revolutionary."

Those things only managed to put my family in danger for

the last eight months, from people like Molloy—jackers that Julian seemed to have no problem working with.

"You don't know anything about me." I yanked open the door of the autocab and slammed it behind me. Hinckley blocked the doorway to the mages' headquarters, installing a metal bar to keep the busted front door closed. He stood back to let me squeeze past.

Inside the converted factory reeked of the gas, and a fine yellowish powder coated everything. A dozen figures in pale green jumpsuits were scattered around the mages' kitchen: on the couch, in the chairs, standing at the sink. I ran toward them, scanning their faces, searching for Raf. Hinckley was the only one not dressed in prisoner garb, still wearing his ratty jeans and the black, long-sleeved t-shirt that he'd had on in the tru-cast feed. He had followed me in and now sat sprawled on the couch, one leg hooked over the end, looking satisfied. I ignored him and dashed in between the circulating mages, peering at every face. Myrtle was standing with a group of prisoners that I didn't recognize. I kept checking everyone, but I already knew.

Raf wasn't there.

I stumbled onto Ava and grabbed her slim shoulders. "Where's Raf? Why didn't you bring him out with you!" I accidentally shook her, which wasn't very mesh, but the trembling had taken hold of my arms.

Suddenly Sasha was by her side. "Leave her alone." His voice was like sandpaper, his lips chapped: symptoms of the gas. One arm wrapped around Ava's shoulders, the other slid between us.

His dark brown eyes were at full attention. I pulled my hands back, remembering what Julian had said about Sasha scribing away a person's entire being.

A pair of hands landed gently on my shoulders. "He wasn't in the prison, keeper," Julian said. "He was never picked up in the sweep."

I shook Julian's hands off me and turned on him. "How can you be sure?"

Hinckley stood with crossed arms right behind Julian's shoulder. "Everyone on the list came out, except the reader," Hinckley said. "No one saw him."

"A reader like your friend would have been noticed right away," Julian said softly. "If he was in there, someone would have seen him. Besides, Vellus had no reason to hold him, especially when he was releasing everyone else on the list."

"Then where is he?" My voice was a whisper.

"I don't know."

My shoulders sagged. If Raf hadn't been swept up in the raid, someone else must have taken him. He was lost in Jackertown, a truly kidnapped reader, just like Vellus had talked about. The idea made my chest so tight I could barely breathe. I stumbled away from Julian and landed on the far end of the couch. Thoughts and images screamed circles in my head.

Raf enslaved to a vile gang of jackers.

My dad lying to me about working for Vellus.

Raf dancing a pirouette, over and over.

My dad doing Vellus's dirty work.

I slowly crumpled into a ball. Ava alighted on the couch, careful not to jostle me. Sasha hovered nearby in the kitchen, watching us. Ava didn't seem to hold a grudge about me grabbing her. Or tasing her earlier with the butterfly, for that matter.

"We'll find him," she said softly. I took a deep, shaky breath, trying to stop the images in my head. I tucked the dark thoughts about my dad back into the deep recesses of my brain. I needed to pull myself together to have any hope of finding Raf.

Julian paced at the far end of the factory, near the couch where I woke up yesterday. Was it only yesterday? My mind blurred the time. He argued with Hinckley about something, but I couldn't bring myself to care.

I turned back to Ava. "I'm sorry," I said. "About before. With the butterfly."

"Sasha says I'm too trusting sometimes." She half-grinned. "I guess he's right about that."

"I just wanted to get back home. To get Raf out of here." My justifications weren't necessary—it seemed like Ava already understood. And they weren't helping me find Raf either. I closed my eyes and reached beyond the walls of the mages' headquarters, using my most featherweight touch to search the nearby minds for any sign of Raf. But everyone was on a high state of alert after the roundup last night and they reacted to my slightest brush.

I pulled back before I set too many of them off. I would have to find another way to search for him. When I opened my eyes, Ava had wandered back to Sasha. She flipped on a screen set on the kitchen counter. It showed a tru-cast with an aerial view of the Vellus Detention Center. Words scrolled along the bottom about the release of the prisoners before the press conference. Senator Vellus came on, mindtalking to one of the reporters, a wiry woman I recognized from the earlier tru-cast. My dad lurked in the background in his gray security jacket, arms crossed. I swallowed down a sour taste that rose up in my throat.

The rescue mission was a complete success. Vellus's thoughts scrolled along the bottom of the screen. Julian stalked over with Hinckley and examined the screen. Sasha's arm snuck around Ava's waist, pulling her close.

What about the prisoners that were released, Senator? the tru-cast reporter asked. *On your earlier tru-cast, you said there had been a mistake made in detaining them?*

Yes, Vellus answered. *Unfortunately, there was confusion about who they were during the initial arrests. While the mission was to recover a single kidnapped mindreader, the police discovered an entire group of mindreaders being held hostage in Jackertown.*

She looked confused, but my mouth hung open in disbelief. *So the prisoners released were actually mindreaders, not mindjackers?* the reporter asked.

Yes! Vellus responded. *Sending a rescue team into a town filled with mindjackers is not an easy thing to do, and there was a lot of chaos during the operation. During the arrests, the mindreaders were accidentally mixed in with the mindjacker clan members that were holding them. I realized this right away when I saw the list Ms. Lopez provided because the warden had already briefed me on the names of the rescued mindreaders.*

Which is why you asked for them to be released immediately?

Exactly, Vellus thought. *It was an innocent mistake, and I don't fault the warden or the police commissioner for this at all. They are heroes today. More than a dozen mindreaders have been safely returned to their families!*

Can you release the names of the mindreaders who were rescued?

I'm afraid not. Senator Vellus looked straight into the camera. *I hope that the press can respect their privacy in this matter.*

"That's a complete and utter lie," I blurted out.

"Yes, it is," Julian said. "I'm not sure how he manages it. The reporter should at least sense his lying, even if the boom mic only repeats his thoughts." But the reporter was simply smiling and nodding.

Maria had managed to keep her thoughts trained on her questions during the interview, and Mr. Trullite had used the other readers' emotions to keep my true name secret. "Maybe Vellus is exceptionally good at keeping his thoughts focused," I said. "He's a politician. They have to keep on message all the time."

"He certainly was charismatic at the station, and he makes for excellent tru-cast material." Julian frowned. "But I'm surprised he can keep up this level of lying."

"Is that why it was difficult for you to handle him at the tru-cast station?"

Julian tore his gaze from the screen. "What makes you think it was difficult?"

"I don't know," I said. "Just seemed like it took some time."

He drew back. "I was trying to make it not quite so obvious that he was being jacked."

I shrugged. I didn't care about how finessed Julian was at handling or how good Vellus was at lying. Apparently my own father could lie to me and I wouldn't even know. I closed my eyes and pressed the heels of my hands to my forehead, trying to rub away the pounding there. I didn't even know where to start with finding Raf, and the images of him being tormented by a clan of jackers threatened to take over my mind again.

"I've put out a message on the short comms." Julian had moved closer, his voice turning soft. "The mage cells are on notice to look for your... friend."

My eyes popped open and I glared at him. "His name is Raf."

"Right." He nodded. "Raf. We'll find him, keeper. I promise."

A quiet tone sounded from Julian's pants pocket. He fished out his phone, frowning at the ID, and activated it by mindlink. A holo image of Molloy floated above the screen.

"Mr. Molloy," Julian said flatly.

"Julian!" Molloy's voice boomed from the phone. "I've seen the tru-cast. Had an interesting morning, did you?"

Julian flicked a look at the tru-caster recapping her report. "Yes, that was us."

"Is little Kira still with you?" he asked. "Or did you leave her in Vellus's playroom?"

Julian scowled. "We managed to recover everyone taken in the raid. Thank you for your concern."

"That's good to hear," Molloy said. "I have someone she might like to see."

Julian stood straighter. "You have him?"

I nearly leapt off the couch and crowded Julian for the phone.

Raf's face floated into view. "Raf!" I grabbed the phone from Julian and held it with both hands. I touched my finger to the holo image, wishing I could reach through the phone. "Are you okay? What happened? Where are you?"

Shadows lurked under Raf's eyes, but he gave me his irresistible smile. He cast an irritated look off-screen, then turned his gorgeous brown eyes back to me. "I'm fine. Kira, I'm sorry, he must have jacked me. I... I wouldn't leave you there all alone. I don't know what happened, I just woke up here a little while ago." He moved a little closer to the phone, and the muscles in his cheek moved. "What are they doing to you, Kira? Please tell me they're not hurting you."

My heart banged against my chest. "No, no, I'm fine." I smiled for him, and suddenly it felt like too many eyes were part of this conversation. I shuffled to the couch and hunched over the phone. "Raf, I'm so sorry," I whispered. "I'm sorry I got you into this."

"Kira, it's okay, I'm fine." He lowered his voice. "Whatever they're trying to get you to do, don't do it, all right? Don't do anything dangerous. Or stupid. Or, you know, like *you*."

A grin stretched my face, but tears filled my eyes. "Your romantic powers are failing if you think that's how to flatter a girl."

"I'm saying stay out of trouble. What about your dad? Maybe he can help—"

"My dad's not—" I didn't know where to start with that. "Look, just tell me where you are. I'm coming right now to get you. And don't do anything until I get there." If Raf still had his taser, I didn't want him taking off through the streets of Jackertown and getting caught by jackers even more unsavory than Molloy.

Raf's face clouded. "I don't know where I am, exactly." He looked around. "It's some kind of basement, I th—" He stopped mid-word and his eyes glazed. The camera dropped, or maybe Raf's hand fell.

"Raf!" I cried.

Molloy's face appeared above the phone again. "He's fine, lass, just taking a little break."

"What are you doing to him!" I gripped the edges of the phone so hard I thought it might break.

Julian appeared by my side, gently prying the phone out of my hands. "We're all a bit tired, Mr. Molloy. What do you say we dispense with the theatrics and you return the keeper's pet, so we can get on with our plans?"

"I don't think so, Julian," he said. "Like I said before, this one's a bit of insurance."

Fear trickled down my back. *No, no, no...*

Julian's jaw worked. "That was not part of our agreement."

"She's key to the plan, and she needs to see it through. If you weren't so soft, Julian, you'd see it my way." Molloy's voice turned grave. "And watch your back. She'll betray you in a heartbeat. She left the last one bleeding in the desert to die. Don't think she won't do the same to you as soon as she has the chance. Don't trust her."

"It's my business who I trust," Julian said. "Right now, I'm not too fond of your methods, Mr. Molloy."

"Whether you're fond of them or not," Molloy said, "she'll not be getting her pet back until she finishes the job. A little extra motivation to keep her focused. You can thank me later, once your sister is free."

My stomach knotted into an icy ball. I wanted to grab the phone from Julian and demand that Molloy release Raf immediately. The only thing that stopped me was knowing it would do absolutely no good and might trigger something worse. Molloy would be happy to kill Raf. More than happy, he would delight in making it painful. Julian briefly closed his eyes, then gave me a strained look that told me he knew it too.

My hands shook. "Julian, please..." My words were barely a whisper. *Please stop him. Please make him give Raf back to me.*

Julian held his finger up and turned back to Molloy. "You will not hurt him." It was a statement and a threat.

"Won't harm a hair on his pretty head," Molloy said. "As long as Kira does her part and brings my brother back out of that horror chamber of Kestrel's."

"Take care that you don't," Julian said very slowly. "Because if the reader is harmed, you will have me to answer to. Are we clear, Mr. Molloy?"

"Aye," Molloy said. "Right as rain."

The floating image of Molloy disappeared. My chest ached and I realized I had stopped breathing. I sucked in a quick breath.

Julian frowned at the now-blank phone, then looked to me. "Seems like we have some planning to do."

chapter THIRTEEN

"Can't we just find Molloy?" I was unabashedly pleading with Julian as he eased next to me on the couch. "Force him to give Raf back? If you all helped me..." I looked around, hoping I had earned some goodwill in helping get the mages out of prison. Ava wrung her hands, and Sasha examined me with his dark eyes, like this was a test. Hinckley studied his fingernails.

"It's not that we don't want to help you, keeper." Julian chose his words carefully, like he was treading a word minefield. "But we have no idea where Molloy is, and I don't think he's a patient man. In spite of his apparent lack of love for you, he's not going to hurt your friend as long as he thinks you'll return with his brother. If we go after Molloy, and he finds out..."

I sagged into the back of the couch. "He would have nothing to lose by killing Raf."

"Precisely." He paused. "The sooner we get in and out of Kestrel's facility, the sooner we get your reader friend back."

They were all staring at me now, waiting.

My stomach twisted in knots. Breaking into Kestrel's facility was like rushing into a burning house to rescue Raf, and Julian didn't even have to handle my protective instinct to get me to do it. Molloy did that just fine by glazing Raf's eyes while we were on the phone. Thinking about that made a scream start to crawl up my throat, so I took a breath and locked that image of Raf away.

"Well." I struggled to push up from the too-soft couch. "I guess we better do this."

Julian's lips drew into a tight line, but he rose up and crossed to a kitchen cabinet. Sasha stopped Julian as he drew out a flex scroll, and they exchanged a silent mental conversation. When Sasha let him go, Julian brought the scroll to the kitchen table, where he spread it out and tapped the corner. A map sprang to life and floated above it. Hinckley watched us with his feet propped up on the table.

"I think we should move our plans up," Julian said, "given the urgency of our situation. Instead of waiting until Monday, I think we can do it today. There will be less city traffic on a Saturday, possibly less staff in the demens ward, and less chance for things to go wrong."

Julian mentally nudged the interactive map and it zoomed out to reveal a good fraction of the city and Lake Michigan. "According to Mr. Molloy, Kestrel's facility is masquerading as a demens treatment facility downtown, near the lake." He zoomed in again. "The Chicago Lakeshore Hospital is, in fact, a containment center for the demens, but our surveillance shows that Kestrel's incorporated these three buildings into a compound." Julian drew a red circle with his finger around the three buildings, then swiped it away. "There are no weapons detectors at the main gate, just a single mindreading guard, but there's a shield in place, and the gate is controlled from the inside."

"So how do we do this?" I asked. "Scale the wall?"

"In theory, you could climb the wall," said Julian. "The disruptor field around the perimeter won't conduct into your mind with a simple touch, but after a while the charge builds up and that makes it difficult to have long-term interactions with the wall without losing orientation."

"Or throwing up," Ava said. She scooted the map aside and placed two plates of sandwiches next to Julian and me. "Guess who got to test that part?"

"You volunteered!" said Julian.

Ava grinned. "I thought you guys were just being pansies."

I contemplated the peanut butter and honey sandwich Ava had made for me. My stomach still twisted with the idea of Raf in Molloy's hands, not to mention the thought of breaking into Kestrel's facility. I decided not to chance lunch.

Julian ignored his sandwich as well. Hinckley leaned over to swipe it off his plate.

"In addition to the shield," Julian said, "there's an electrical field sitting on top of the wall like invisible razor wire. The compound is dressed up like a mental facility, but it's definitely a prison. No, you'll be going in the front gate."

"Are you sure this is Kestrel's facility?" I asked. "Because I'd rather not just go on Molloy's word, if you don't mind."

Julian looked up from the map. "There's not much love lost between you, is there?" he said. "What truly happened in that prison camp, keeper?"

"It doesn't matter. It's between him and me."

He fixed me with those unnerving clear blue eyes. "I'd rather know a bit more about it," he said. "If you don't mind."

I crossed my arms, not really wanting to tell Julian the whole story, especially given that I had completely betrayed Molloy. So, keep it simple.

"I was trying to escape the camp. Molloy sent someone with me, a boy." I stopped. I hadn't talked about Simon in so long, I was surprised how the words seemed to stick in my throat. "He ran out to distract the guards and their sniper rifles, to give me a chance to escape. I made it, he didn't. Molloy thinks it should have been the other way around. That's all there is to it." I unfolded my arms and pretended to study the map, so Julian wouldn't see the tears welling up in my eyes. I cleared my throat. "Are we going to do this, or what?"

Julian placed his hands on the table and leaned forward. "Can I trust you, keeper?"

I met his stare, but looking up only caused the tears to race down my cheeks. "You should trust that I will do what it takes to get Raf back alive."

Julian eased back and nodded.

I wiped my face. "Which brings me back to my point. How

do we know Kestrel's even in there? Or that he has Molloy's brother?" That was the prize I had to get, to save Raf, and I was keeping my eye on it. Although Julian was right about getting the changelings out and making Kestrel pay for everything he had done. As long as I was going in anyway, that was unfinished business I needed to make right. I wasn't so sure about letting the rest of the jackers go, but Julian was probably right about that too—no one deserved to be tormented by Kestrel's needles.

"We have surveillance set up across the street, monitoring the entrance," Julian said. "Hinckley will review the surveillance files to make sure he's inside." He nodded to Hinckley, who pointed to the half-eaten sandwich in his hand. Julian jerked his head to the back, and Hinckley reluctantly heaved himself up from the table and clumped toward the racks.

"Do we have any idea of the security on the inside?" I asked.

"Unfortunately, no," Julian said. "The shield extends above the wall and keeps us from getting a good look inside. If it weren't for that, Ava could peek on it from here, if she stretched."

"Tried," she called from the couch, where she and Sasha were eating their lunch.

"So we're going in blind," I said. "Fantastic. I don't suppose you have more of those butterflies lying around? I promised myself if I ever broke into another jacker prison, I would bring more than just my wits. A dart gun would be even better."

Julian's grin grew wide. "We definitely have weapons for you, keeper." He strolled to a low kitchen cabinet. Instead of pots and pans, it was stocked with guns, all shiny, black, and dangerous-looking. He brought back a flat paper box, which he gently set on the table, and a miniature gun that he placed in my hand.

"You're kidding, right?" It was surprisingly heavy.

"It's a fast-acting dart gun with four rounds, effective at more than one hundred meters," he said. "You should be able to keep it hidden under your clothes, unless you're patted down. Or did you want a more deadly weapon?"

It felt cold and plenty deadly in my hand. Anything more and I wasn't sure I would be able to pull the trigger. "I think I can take Kestrel with a dart gun." With a twinge, I realized I was looking forward to shooting him again.

"If you can get a shot," Julian said quietly, "that will work. But if not, I have a present I've saved just for Kestrel." He lifted the lid of the slender box to show me three tiny, silver bullets inside. The metal of the bullets looked wrinkled and delicate, almost like foil.

"You want me to shoot Kestrel with aluminum-foil bullets?"

A mischievous smile snuck onto Julian's face. "These aren't bullets." I poked a finger into the box to see if they were as flimsy as they looked, but Julian slid it out of reach. "I wouldn't touch, if I were you. They're not that sensitive, but I wouldn't like to waste one blowing up our minds."

"What?" I snatched my hand away. "Are they miniature bombs?"

"I call them thought grenades," he said. "They're not bombs, except to the unfortunate jackers who happen to be in their path."

"They only work on jackers?"

He nodded. "They have the same technology that the butterflies do, only they emit an electromagnetic pulse that wipes the mind of any jacker caught in its wave."

I leaned back.

"Don't worry," he said. "It's just temporary and they have to be crushed to be activated."

"Crushed?" I asked. "That doesn't sound like a very good grenade. I mean, won't it blow up the mind of the person crushing it?"

"Yes," he said, leveling a stare at me. "Unless, of course, you're a reader. Or a jacker whose mind is impenetrable to normal jacker mind fields."

I gulped.

"The plan is for you to get close to Kestrel and use this on him," Julian said. "It's a weapon he wouldn't expect, even if you're caught. And you alone will be unaffected by it."

"Are you sure about that?"

"Anna tested one and said that she was able to endure it."

"Endure it?"

"It's not without side effects." He shrugged. "I only have three, and those were very expensive to obtain, so I'd rather not test it again. Plus, we don't have time for you to recover if we're going to get this operation done quickly."

"Okay." I wasn't sure if not testing the thought grenades was a good thing or a bad thing, but I wasn't exactly eager to try them out.

"You'll have to get close to Kestrel before you use it on him."

"Will it hurt?" I asked. "Kestrel, I mean. Will the thought grenade hurt him? I kind of want it to."

"Yes, it hurts," Julian said with a laugh. "But not enough for what Kestrel deserves. Which is why I want Sasha to have a few minutes alone with him." Julian slid a look to Sasha, who met his stare from the couch and nodded.

How long would it take Sasha? A minute? Two? Then the Kestrel that I knew and loathed would be gone. Not dead, just... gone. My skin prickled with the idea, even though there was no doubt Kestrel deserved it.

"So, how do I get in?" I asked.

"Hinckley will make you a badge." Julian tapped the flex scroll and it popped up an image of a girl who looked like him. She had the same creamy brown skin, and her blue eyes were unmistakably Julian's. Her face was framed with a badge stamped *Chicago Lakeshore Hospital*. "Anna planned to be our Trojan horse, but you'll take her place."

"I still can't believe you were going to send your sister in there."

"It was actually her plan." His eyes lit up. "She hacked the facial thermography system at the gate, but she knew that navigating the security inside would be difficult without reliable intelligence. Which is why she planned on getting caught."

"What?" Getting caught was *not* part of my plan.

"That way she could get close to Kestrel."

"If it's all the same to you, I don't plan to get caught."

"If you can shoot Kestrel, that will work as well," he said. "But if you get caught, don't panic. As long as you have the thought grenade, you'll have the upper hand. You'll have two, just in case. I'll keep the third. And there're these."

He fished a dozen med patches out of his pocket, each about a half inch square, and set them on the table. They were covered with a transparent film to keep the medicine from dosing before it was time.

"These are specially formulated adrenaline patches," he said. "They will bring a person back to full mental strength, even if they're on the gas." He inclined his head. "I know you can fight the gas off on your own, keeper. I saw you do it during the raid. But this is quicker, plus there's extras for the prisoners inside, who might be quite helpful should you get stuck."

I took several of the patches and tucked them into my running shoes. "What if they lock me up and I can't get near Kestrel? Your thought grenades won't do me much good then."

"Getting close to Kestrel won't be a problem for you, keeper." He tapped another section of the flex scroll and popped up a picture of me with long brown hair and no tattoo—and the word *REWARD*. It sent a chill down my back. I knew a lot of jackers wanted me dead, but I thought it was only for revenge. I didn't know they would also get paid to do it.

"This has been circulating around the jacker chat-casts for a few months," he said. "Anna traced it back to a server at the Lakeshore Hospital. That was our first break in hunting down Kestrel's new hideout. He's been looking for you for some time, and we're going to deliver you to him, wrapped in a bow. Believe me, he won't be able to resist visiting you."

Molloy's words floated back to me. *We're using you as bait Kestrel can't resist.*

Yeah. I was running straight into a burning building.

chapter FOURTEEN

Julian's perch in the thirteenth floor of an abandoned apartment building had a nice view of the interior of Kestrel's facility, as well as the placid Lake Michigan shorefront. Kestrel had simply walled off a section of the street to create his latest jacker compound. A weathered wooden shack guarded the front gate, which was large enough for cars to drive through, and a skinny parking lot ran between two front buildings. Each was four stories high and stretched to a shorter brick building in the back. A series of elevated tubular hallways connected the buildings to each other. *Chicago Lakeshore Hospital* shone in white letters on the far building.

We were right across the street, so my reach would normally have stretched the length of the compound, but I ran smack into the same shield barrier that had protected the SWAT team. In the heat of the raid on Jackertown, I hadn't had time to investigate the shield, but now I took a minute to skim the surface of it. A clammy feeling crawled along my skin and made the hairs on the back of my neck stand up. The perimeter shield stretched well above the physical wall, blocking my reach even from thirteen stories up. I felt around the edges, wondering if I could somehow go over or under, but apparently my reach was straight-line only, which was a new discovery. I had always been able to reach whatever I wanted, roaming high and low, but I had never had something that could block me before. Very interesting.

Oh man—now I was starting to think like Julian. My brain vibrated with the energy pulsing through the shield, so I pulled away. Vellus had called it a mindwave disruptor field—it certainly felt like it could shake my brain apart.

Hinckley was camped in the corner of our apartment hideout, watching the Cubs game on a handheld screen. Sasha and Ava talked quietly at the end of the barren room, with Ava shaking her head and Sasha looking frustrated. I suspected he was trying to talk her out of the mission. Everyone was pretending not to hear their whispers, giving them privacy—which I imagined was in short supply at the mages' headquarters. Myrtle was studying the complex, peering through a far window she had rubbed clean of the grit that seemed to coat every surface.

Julian had said the guard didn't control the gate, but I checked anyway. He was a mindreader, sitting in his shack outside of the shield's protection. Apparently the disruptor field blocked mindwaves as well, because he wasn't sensing anything from the other side. He thought the disruptor shield was intended to keep jackers from breaking into the ward and setting the most violent demens loose on the downtown offices.

Why jackers would want to do this didn't seem to have crossed his mind, just another wild story that readers too easily believed about jackers. His thoughts also showed that a central controller inside checked IDs and facial therms. I hoped that Hinckley had been successful in updating their facial thermography database with my image, or this was going to be a very short mission.

Myrtle had sewn one thought grenade capsule into the front neck of my scrubs and another under a logo on the pocket. The one along the neckline itched, but I couldn't tell if it was actually poking me or if the itching came from the idea of having a thought bomb located so close to my brain. They were small enough that they shouldn't be discovered in a pat-down and yet within reach when I needed them. I decided they just loomed larger in my mind.

The disguise Julian had provided made it plausible that I could rook as a hospital worker, although my pink scrubs stamped with tiny elephants looked slightly alarming with my bright white hair and tattoo. I would probably fit in better with the demens. The pant legs pooled around my sneakers, but they covered the dart gun pretty well, and the adrenaline patches were safely tucked into my shoe. The silky material of the scrubs draped smoothly over the t-shirt and shorts I wore underneath, making the too-big uniform look like it was close to fitting. I guessed that Anna was blessed in the height category, like her twin brother.

According to Julian's surveillance, a lot of the staff arrived by autocab, so he had one standing by for me. "Once you're inside,"

Julian said as he scanned the facility with a televiewer, "you should be able to reach the rest of the compound, right?"

I surveyed it quickly. "Yeah, no problem."

"Good. You'll have an advantage that Anna did not, since she was only a keeper and you..." He lowered the televiewer to look at me. "You have many talents."

Before I met the mages, I used to think that my talents were special, not just another flavor on the spectrum. "You know, back in the hospital, when I was rescuing the changelings, I found vials with my name on them. At the time, I thought Kestrel might have injected me with something that made me extra mutant."

"You *are* special, keeper," he said. "But your abilities are just a variation on the genetic mutation that is changing people into jackers all over the world."

I wasn't sure what he meant by "special" then. But whatever. "Well, maybe Kestrel didn't create *me*." I gestured to the compound with my chin. "But maybe he's trying to make other mutants."

Julian studied the compound, without the televiewer. "Perhaps. At the least, he's trying to find out how mindjacking works," Julian said. "He's not that much different from my parents, I suppose. Using science to figure us out. Except that he's completely amoral and willing to torment people to get his answers. I think he plans to use that knowledge to destroy us, one way or another."

"If he wants to get rid of us, why doesn't he just kill us?" I said. "I mean, he had no qualms about kidnapping all kinds of jackers, even changelings, and sending them to a prison in the desert. A lot of jackers died there." I stopped. The image of Simon lying in a pool of his own blood flashed through my mind. I could almost taste the grit of the desert, feel the heat on my skin. I shook my head clear. "I can't imagine killing jackers would bother Kestrel any. What if he's trying to do something different? What if he's trying to create more jackers like the mages?"

"Now that jackers have been exposed to the world, it would be difficult to kill them outright," Julian said. "There's too many of us; more every day. Not that Vellus isn't heading that way with his Detention Center." Julian stared down at me. "I don't know precisely what Kestrel is doing, but whatever it is, it has to be stopped."

I nodded. I was going in to get Molloy's brother and to save Raf, but one way or another, I was going to stop Kestrel, once and for all.

Julian gave me one last look-over, ostensibly checking my uniform. "Do you have your phone?"

I patted my pants pocket. "Got it." I had erased any identifying information, just in case.

"Call us when you've dropped the shield," he said. "Or if you have Kestrel and can't get the gate open. If necessary, we'll break it down and come get you."

"I thought that was too theatrical for you."

Julian gripped his televiewer tighter. "I'm willing to blow a few things up, as long as I'm sure we have Kestrel. I just don't want him slipping away while we're crashing down the front door."

I gave a sharp nod, and his hold on the televiewer relaxed. He lightly tapped me on the forehead. "Or you could reach out and give us an all-clear nudge."

"I'll nudge Ava," I said. "I'd like to avoid your brain, if it's all the same to you."

A smile lit his face, then he went serious. "Be careful, keeper." There was more worry in his voice than I wanted to hear moments before I was about to break into a jacker prison. I didn't say anything, just smoothed down my scrubs and turned away. The rotted-out wooden stairs creaked under my footfalls as I went down to the waiting autocab below.

The autocab dropped me in front of the main gate. A half dozen other orderlies in flat green scrubs lounged outside the guard shack, waiting for the shift change. Most of them were substantially larger and beefier than me. I stood a little taller and tried to look tough as I linked into all their heads. Their musky mind-scents overwhelmed the fresh-water breeze coming off the lake, and they tossed thoughts of dread about the work day back and forth, but nothing unusual.

Just another day working in the demens ward.

I always thought the workers at mental hospitals would be zeros who wouldn't be plagued by the chemically altered thoughts of the demens. It was exactly the job I once thought I would have: a zero on the lowest rung of the social ladder, consigned to working in the demens ward. There must not be enough zeros to go around, because these orderlies were all readers. At least they were doing respectable, law-abiding work, while I was committing criminal acts and rooking to break into a demens ward. Turned out there was an even lower rung than I had thought possible.

I straightened my scrubs and focused on the people ahead of me in line.

One by one, they swiped their badges through a scanner and looked into a wide-barreled thermal camera behind the glass. The guard barely looked up from his screen, his thoughts bound up in catching and sorting the pieces of his game. When the orderlies ahead of me were cleared, a side door next to the gate sprung open, then closed behind them once they'd gone through.

I shuffled forward when it was my turn and swiped my badge. I stared at the camera, wondering how long I was supposed to do that and if I would mess it up by blinking. Julian had taken a picture for the facial therm database and my badge, but were they checking my retinas too?

The guard glanced up, then did a double-take. He set down his game and his thoughts were awash in curiosity. *New here?* He was more excited than suspicious, so I decided it was better not to jack him. Maybe his thoughts were being monitored by a hidden boom mic. I didn't want to set off any alarms before I'd even gotten inside.

Today's my first day, I linked to him. *Is it as bad as I've heard?*

Worse, probably. Was he trying to scare the newbie? He eyed my tattoo and had a fleeting thought about asking me out for coffee. He pressed his face close to the glass between us. *Stick to the west wing.*

Why? What's in the east wing?

The hard-core demens are there, he thought. *If you get stuck doing a rotation in there, come back and find me. I'll make sure you get swapped out.*

Thanks. I smiled my fake appreciation and glanced at the gate. *What about the north wing? Who do they keep in there?*

Oh, you won't get sent there. He shrugged. *That's only for medical treatment and recovery. Mostly empty.*

North wing it was. Anna's original hack and Hinckley's swap of my information must have worked, because my ID came back approved. The door clicked its unlock and I hurried toward it.

Hey, maybe we can have coffee after your shift?

I threw a smile back to him. *Maybe.* If I was lucky, I would be out long before the shift was done. As I stepped over the threshold and through the shield, a slight electric buzz bristled my hair out. I smoothed down my electric hairdo, and the gate swung shut behind me, clicking into place. The orderly ahead of me disappeared into a side entrance to the east wing.

I paused in the parking lot and did a quick scan of the west wing. The guard was telling the truth—not that I expected anything different from a reader. It was filled with orderlies, several doctors huddled in their offices, and almost a hundred demens. Their minds were like a witch's brew of peppermint-scented thoughts—fear, anxiety, panic—and even the light brush on their minds was disorienting. I pulled back and scanned the east wing. It was more of the same, only worse. Many of the demens there were sedated, but the ones that weren't had violent, murderous thoughts. There were more orderlies and locked cells and fewer doctors. I drew back before their thoughts could make my stomach churn.

I scurried down the center of the parking lot, past a fleet of electric carts and a couple of shiny hydro cars, and reached for the north wing where Kestrel probably kept his jacker prisoners, but I was stopped cold by a disruptor field that surrounded the entire building. There was no gate controller in the other wings, and it made sense that he would be secured behind the shield. The trick would be getting in. I searched the perimeter of the shield as much as I could stand without the clamminess overtaking my brain, then pulled back to scan the tunnels that connected the east and west wings to the north wing. I brushed against a mind as hard as a rock in the access tunnel, and jerked back before he was alerted to my presence.

A jacker guard.

And not just any jacker guard. I hadn't felt a mind barrier that strong since I'd tangled with the jacker guard at the Great Lakes Hospital, back when I was liberating the changelings. If this guy was the same Granite Guard that had nearly choked me to death then, it was a good thing I was armed. There was no way I would get past him otherwise.

The dart gun strapped to my ankle was reassuringly heavy as I approached the main entrance of the east wing. Hovering by the door, I scanned the minds ahead of me. If I was going to take on the guard, I needed access to the tunnel at the far end of the building. Most of the demens rattled in their locked rooms on upper floors, while the main floor held a large grouping of demens together. Some were sedated, others awake but confined to their beds. I slipped through the door and tiptoed up the three marble steps to the interior double glass doors that walled off the ward. A stale stench of sweat and antiseptic filled the air. A large orderly in terrifying pink scrubs like mine waved at me from behind a glass-enclosed nursing station that guarded the ward. I linked into her mind.

What'cha doing there, girlie, standing around like you've got nothing to do? she thought. *My lord, I swear the people they send me. Get your butt over here, child.*

I jacked her to open the door to the demens ward. Her thoughts echoed my command and she buzzed me in. When I opened the door, the smell of antiseptic grew exponentially stronger. I started breathing through my mouth and searched the orderly's mind, but she didn't have access to the restricted area at the back of her ward.

No matter. I was pretty sure the jacker guard did.

I crept through the ward, keeping an eye on the demens. I brushed their minds very lightly, trying to not soak up too much of their madness. It caught me off guard when one of the minds I swept was a jacker.

His withered body was strapped to a cot, eyes shut and mind barely conscious, but awake enough to push back. Why was Kestrel keeping jackers sedated in the demens ward? Didn't he worry about them escaping? I made a mental note to check on him on the way back out, but I had to find Kestrel and get him immobilized before I could worry about coming back for inmates in the demens ward. Still, I slowly checked each mind as I passed by, searching for more jackers hidden among the demens.

I stumbled to a stop when I saw a shock of red hair lying on a pillow. The inmate was younger than the other jacker, maybe mid-twenties, and asleep. His fitful dreams were like any demens waking nightmares, filled with needles and voices and nightmarish creatures. I couldn't tell for sure if he was a jacker, but the resemblance to Molloy was unmistakable: wild red hair, body too large for the cot, meaty hands flopped over the edges.

I jacked him out of his sleep, speeding up his heart, but it took him a long minute to come to. As I probed around in his mind, I found the soft dead spots that were the result of Kestrel's heinous experiments. The man's name should be popping up by now, as it did for even the demens, but his thoughts were too jumbled. I wasn't sure if *he* knew who he was. The man held tight to a floating image of Molloy, like it was a life raft in the stormy seas of his mind.

That was all the confirmation I needed.

Molloy's brother was fully awake now, which was still a confused state for him. I ordered him to come with me, and he was as compliant as a dove, offering no resistance whatsoever, in spite of being a jacker. I needed to keep him close—I wasn't going to take any chance of losing him in whatever craziness would happen when it was time to get out of here.

I stalked toward the back of the ward, Molloy's brother stumbling behind me. The connecting tunnel was on the second floor, so we climbed the steps and to my surprise, my badge worked to swipe us in. I quickly knelt down, pushed aside the extra fabric of the scrubs, and unstrapped the gun from my ankle. Holding it forward, I pulled open the door. The hall was close to a hundred feet long between the two buildings, and at the far end was Granite Guard. Same military-grade haircut and fatigues, and apparently still doing Kestrel's dirty work. I knew it would be futile to try to jack in, but I surged against his mind barrier anyway to test his reach. He pushed me away, but his reach wasn't as far as mine, and at its limits he wasn't so strong.

He started sprinting toward me.

I aimed my dart gun at him and fired, the pop echoing off the hard walls of the hall, but he kept coming. I let out an exasperated breath and aimed again. He had covered almost a third of the distance between us already, and the intensity of his mind on mine grew.

He also had a gun.

I fired again and twirled behind Molloy's brother, using him as a bulky and confused shield. The guard cursed, but his footsteps kept coming, so I peeked under the hairy arm in front of me. Suddenly the pressure on my head ceased, and Molloy's brother knocked me to the ground with his massive arm. Granite Guard was in his head! Rather than trying to fight him in Molloy's brother's head, I twisted on the cold tiled floor and fired again. Granite Guard stumbled, the shot went wide, but he fell and slid to a stop. I wasn't sure which shot had gone in, but I'd used up three darts taking him down and I wasn't even inside the north wing yet. Molloy's brother's shoulders went slack, and he stared at me as if I were a curious bug he had just found lying on the floor.

I got up before he decided to squash me.

The clock was ticking now before someone discovered what had happened. For all I knew, there were security cameras that had already taken in our little scuffle, and more guards with guns were on the way. I snagged the badge off Granite Guy and noticed that the gun lying near his hand wasn't a dart gun. I hesitated, then picked it up and tucked it in the back of my pants. Jacking Molloy's brother to follow me, I hurried down the hall toward the north wing.

Granite Guy's badge granted me access through the checkpoint scanner. As soon as we stepped through the disruptor field, I lightly swept the building, searching for Kestrel. If I had any chance of taking him by surprise, I had to do it fast.

The north wing looked just like the hospital it formerly was. We dashed down a sterile white hall with speckled industrial carpeting while I scanned all three floors. There were patches of disruptor-shielded rooms interspersed with unshielded rooms that held sedated jackers. Several of the orderlies were jackers, but most were regular readers. I couldn't find anyone who was in charge of the gate at the entrance. Dead center on the bottom floor was a square shielded room that seemed centrally located enough to be a command center.

I found a concrete stairway at the end of the hall and Molloy's brother's bare feet padded behind me. On the first floor, I creaked the stairwell door open, dart gun held at the ready. We jogged through the main hallway toward the center of the building. The shielded section had a door with no markings and no one nearby. In fact, we hadn't seen a soul since we entered the north wing, even though jackers and orderlies filled the rooms and floors around us.

I swiped Granite Guard's badge, but of course it didn't work. As I reached to find a jacker guard who might have access, the door swung out fast, clipping me on the chin and sending me reeling into the lumpy chest of Molloy's brother. He held me up, with an odd look on his face, like he had just woken from a dream and found me there, crumpled against him.

Coming from the door, I saw another flash of red hair.

Molloy!

I tried to jack him and swung the dart gun his way, but he pushed me away from his mind and batted the gun out of my hand. It tumbled down the carpeted hallway. I reached for the gun tucked behind my pants, but Molloy's brother grabbed my wrist and painfully twisted it, holding the gun high in the air and nearly lifting me off the ground. I tried jacking him to let me go, but Molloy's presence was firmly in control. Molloy's brother looked down at me, like a giant teddy bear that was confused why his owner was playing with guns.

Molloy wrenched the gun from my grasp, but his brother didn't let me go, just left me dangling there. The door swung closed behind Molloy as he studied me with a crooked smile.

"Ah, lassie," Molloy said. "It's about time you showed up.

Kind of you to save me the trouble of rounding up my brother Liam, as well."

Molloy was here, in Kestrel's facility. Jacking his brother Liam to hold me captive. *Waiting for me.* My body buckled under the weight of a thousand lies.

I wasn't the bait. I was the prize.

chapter FIFTEEN

Molloy banged on the control room door with the handle of Granite Guard's gun, while holding my hands behind my back in his other enormous hand. His brother Liam stood limply next to us. The door swung open. I should have completely expected it by now, but my heart still sank.

Kestrel.

I struggled against Molloy's hold, but he just tightened his grip until I gasped. The pain nearly brought me to my knees.

"Bring her in," Kestrel said.

Molloy shoved me through the doorway, still clutching my hands. His brother Liam followed, Molloy's presence in his mind driving him forward and providing a sort of comfort that I would have found heartwarming if Molloy hadn't just delivered me into Kestrel's hands. The door clicked behind us. Kestrel crossed the room to sit on the corner of a pale metal desk. I tried to slow my breathing and keep calm. What did Julian say? *If you get caught, don't panic.*

I wasn't panicking, but keeping the anger at Molloy under wraps was more than I could do. "What did you do with Raf?" I wrenched around to throw my accusation into Molloy's face and shoved into his mind as well. The surge of my thoughts into his summoned up an image of Raf lying on the floor, like a broken doll, his limbs poking into the air. I only saw it for a split second before Molloy pushed me out of his mind, but all the air went out of me with it.

"Easy there, little Kira." Molloy's lips curled up into a cruel smile. "Your pet is dead, so you needn't worry about getting him back now."

All energy drained out of my body with his words. *Raf is dead.* A dull roar of protest filled my mind. *No!*

Molloy was saying something, but not to me. "She's no doubt still armed, Kestrel."

"Well, go ahead and pat her down," Kestrel said with a bored expression, like this was the least of his concerns.

Molloy slid open a drawer on Kestrel's desk, placed the gun inside, and shut it. His hand was now free to pat me down while keeping a vise grip on my wrists. He found my phone and tossed it on Kestrel's desk. Molloy's rough hands kept up their invasive search, nearly toppling me over, but my mind was seized by that image of Raf, crumpled, lifeless. Maybe he wasn't dead. Maybe Molloy was lying...

All of a sudden, Molloy was lifting the hem of my scrubs up and over my head and dragging my arms up with it. I struggled against him, desperately searching for the thought grenade capsules, but the smooth pink fabric slipped through my fingers. I was left standing in my t-shirt. Kestrel tore his gaze from the screens and raised an eyebrow.

"She has more stashed somewhere," Molloy said. "I'm sure of it."

Kestrel nodded and returned to studying the screens. Molloy discovered the patches in my sock, so I kicked him. He growled, yanked my shoe and sock off in one painful scraping motion, and tossed the patches on Kestrel's desk.

"Come on now," Molloy said. "Off with the rest."

My body stiffened. There was no way I was taking off my clothes for Molloy. I eyed the crumpled scrub shirt he still held in his hand, wondering if I could find the capsule and crush it fast enough if I lunged for it. I decided I had to wait for the right moment, so I slowly took off the other sock and shoe. There wasn't anything in there anyway.

I threw it at him, but he easily caught it. "I'm not stripping for you, praver."

Kestrel let out a chuckle. "She's fine the way she is."

I glanced around the room. It wasn't so much a control room as Kestrel's personal office, complete with a beaten-up desk, a rickety metal chair, a stack of scribepads neatly squared with the corner of the desk, and a dozen monitors lining the wall. I stared openmouthed at the screens. He had almost certainly watched me the entire way in.

It was an elaborate trap. Too elaborate. I closed my mouth and examined Kestrel. Same cold blue eyes from the last time I saw him handcuffed to his bed post. Same hollowed cheeks that looked like they had been scarred. He ignored me, flicking looks across the screens. Why had he gone to so much trouble to lure me here? Molloy, who was obviously working for him, already had me in his grasp two days ago. At the diner.

He could have taken me then and left Raf alone entirely.

Raf. That image of him dead on the floor reared up in my mind again, and my knees went weak. What was going on? I began to think *now* was an excellent time to panic. Molloy was looking me over again, as I stood in front of him with bare feet, a t-shirt, and too-long scrub pants. He must have decided I wasn't hiding anything else, because he walked my scrub shirt and shoes over to a high shelf that held a dead plant and a chipped coffee cup. Kestrel was pretty spare in his decor. His apartment had been the same way, empty of anything personal, no memory films or personal items. It was like the guy didn't exist outside of his work. I tried not to stare at the scrubs too long, afraid to give myself away. I would have to wait for my chance to get to the capsules.

"She's all yours," Molloy said to Kestrel. "I kept my end of the bargain. Time for Liam and me to make our exit." His hand rested on a dart gun holstered at his side, and I wouldn't be surprised if he planned to shoot his way out if Kestrel reneged on whatever agreement they had made to bring me in.

"Not yet," Kestrel said. "Besides, I don't think you'll want to miss the show." He turned to me. "What do you think, Kira? How long will it take your friends to come in after you?"

"What friends?"

Molloy snorted and Kestrel gave me a look like I was being a silly little girl. My face heated up. Molloy knew Julian and all the mages. Knew about all their plans. Of course Molloy had told Kestrel everything.

"Well," Kestrel said. "I don't want them to break down the front door, so we might as well let them in." Kestrel tapped his ear, using some kind of com system. "Drop the disruptor field at the front gate."

A full minute ticked by with Kestrel and Molloy scanning the screen images of the front gate, the demens wards, and the connecting tunnels. The other screens held images of prisoners in their cells, asleep on cots in sterile white rooms. They didn't look peaceful, more like simply unconscious. There were hundreds of jackers in the building. What made these prisoners so special? I had more pressing things to worry about at the moment.

Maybe Julian wasn't coming because he had figured out that it was a trap. If I had been the one to drop the shield, I would have linked to Ava or called on the phone. The phone! It was still sitting on Kestrel's desk. I quickly jacked into the mindware interface: Molloy had left it on! I pulled up Julian's number and hastily tried to scrit him a message—just a single word, *trap*—but the phone had lit up and Molloy quickly snatched it up. While he fumbled to turn it off, I darted behind his back toward the shelf, but he caught my arm and yanked me close, my bare feet dragging across the rough industrial carpeting.

He stared down at me. "Don't be trying anything, lassie."

Molloy pocketed my phone, then twirled the desk chair around and shoved me into it, keeping a hand on my shoulder. Had the message gone through? Maybe that would be enough to warn Julian. Kestrel's gaze never wavered from the screen with the gate. A movement on the screens caught my eye, and a boy with dark hair—Julian—led a crew toward the guard. The gate sprung open as they neared and Julian paused.

I wanted to scream and reflexively reached out, but was stopped by the chill of the field surrounding Kestrel's office. Julian signaled to the mages behind him, and Ava, Sasha, Hinckley, and Myrtle crept forward, following his lead, right through the gate.

Kestrel tapped the com link again. "No," he said to whoever was on the other end. "Wait until they're inside the tunnel."

No, no, no. Think!

I couldn't jack Kestrel or Molloy on my own. Maybe I could jack Molloy's brother, just long enough for a distraction. It might buy me a second of time so I could reach the scrubs and activate the thought grenade.

Whatever I was going to do, it had to be now.

I plunged into Liam's mind, which churned with confused thoughts even as he was fascinated by all the colors on the screens. Molloy was still there, holding tight onto Liam's mind. At the same time, I wriggled out from under Molloy's grasp and lunged up from the chair, past Liam, heading for the shelf. Molloy growled and caught me by the wrist. It was the same wrist that Liam had twisted before, and I let out a yelp that finally drew Kestrel's attention.

"Hold her still," Kestrel said to Molloy, then returned his gaze to the screen. Molloy forced me back into the metal chair, his two hands welded to my shoulders and jamming me farther into the seat. I tucked my injured wrist against my chest.

"There will be no more escapes, Kira." Kestrel's eyes remained glued to the screens. "No more rescue attempts." I watched helplessly as Julian and the mages worked their way through the demens ward. "Now that you've brought all the most dangerous," he said and flicked a look to me, "and the most unusually talented jackers to me, there won't be anyone left to come get you."

Julian and the mages found the door to the access tunnel that I had left open. I could hardly pull in a breath. Julian examined the inert body of the guard. A smile lit his face when he found the dart sticking out of his chest. My dart. From the gun Julian had given me. He must think I was simply waiting for him.

I was suffocating on the need to scream out. Warn him. Do something.

Kestrel tapped the com link again. "Now." Orange mist floated down from the ceiling of the connecting tunnel. My shoulders caved further under Molloy's weight. Ava spotted it first. Her shout—soundless on Kestrel's monitor—alerted the others. They covered their noses and mouths with their hands, but they were already stumbling. A tear leaked down my cheek as, one by one, the mages fell. Julian was the last. He almost made it to the door, his fingers fumbling adrenaline patches from his pocket, but the gas took him. The patches lay scattered on the floor, and Julian's hand fell open next to them.

An animal sound rumbled deep in my chest, and I struggled vainly against Molloy's hold. I twisted around, trying to scratch his face, grab his ears, get hold of anything to make him pay. He held me at arm's length with a sour look on his face.

"Would have been better if I'd killed you too, lassie." Molloy's teeth glistened white when he smiled. "Better for you, in any event."

"And for her friends," added Kestrel matter-of-factly. "I haven't forgotten those three darts you put in me, Kira, even if I can't remember how you got them there. But I assure you, this is nothing personal. This is much bigger than you. It always has been."

Kestrel's voice was closer now. The needle stung as it went in. As the juice clouded my mind, Molloy's leering face blurred into a patch of white and red. My last thought before the juice pulled me under was about Raf.

I hadn't been able to save him after all.

chapter SIXTEEN

When I woke up, the familiar orange anesthetic taste of the juice stung the back of my tongue. A sterile white sheet crinkled under me. My room looked identical to the ones on the screens in Kestrel's office: bare white walls blending into the white tiled floor; the cot standing opposite the thin outline of a handleless door; diffuse light raining down from overhead panels. I swallowed down the dryness that came from the juice and sat up. My wrist couldn't take any weight, still sore from Molloy and his brother Liam.

I slumped on the edge of the thin cot, tempted to lie down again. I was trapped. Julian and the mages were caught. Molloy had to be long gone by now, having finally gotten his brother in exchange for the rest of us.

I should find a way to break out.

I should try to escape.

All I wanted to do was lie down and wish it all away.

A cloud of anger boiled in my chest. It was my wishful

thinking—that I could go home, that Raf and my family would be safe from the likes of Molloy and Kestrel—that had landed me back in Kestrel's grasp.

And Raf...

Tears stung my throat even more, making me cough and sob at the same time. The image in Molloy's mind of Raf sprawled on the floor haunted my thoughts. If Molloy was telling the truth, Raf was dead. If not, he would either kill him now or maybe trade him to some praver in Jackertown. Then Raf would live, although I wasn't sure if that was better or not.

My shoulders caved and my knees slowly tucked up until I tipped sideways on the cot, a tight ball of pain crushing me from the inside out. Tears dripped onto the starched pillowcase and clouded my head, a fog descending on my brain. Maybe I could just slip into it, fade away—

A click sounded from the door. I mentally lunged at whoever was coming through, only to find it was Granite Guard. He easily batted away my juice-hindered mental reach. I rolled up to face him, bracing my bare feet on the floor. Maybe I could make a run for it. I reached through the open door, but it was blocked by the disruptor field, same as the rest of the room.

Kestrel came in with a scribepad in hand and two orderlies in tow. One was tall and thin, his hands twitchy at his sides. The other was carved from the same square-jawed, muscular gene pool as Granite Guard, with no neck and the shoulders of a grizzly bear. Grizzly Man closed the door with a mechanical thunk that I was sure meant it was locked. Not that I had any chance of getting past Kestrel's entourage anyway.

Kestrel didn't say a word, just nodded to the other three. The pressure of their minds hit me like a blow and knocked me back on the mattress. I pushed up with my weakened wrist, but I could barely sit up under the onslaught.

The pressure ramped up further. I clutched my head, as if that would ward them off. The intensity kept climbing. I had to stop them before my skull imploded. I launched myself off the cot, running smack into Grizzly Man. I flailed my hands against his chest, but it was like pounding a concrete wall. The pressure grew worse. I crumpled to Grizzly's feet. A sound keened in the distance, echoing off the bare hard surfaces of the walls. It bounced back to me, inside me, inside my head. Screaming, screaming, I rocked back and forth on the biting cold of the tiled floor.

The pressure cut off like a switch.

I panted against the floor, my mouth dry and buzzing. Stars twirled in front of me. I pushed myself up to sitting, gingerly touching the side of my head and half expecting to see blood on my hand, but it came away clean. Kestrel made a notation on his scribe pad, then he tilted his head toward me, giving a silent order to Granite Guard. I heaved myself off the floor and scrambled back to the cot, but there was nowhere to go. Granite Guard pinned me down while the gangly orderly came at me with a needle. I kicked and twisted, making it difficult for them to find a spot to stick me, but Granite Guard leaned his knee into my stomach, knocking the wind out of me and momentarily holding me still while the needle pierced my skin.

They both quickly backed away.

Whatever they injected into me raged like fire through my veins and boiled off the fog in my head. Blood pounded my ears, and my legs twitched with the need to run. I fought to gasp in enough oxygen to feed whatever was pulsing through my body. They had put some kind of adrenaline in me, like Julian's patches, but why?

The answer came with another onslaught of pressure. This time, hyped up on the drug, I was able to push back. I forced them slightly back from my head, stepping down the pressure and pain. After a moment, they stopped, and I shoved them back into their own minds. Granite Guy's head was too hard, and his cousin Grizzly was the same, so I concentrated on the orderly with the relatively weaker mind barrier.

I poured my anger and frustration into jacking him, and his knees buckled.

"Enough," Kestrel said calmly. He shoved me out of the orderly's head and back into my own. I scuttled back on my cot. My ragged breathing was the only sound for a moment as Kestrel regarded me.

"I'd like to do a few baseline tests." Kestrel's sharp gaze looked like he wanted to pierce my skull to take a peek inside. "It will go much easier if you cooperate."

No doubt it would be easier on Kestrel if I cooperated. I had no intention of doing any such thing. I just stared back at him.

If he came close, I was contemplating biting him. I gagged, not liking that thought very much and feeling way too trapped. I needed to think my way out of this, now that my head was clear of the juice.

Kestrel nodded, as if he could hear my thoughts, and for a short paranoid moment I thought maybe he could.

I seriously needed to pull myself together.

Kestrel tapped his ear. "Pemberly is coming out for trial two." The door clicked and swung open, and with a wave, Kestrel sent Pemberly out of the room. Another guard was stationed outside the door, his hand resting on the bulky dart gun at his hip. They weren't taking any chances—even with the door open, the disruptor field was firmly in place. Pemberly walked right through it, and the door swung shut behind him.

Escape looked impossible.

The part of my heart that hadn't hit bottom yet sank a little further.

Kestrel folded his arms, tucking the scribepad under one. "I'd like you to try to jack into Mr. Harrier's mind." He flipped his hand to Granite Guard. "Please try hard."

I drew up my knees and held them tight to my chest. "Do it yourself, if you're so interested in what he's thinking." Granite Guard looked like he was relishing whatever Kestrel expected me to do. Grizzly stared at me like he expected me to make a sudden move. I wasn't sure what Kestrel was getting at, anyway. If I could jack into Granite Guy—Harrier, whatever—then I would have already done it.

Kestrel smirked. "You're one of the few here whose thoughts are truly private, Kira," he said. "I'm not so much interested in what's in his head as what's in yours."

Well *that* he wasn't going to get. I was determined about that if nothing else.

"For now I'd like to simply know the extent of your abilities." He untucked his scribepad and continued in a clinical tone. "For example, your mind barrier seems exceedingly strong, even harder than Mr. Harrier's. And yet I seem to be able to push you out of Agent Pemberly's mind rather easily. So I'm wondering just what is the extent of your jacking strength?"

"I guess that's going to be a mystery for you."

A light knock at the door drew Kestrel's attention. He tapped his ear. "Yes?" He listened for a moment. "Bring her in." The door swung open. Pemberly had returned, now gripping the arm of a girl. She stumbled as she crossed the threshold, her feet bare and her straggly blond hair hiding her face. Pemberly left her standing in the middle of the room and closed the door behind him. When she looked up, her fine features were shadowed, her eyes sunken and dark.

Ava.

I uncurled and clutched the edge of the cot. What was Kestrel doing?

"Ah, good," he said. "I see that you recognize her. Now, please. Jack into Miss Trinkle's mind so we can have a sense of your uninhibited jacking strength."

"I'm not interested in your games, Kestrel." I threw my words at him, but I couldn't take my eyes off Ava. She seemed thinner. How long had I been out? What had Kestrel done to her?

"Mr. Harrier, if you would."

Ava's eyes clamped shut, and she fell to her knees in wordless pain.

"Stop it!" My body tensed, ready to fly at all three of them again, even though it would do no good.

"That's up to you," Kestrel said. "Are you going to stand by and watch her suffer, Kira? That doesn't seem to be your personality type. You're more the kind that pokes your nose into places it doesn't belong. Surely you'd like to stop the suffering of your friend."

My hands bunched the thin sheets of the cot, but what choice did I have? I jacked hard into Ava's mind and found Harrier there. He was digging through her memories, causing the kind of internal pain that comes from mental violation. I grabbed hold of Harrier's presence and managed to pull him out of the cavern of her memories to wrestle with me full time. Ava tried to help, but she was weak. Her strawberry mindscent was tinged with orange—was she normally this weak, or was she still under the influence of the juice? I didn't have time to figure it out; I was too busy trying to get Harrier out of her head.

When I finally moved the solid spot of his presence a little, he fled her mind.

Are you okay? I asked. *I'm sorry, I just... I'm sorry.*

It's okay, she thought. *I'm okay.* But I could tell she wasn't.

I lightly searched for the dull, dead spots that were in Liam's mind and let out a sigh of relief when I didn't find any.

Where are the others? I asked. *Have you seen them?*

No. Her thoughts were fragmented and tired. I backed out slowly, trying not to cause her any more pain.

"About a five or six," Harrier said impassively, and Kestrel made a note on his scribepad. The desire to make them pay for what they were doing was a hot fire in my chest. How much of this pointless pain and suffering had they already inflicted on innocent jackers like Ava? But there was no way I could jack Kestrel or Harrier, much less Grizzly, standing by like a Roman centurion. Even hyped up on Kestrel's drug, I could barely take on Pemberly.

Which was almost certainly why they were all here: to test me, but keep me safely caged.

I smothered the fire threatening to flare up and consume me so I could think. There had to be a flaw in their system. I needed more information.

"So, did you get tired of torturing children, Kestrel?" Ice dripped from my voice. "Graduated to twenty-year-olds? How civilized of you."

He didn't even look up from his scribepad and silently consulted with Harrier, who took Ava by the arm and steered her toward the door.

Kestrel held a finger to his ear. "Harrier and patient 603 are coming out." They seemed to have an elaborate checking system. The room was almost certainly monitored, like the other patients' rooms had been. Was the person on Kestrel's com link watching us to make sure everything was going according to plan? Or was Kestrel talking to the guard outside the room?

The door swung open and Harrier led Ava out. I wanted to link back into Ava's mind and find out if there was anything she knew that could help, but she was already through the disruptor field in the doorway, clutching her stomach as she went. I hoped against hope that they would leave her alone now that they had done their test.

"Ready for trial three," Kestrel spoke to the com, then finally looked at me. "I suspect, based on what I know of your previous escapes, that your reach extends beyond most jackers'. Is that true?"

I just stared at him. *My previous escapes.* How much did Kestrel know about me? I had to be careful not to tip my hand. It might be my only advantage.

He tapped his com link again, this time holding my stare. "You may proceed."

My heart stuttered.

To me he said, "There's a changeling somewhere in the building. He's receiving painful electrical shocks from Mr. Pemberly, carefully tuned to his jacker mind. I suggest you find him."

My mouth fell open. What kind of sick game was Kestrel playing? "I won't do it."

"The shocks will continue until you do. I'm in no hurry."

I didn't for a second doubt that Kestrel would do as he promised and probably make it worse if I delayed. I clenched my fists and mentally pushed out. Sure enough the disruptor field was down. I quickly brushed through the hundreds of minds in the hospital, searching for the changeling. I found Pemberly intent on administering the shocks. He wasn't expecting me, so I easily knocked him out.

I linked into the mind of the changeling. *Are you okay?* He was so disoriented by the jacker-tuned shocks that I had to pull out of his mind for fear of getting trapped in the swirling electrical field. I roamed the building, searching for Ava or Julian or the other mages. Kestrel must have them locked behind disruptor-field-reinforced rooms like mine, because I couldn't find any of them.

"Pemberly!" Kestrel's voice made me start. "Control, this is Kestrel. Shield!" Suddenly the disruptor field sliced through my mental reach, like a knife had cut through part of my brain. I gasped with the pain of it, my hands holding my head. The agony of having my thoughts chopped in half made me double over. I staggered back to the cot, catching myself before I fell. I reached to the door. It was sealed with the mindwave-disruptor field again.

When I finally shook my head clear, Kestrel's face was on fire with an excitement that made me shrink back. "I see. You can jack at that distance. Very interesting."

He scribbled furiously on his scribepad. Kestrel had only told me to find the changeling. He must have expected me to link a thought to Pemberly to tell him to stop. It didn't occur to him that I could stop the experiment, which was at least a couple of hundred feet away, by knocking Pemberly out. But how could I keep from revealing what I could do, when he was torturing people in front of me?

My fists curled up. The only one who was getting any information here was Kestrel and I needed to change that. What *was* Kestrel really after? Was he trying to create a legion of super jackers, like I thought? Thanks to me, he now had the mages and a wide range of DNA samples to choose from. So why the heinous experiments?

"Look," I said. "Why don't you just take our DNA and let us go?"

Kestrel frowned slightly and seemed to consider something, then said, "I've had your DNA from the beginning, Kira. I do appreciate you bringing the others in, though. That will certainly speed things up."

"Speed up what things?" Kestrel ignored me and went back to his scribepad.

Did having the mages' DNA speed up his quest to create super jackers? Or had I simply delivered more subjects for his experiments to discover a medical way to destroy us all? Was he trying to damage parts of our brains with his serums or was that just a side effect? He said he wanted to see what I could do. A *baseline test*, he said, before whatever serums he had planned for me.

I pressed my back against the smooth wall behind the cot. The chill from the wall and the situation seeped into me. Whatever Kestrel had planned, there was no way he would ever let us go. He'd use us up in his experiments and then we'd waste away in the demens ward. I searched for something I could use to bargain my way out, but I was locked in his cell with no leverage whatsoever. He already had my DNA. He had *me*. What else could he want?

Then I realized he had already told me: he wanted inside my head.

"You want to know what I can do?" I asked. Kestrel looked up, mildly interested. "I'll tell you everything I can do, how it all works, why you can't get into my head. That is, if you want to know." I would make up stuff if I had to. The trick would be getting Kestrel to believe me. "I'll do whatever little demonstrations you want to prove it, but then you need to let us go—all of us."

He laughed a little. "You're far too useful at this point to release." He had that clinical tone again. "You were too old for the experiments before, but now that my research has advanced, you and your friends are the perfect test subjects. You may not like it." A cruel smile twisted up his lips. "But like I said before— if you cooperate, things will be much easier."

Easier. He meant easier on *me*. Easier on the changelings or Ava or whoever was the other party to his experiment. The chill settled into my stomach and made it seize up.

Kestrel nodded to Grizzly, who produced a syringe filled with a clear serum. He came toward me slowly, gauging whether I would put up a fight.

I wanted to.

Every part of me screamed out to fight him.

But I didn't.

I hardly felt the pain of the needle.

"Very good." Kestrel checked his scribepad one last time, then turned to the door. Grizzly went out first and Kestrel paused at the threshold. "Don't worry. I'll be back later to see if it worked." The door clicked shut behind him.

Whatever Kestrel had injected in me coursed painlessly through my veins, probably heading straight for my brain to do its damage there. I didn't feel a thing.

I was completely numb, inside and out.

chapter SEVENTEEN

Time crawled by.

I forced down the morning delivery of flavorless oatmeal from Pemberly. At least I thought it was morning. Oatmeal seemed like it should come in the morning. When I returned to my cot, an indentation the shape of my body remained pressed into it.

The lights in my cell never dimmed and the air never stirred, always warm enough to not be cold. I wasn't sure if time was ticking by in days or weeks. I spent most of it curled up on the cot. Kestrel came and went. Sometimes there were more injections. Sometimes it was just tests. Mostly there were long stretches when nothing happened.

That was when I probed around in my own mind, wondering what Kestrel's injections were doing to me. Searching for dead spots. Would I be able to sense them? As time dragged on, I became more and more certain that I wouldn't get out of Kestrel's torment room except to head to the demens ward, to slowly become addled like Liam. How long had Liam been under Kestrel's care? He hadn't been at the camp, that much I was sure of. He would never have lasted, and Molloy would have found him.

Molloy. Part of me clung to the idea that he had traded Raf, rather than killed him. I wanted to believe it. Except then my mind drifted to the horrible things that would happen to Raf as a slave to jackers, and I hoped that Molloy had actually killed him instead.

Then my brain shut down, because I couldn't keep that thought without going insane.

I should have slipped away after I escaped the camp, like Simon wanted. Stayed far from everyone I loved and survived as a jacker hidden among the readers. That was the only way any of this could have turned out okay.

But I wasn't strong enough to do that.

At least with me locked up in Kestrel's facility, my family was relatively safe. Molloy had no reason to go after them, not with his revenge already exacted on me. He would dispose of Raf's body and go on his way.

I rolled over and faced the wall. My body ached from being on one side too long. My mind didn't feel different, but I decided there was no way for me to know if it was spotted with dead zones. Maybe they were already there.

The door clicked open, but I didn't bother to move. The scuffle of feet on the linoleum told me there were three of them. There were usually three—Kestrel, one of the strong jackers like Harrier or Grizzly, and an orderly or agent like Pemberly. Hard-soled shoes tapped the floor. Those belonged to Kestrel. I kept my eyes shut, wondering if there was any point in resisting this time. Most times I didn't. They came and went so quickly it was better to get it over with. Sometimes I did, when I couldn't stand it anymore and anger climbed out of the deep well of my despair. Those times were worse, lasted longer, and were usually more painful for everyone.

Kestrel was right about that—it was easier on me if I cooperated.

"Kira?" Kestrel's voice was quiet. Did he think I was sleeping, just because my eyes were closed and I was ignoring him?

"Kira's not home right now," I said, mustering my best gallows humor. I opened my eyes to stare at the wall. "Please check back later."

"I'd like to test your strength today," he said stiffly.

I took a deep breath and rolled over. This time he'd brought a changeling along to be the object of my "strength" testing. I eased my body up to sitting and stretched. Were the aches from my voluntary bed rest or were Kestrel's chemicals wasting away my body? I supposed it didn't matter.

"I thought you gave up testing changelings." The sarcasm was weak this time. I just didn't have it in me, staring at the dull look in the changeling's eyes. He was maybe fourteen and looked like he'd been through a lot more of Kestrel's tests than I had. If there was any justice in the world, Kestrel would suffer a long and painful death. At that moment, I would gladly be the person to make that happen.

Kestrel nodded to Pemberly, his freaky little assistant, who obliged him by jacking into the changeling's mind. The boy winced, but bore whatever was going on in his head with an infinite amount of patience. Like a dog that's been beaten so many times he doesn't even pull away anymore. My hatred for Kestrel stirred, rising up from the depths and hurling me off the cot. I ran straight at Pemberly, shoving him hard and fast. My weight and speed weren't much, but it was enough to surprise him and he stumbled backward. At the same time, I jacked into the changeling's mind and found Pemberly inflicting imaginary stomach pain. I flung him out.

Pemberly immediately pushed back in and wrestled with me in the changeling's mind. I took a threatening step toward Pemberly, fists raised, but Harrier caught hold of my arm. I tried to push Pemberly out again, but I was weaker than I had been in our countless previous sessions. I couldn't move him at all.

I struggled against Harrier's grip and he let me go. At the same time, Pemberly fled the changeling's mind. Air gasped out of me. My head swam. I pulled back to my own mind.

I was weak. Weaker. I could feel it.

A full-body shudder shook me. I stumbled backward and grabbed the cot to sit back down. The injections were finally finding their mark. I tried not to let the panic show on my face, even though Kestrel wasn't looking at me. He and Pemberly were having a wordless conversation while Kestrel wrote on his scribepad.

They left in a scuffle of feet, just like they had come, taking the changeling with them.

I flopped down on the cot, my stomach threatening to hurl up the oatmeal. I thought I could rescue changelings like the boy with the dull eyes. I thought I could finally stop Kestrel. Instead, I was trapped playing Kestrel's games, while he slowly worked his way into my head. Bit by bit, with serums and tests, he was getting inside me. He couldn't jack in—yet—but it was only a matter of time before he would find a way to crack open my head.

My mind fled that thought and landed on the first time I woke up in one of Kestrel's cells. That was when I discovered I could reach inside my own mind. It was by chance, as I was desperately trying to escape Kestrel and his no-win options of going to the camp or sending jackers there. I found I could speed up my own heart rate to fight off the juice.

Maybe I could do the opposite too.

Was it possible to slow my heart until my mind turned dark and empty, like Simon's when he died? His mind had hollowed out at the end, empty except for echoes of my thoughts searching for his. Somehow I didn't think it would work—I would just drive myself unconscious. Maybe I could make my heart stop all at once. By the time I passed out, maybe I would already be dead. Could I do it? Was that the only way out of Kestrel's trap?

I curled up on the cot, facing away from the door and reaching inside my mind. My body quivered even though I hadn't done anything yet. I gingerly probed inside my head, suddenly scared of breaking something. Just thinking about what I could do to my own mind sent a part of me howling in protest, like a crazed fiend banging around in my brain. But I didn't want to be Kestrel's guinea pig any more. I wanted to stop him before it got to the point where I no longer could. Maybe I couldn't rescue anyone, not even myself. Maybe I couldn't stop him from experimenting on other jackers. But I could stop him from using *me*.

I pulled out of the exploration of my head, took a shaky breath, and ran my hands along my face, scrubbing some feeling back into it. Could I do this? I stared at the wet streaks along my palms. I hadn't even realized the tears were leaking out. I blinked and the synth tattoo on my wrist seemed to jump through the blurriness of my vision, as if the red lines of the Celtic knot were alive and the two pieces of the heart were reaching for each other with their tangled strings. Somewhere, Raf's tattoo was the same—two halves, reaching for each other. I touched the lines on my skin, drawing them closer together.

All the running, all the hiding, all the changing of our names, my hair, my looks. All of it was my attempt to keep the people I loved safe from the danger I had brought into their lives: the haters who vented their fear with bricks through our front window; the jackers who attacked us in Gurnee; Molloy, the clan leader who delivered me back to Kestrel for revenge. All my attempts to hide, to be someone else, to keep everyone safe, and Raf *still* ended up in Molloy's hands. The changelings were still in prison, and now the mages were too. All of it... for nothing.

Kestrel had won.

If I slowed my heartbeat down until my mind emptied... that was just another way to hide.

Another way to let Kestrel win.

As long as I was alive, as long as my mind was intact, there was the possibility of getting out and finding Raf—even if it was only to bring his body home to his family. I might never get out of Kestrel's cell. I might end up wasting away like Liam in the demens ward. But I would fight Kestrel every step of the way, with everything I had, until I had no fight left in me.

I wouldn't let him win by giving up.

The door swished open behind me. I frowned at the wall. It was unusual for Kestrel to return so soon.

"Kira!" That *voice*. It didn't belong to Kestrel. I rolled over fast. Kestrel and Harrier flanked a new jacker prisoner.

Julian.

chapter EIGHTEEN

"**K**ira, sweetheart, thank God you're all right!" Julian crossed the six feet between the door and my cot in two long strides.

Sweetheart?

Before I could say anything, Julian went down on one knee, took my face in his hands, and kissed me. It was over before I could react. His hands slid around my back and he crushed me in a hug, his cheek pressed to mine.

"Kira, darling," he said. "I was so worried about you."

I had no idea what Julian was up to. I tried to play along by patting his back, but my arms were trapped in his embrace. His lips hovered near my ear and breathed a whisper across it. "Link with me, keeper."

What? I reflexively stiffened and tried to pull away, but he just held me tighter. My body twitched as I slowly reached for his mind. Instead of being gripped by an unfathomable horror, I was enveloped in an amazing sense of belonging. Of being loved. It was a warm bath of happiness that filled me with light.

And suddenly I realized that I loved Julian.

I closed my eyes and bunched his shirt in my fingers, pulling him closer. I had always loved him, from the first moment I saw him, waking me up on the couch with that gentle touch. I knew down to my core that he loved me too, and his love was all that I needed to live and breathe and exist. It completed me in a way I hadn't even known I was missing.

I love you, Julian. I twisted in his arms to plant kisses on his cheek and tried to wiggle out of his grasp so that I could reach his lips.

He gripped me so hard that his hands dug into my back. *I'm sorry,* Julian's thoughts said. *I'm sorry, Kira, I didn't know.* His words didn't make any sense to me. What could he be sorry for? He was wonderful and perfect and—

The blissful feeling of being in his arms dialed down, and my own rational thoughts fought through the haze. How could I possibly love Julian? He was the demens revolutionary who had dragged me into this mess with Kestrel. My shoulders hunched up as a chill ran down my back. Was Julian in my head? What was he *doing* to me?

Kira, I'm so sorry, Julian's thoughts cut through mine. *I didn't know the effect would be so strong, but we only have a few moments. Whatever Kestrel asks of you, just do it, okay? Play along. I have a plan.*

Julian pulled back, opening a narrow space between us. I

forced my eyes open, but had a hard time focusing. He looked down at my t-shirt. *They took your scrubs, didn't they?*

I blinked, my mind befuddled by whatever Julian had done. *Handled* me. I recognized it in my mind, but my instincts still told me that Julian loved me. That I had let him down by not keeping hold of the thought grenades. *I'm sorry. I tried Julian, but I couldn't reach the tablets...*

It's okay. He gently took my hand and pressed it over his heart.

Something hard underneath his shirt poked into my palm. Something small that didn't belong there. The third thought grenade!

It took everything I had not to show the recognition on my face.

Just play along, Julian thought again.

"That's enough, Mr. Navarro." Kestrel's voice cut through our thoughts and Harrier grabbed Julian's arm, yanking him up from the floor. My hands clutched at Julian to keep him in my arms, but his slick shirt slipped through my fingers. That false feeling of transcendent love had faded, but the whisper of it still tugged my mind and seemed to control my body.

Was that what Julian wanted? For me to act like we were lovers?

Harrier wrenched Julian away and mentally slammed me back into my own head. Kestrel took a step back and nodded to Harrier.

Julian's striking blue eyes captured me in a way that wouldn't let me go. "Everything's going to be all right, sweetheart."

Hearing Julian call me sweetheart caused an emotional vertigo that had me bracing myself on the edge of the cot. The feeling of overwhelming love surged up again and crashed into the rational part of me that knew it was only a lie he had told Kestrel. Was that how Julian managed to get to my cell? Kestrel was just the type to use that information against us in his twisted experiments.

Harrier focused on Julian, making him drop to his knees, eyes squeezed shut.

"Stop!" My hands flung out, the reflex still strong and sudden inside me.

"By all means, please do try." Kestrel barely looked up from his scribepad.

I closed my eyes and plunged into Julian's mind, expecting to find Harrier tormenting him deep inside, but instead I was enveloped in that bath of happiness again. It surprised me how much I craved it, how I soaked it up into every corner of my mind. Only there wasn't enough of it. The bath had turned lukewarm, the kind that gives you the chills even though it still has warmth. The disappointment was like a hole in my chest. Beyond the lack of fake instant-love, Julian's head was strangely empty of thoughts as well. Harrier chased a sim at the edges of Julian's mind.

While he's distracted, we have to talk quickly. Julian's thoughts echoed, as if being projected in from the outside. I had to open my eyes again to check. On the outside Julian was writhing in a false picture of torment. On the inside, Harrier believed he was actually inflicting pain. But Julian's thoughts were as calm as a mirrored lake.

How do you do that? I asked, then remembered I was supposed to be wrestling with Harrier. I closed my eyes again. Watching Julian curl in pain while I mindtalked to him made me dizzy. *Does Harrier think I'm in here?*

He's busy, Julian thought. *I'll explain later. As soon as Kestrel is done, he'll open the door to leave. Before he can get past the disruptor field, I'll crush the thought grenade.*

That will knock everyone out, including you. What am I supposed to do then?

Do you still have the adrenaline patches?

No.

Can you find some?

Molloy had confiscated the patches stashed in my sock. I would have to jack someone to find the adrenaline-like drug that Kestrel used on me before.

Yes. One way or another. I prayed my jacking strength would be enough to get the job done.

Then get it and come back for me, Julian thought. *We'll get out of here together.*

Julian gasped out loud and my eyes popped open. Harrier had a smirk on his face, as if he had just won our wrestling match. The false pain that etched Julian's face had lessened, as if his internal torment was mostly over.

I had to wrench myself out of Julian's head. Part of me didn't want to leave that pool of joy in his mind. A shudder shook me when I was finally free of that feeling. Whatever Julian had done to me—handled me—it left a creepy hangover that made for a confusing cocktail of love and hate. I would sort it out with him later.

"She's weaker," Harrier told Kestrel. "Probably a four or five now."

I scowled at them both, not sure if that was the proper reaction, but they weren't paying attention to me anyway. Julian had his hands on his knees, panting and concentrating on the floor, as if trying to recover. The love reflex surged again, making me crave another link into Julian's mind to ask if he was okay.

Kestrel looked up from his scribepad and studied me for a moment. Maybe deciding whether he wanted to put me through more tests with Julian. He nodded to Harrier, who hauled Julian up from the floor. Julian made a show of wincing, but didn't fight Harrier.

It seemed like I should protest. "Wait!" All three looked at me. Julian kept his face neutral. "Can't you just... leave him here for a while?"

"He needs to rest," Kestrel said coldly. "For the next round of tests. Don't worry, I'll bring him back when I need to test your limits again." He tapped his ear. "Patient 607 is coming out with Harrier." When the door lock clicked, Kestrel held the door and Harrier jostled Julian toward the threshold. Julian coughed. He bent over, coughed again, and then slammed his fist to his chest.

Nausea rippled from my stomach up to my throat, making

me curl over, but Kestrel, Julian, and Harrier dropped like stones. I grabbed the cot to keep my balance and then shuffled to the bodies sprawled on the floor. Harrier had landed on Julian, crushing him under his bulk. An urgent feeling welled up and begged me to push Harrier off and check that Julian was all right, but my rational thoughts beat back the lingering love-concern. The clock was ticking before we were discovered, and I needed to get the adrenaline to revive him.

My hair bristled as I passed through the disruptor shield. Another jacker orderly lay in the hallway. The thought grenade blast must have reached through the disruptor shield. I snagged the orderly's dart gun and hastily tugged his passring off his hand. The ring spun on my finger, so I closed my fist and passed it by the electronic lock on my door. It clicked.

Excellent.

A cluster of shield-protected rooms surrounded mine, limiting my reach, but shields didn't matter if I had the passring. These cells must hold the mages or other special prisoners of Kestrel's. Maybe I should let the mages out first? But Julian had told me to get the adrenaline first. I wavered. Which was the rational thought and which was the residual love-handling? I clenched the passring tighter, uncertain of what my own mind was telling me.

Footsteps echoed off the walls, coming my way from down the hall. The shielded rooms stopped me from reaching whoever was coming, so I pressed flat against the wall. A strange buzzing feeling crept along my back as shield energy bled out from the wall and raised the hair on my neck. I leaned slightly away from the wall. Maybe my Impenetrable Mind wouldn't be as affected by the shield, but now wasn't the time to test it.

An orderly skittered around the corner. As soon as he was in my line of sight, I jacked into his head. He was a reader, so I made him stand still while I searched his mind. He didn't have any wake-up meds, but he knew where they were kept—downstairs in the main medical treatment room, which was also the control room that monitored the cells. It was next door to Kestrel's office, protected by the shielding there.

Going all the way to the first floor by myself, with Julian lying prone, seemed like a really bad idea. Maybe I couldn't trust my instincts anymore, but I didn't have time to think it through. Getting help seemed like a rational choice. I unlocked the nearest room with a wave of the passring and pushed open the door. A girl with long, blond hair was curled in a ball on her cot, tall but wafer thin.

"Hey!" I whispered, my voice hoarse. "Ava? Is that you?" When she didn't move, I jacked into her head. The thought grenade had knocked her out, and her mind still swirled with the electrical vortex it had induced. I tried to wake her, but I couldn't stay in her head without getting caught in the sparking mental storm. I pulled out and searched for something to prop the door open, but there was nothing.

I reluctantly closed the door again. How far had the effects of the bomb reached? Not far enough to knock out the downstairs guard, but far enough to reach the inmates nearby. I needed adrenaline shots *now*. And a lot of it, depending on how many prisoners had been affected.

I jogged toward the frozen reader guard, gaining distance from my room and the center of the bomb blast. The passkey worked on the last shield-protected room in the hall. Inside was a dark-haired girl doing pushups in her hospital gown. The sleeves bunched up on her muscular shoulders, and the gown pooled on the floor beneath her. She paused, put a knee down, and lunged at me with her mind. It wasn't the greatest pressure I'd ever felt, but it wasn't soft either.

"Hey! I'm a friend." I pushed her away, and recognition dawned on her face.

"Oh! Kira! Of course." She tucked her legs and sprang up from the floor.

I backed into the hall as she dashed toward me. How did she recognize me so fast? She stuck her head straight through the disruptor field in the doorway without slowing down, glancing quickly up and down the corridor. She nodded in satisfaction at the guard standing nearby, staring at his shoes.

"Well done." Our faces were now close, her blue eyes piercing mine. "Is my brother with you?"

Of course. I should have recognized Anna from the fake hospital ID Julian showed me.

"Yes, but I need to find some adrenaline to revive him. And I'm pretty sure they know what's happened." We were running the same plan that Anna had originally hatched, so she should know what I meant.

"Right," she said. "Wait, don't you have it with you?" She glanced down at my bare feet, frowning as she saw there were no shoes or socks. Then she took in my appearance a little more slowly. "What happened to you?"

I must look worse than I thought. I certainly hadn't been doing pushups in my cell for the last however many weeks that Anna had been imprisoned here, being experimented on.

My face ran hot. "Things didn't exactly go according to the plan." Which was the understatement of the year, but time was a demon breathing hot down my neck. "Ava is in the room across from mine. She was knocked out by the grenade. I don't know how many of the others are conscious. We need a bunch of adrenaline doses. This guy," I said and tilted my head to the inert guard, "seems to think the drug lockup is downstairs."

She examined my hand with the passring. "Is that how you got into my room?"

I nodded.

"Give it to me. The gun too." She jutted her chin to the guard, who also had a passring and a holstered dart gun. "Take the guard's passring and gun with you. I'll check on the others and keep watch until you get back. You find some doses and bring them as fast as you can." She said this like she expected no protest from me, as if she was used to giving orders and having them immediately obeyed. All along I had thought Julian was the one in charge.

But I wasn't going to question it.

I handed over the passring and gun. The guard's fingers were skinny so his passring fit a little better as I fumbled to slip it on. Gripping the guard's dart gun, I dashed around the corner to get free from the shielded corridor. I skimmed the surrounding hallways and spied a stairwell a split second before I heard feet clanging up the metal stairs and felt a mental surge slamming against my head. I took cover behind the corner, careful not to touch the wall, and jacked the reader guard to amble over. Then I leveled my gun at the stairwell door.

"Anna!" I whispered loudly over my shoulder. "There's more coming!" She was unlocking doors along the hall. The stairwell door was yanked open, and I pulled back again, out of sight. Anna had disappeared into one of the shielded rooms. At the end of the hall, orange mist curled out of my room, the door still propped open by Kestrel's body.

They were gassing the rooms.

If Anna was inside a room, she might have gotten caught in the mist.

I tried to quiet my hyped-up breathing. The footfalls had gone silent. I hadn't seen anything but dart guns since landing in Kestrel's cell, but Harrier had a real gun when he was guarding the tunnel. It was possible that whoever was around the corner would have guns with real bullets, too. I wrapped my fingers tighter on the gun. What I needed was a clear shot, without getting shot myself. I jacked the reader guard to charge around the corner. As soon as he was in their line of sight, two jacker guards plunged into his mind, wrestling with me for control of his body.

Which was just the distraction I needed.

I let them shove me out of the reader's mind, then peeked out and fired my dart gun, quickly jerking back behind the protection of the wall. A shot popped the air and something whooshed past me to clatter on the floor down the hall. So they had dart guns, and from my quick look around the corner, I knew the guards were Grizzly and Pemberly. That made two against one and Grizzly was a much stronger jacker, plus they were armed.

Time to run.

I dashed toward my room as fast as my bare feet would carry me. Another shot whooshed past me. I dodged the fallen guard outside my door, kept running, and flung myself around the corner at the end of the hallway. Out of the shielded corridor now, I reached out as I sprinted down the hall. Just one reader guard pounded up a nearby stairwell, desperately checking his dart gun to see if it was loaded. I froze him and searched his mind while I used my passring on the stairwell door. The controller in the shielded medical area next to Kestrel's office had put the compound in full-scale lockdown and had gassed the tunnels between buildings as well as the cells. Apparently, he also controlled the perimeter shields and the gate.

The shielded control room was definitely where I needed to go. I knocked out the guard and swept the first floor before I reached the bottom of the steps. All the guards were either knocked out, hidden behind shielded rooms, or hot on my tail, like Pemberly and Grizzly. I dashed through the maze of the first floor, working my way to Kestrel's shielded office by feel.

I swiped the passring by Kestrel's door and said a silent

prayer of thanks when it worked. Locking the door behind me, I quickly scanned his office. His desk was bare except for a scribepad, but the shelf still held my scrubs and shoes from when Molloy had stashed them there! My heart raced as I ran across the room. I tugged on my shoes and snatched my scrubs off the shelf, gently fingering the cloth of the scrubs until I found the thought grenades. With these, I could take down Grizzly and Pemberly and anyone else that I couldn't jack my way through to get the adrenaline. A thrill pumped through me until I realized I would have to stick my head out the door to see if Grizzly and Pemberly were nearby, which would only give them a chance to shoot me.

If the thought grenades were still here, maybe Kestrel had forgotten about the adrenaline patches as well. I tugged open the top thin, metal drawer of his desk, thinking he might have stuffed them inside, and jerked my hand back when I saw a gun there, black and shiny. Then I remembered Molloy had put Harrier's gun there when he was frisking me. I picked up the gun, and it weighed heavy and cold in my hand. I tucked it into the back of my pants, but I was still missing the adrenaline doses that I really needed.

Kestrel's screens caught my eye, lit with scenes around the facility, including shots of the access tunnels, both tinged with mist, and one of the ground-floor entrance. One showed my cell, where Kestrel, Harrier, and Julian lay in a swirling orange-tinged mist. Half a dozen other cells held sleeping jackers, including one with Anna sprawled on the floor in Ava's room. Her arm stretched toward the door, like she had been trying to get out.

There were no shots of the hallway outside Kestrel's door, or the rest of the shielded area, which held the medical facility and the central control room. How many people did they have inside that area? I could tell by feel that it was about five times the size of Kestrel's office. If the thought grenade could reach through the disruptor field, it might be able to reach everyone in the control room. I could knock them out before they knew what hit them.

But I needed to get rid of Grizzly and Pemberly first, before they got me.

I scurried to the door of Kestrel's office, fingering the thought grenade with one hand and holding the dart gun in the other. I flung open the door, keeping my head safely in the room and propping the door with my foot. A shout came from down the hall, followed by running footsteps. My heart climbed higher in my chest with each banging step that brought them closer. When they were nearly on me, I crushed the thought grenade in my hand.

Nothing happened.

I slammed the thought grenade against the frame of the door. Once, twice... on the third hit, something connected and at the same moment, Grizzly reached me, closing one giant hand on my arm, the other on my throat. The grenade sent a wave of nausea through me and Grizzly's hand reflexively squeezed my throat. I choked and tore free of his grasp as I tumbled to the floor on top of him.

Once down, he didn't move. Pemberly had landed facedown, five steps behind him.

I climbed over Grizzly, dragging the scrubs and dart gun along. The trembling in my hands made it tricky to find the second thought grenade. Finally, I curled my fist around it. I needed to make sure I had a good strong strike the next time. That had been *too* close.

Had the thought grenade already reached into the control room? Had I given myself away by only blasting half the room? I lumbered down the hall until I was as close as I could get to the center of the shielded area. At the far end was a door, and just as I was thinking about trying it, a guard flung it open. He was surprised to see me, but quickly reached for his gun. Before he could pull it from the holster, I smashed the thought grenade against the wall with all my might.

This time the nausea brought me to my knees, and I almost threw up on the industrial carpet. I had to gulp several breaths of air before I could look up. The guard was down, sprawled in the doorway.

Propping it open.

I staggered to my feet and stumbled to the door, holding my stomach so it would keep its contents. I peeked inside, dart gun at the ready, in case anyone was still up. An orderly stood in the middle of the room, next to a gurney, staring at the fallen bodies all around him.

I hastily shot at him with the dart gun. I managed to hit him, in spite of my hand shaking like an earthquake had struck. He fell on top of the two doctors in scrubs who were already heaped on the floor. They lay next to a gurney with a prisoner strapped to it. Behind a glass wall in back, a bank of computers lined the wall. A guard was slumped over what must be the control center.

I stood in the doorway for a long moment, afraid one of them would pop up again like a zombie, but they were all completely still. I crept in like I was stealing into a graveyard and then tiptoe-ran to the prisoner on the gurney.

It was Sasha.

chapter NINETEEN

Sasha lay unconscious on the gurney. He must have been caught in the pulse from the thought grenade like the rest of the jackers in the medical room. I knew better than to jack into Sasha's head in that state, so I tried to shake him awake, which was stupid, then I searched around for the wake-up meds. I stared at the shiny cabinets of medical supplies. I had no idea what I was doing.

I floundered, then I realized the orderly—the only guy left standing during the thought grenade blast—must have been a reader.

And I'd shot him full of juice.

I sighed and jacked into his head, bringing him slowly awake. He groggily peered up from where he had fallen, then jolted when he saw the doctors' bodies he had landed on. He winced while I searched his mind for the information I needed. I didn't care. He was one of the monsters doing heaven knew what to Sasha and the rest of us.

Thankfully, he was a medical orderly, not just a goon for Kestrel, and knew how to prepare the adrenaline doses. I jacked him to get a dose for Sasha out of the locked medical cabinet in the corner. While he lurched up from the floor to obey my command, I counted the rest of the bodies: three doctors on the floor, the command controller behind the glass, the guard at the door, and two other jacker guards slumped in chairs, probably waiting to take Sasha back to his cell. What were the doctors doing to Sasha? I thought it was bad with the tests in my room, but at least I hadn't been taken to this medical torment chamber with trays of serums and gleaming metal cabinets.

When the orderly had the syringe ready, I injected it into Sasha and jacked the orderly to prepare doses for the other mages. Then I hurried to the control room to find a way to open the gate. I jacked into the control panel mindware and found the switch for the shield just as an urgent message came in from the guard at the gate, the one who had warned me away from the east wing. His thoughts scrolled across the heads-up mindware display, asking if the patient breakout had been contained and saying he had sent for backup.

Just what I needed.

I mentally flicked the switch to drop the gate shield, but my reach was still blocked by the shielded control room, so I hunted for that too. Once the control room shield was down, I reached out of the building, across the parking lot, all the way to the front gate. I could knock out the guard, but the damage had already been done. Did he know we were jackers, not just demens breaking out? It would make a huge difference if he had sent for the local police or the FBI. I probed his mind—he didn't know anything about jackers, but he had a special number to call, a failsafe in case of a lockdown.

Kestrel would have made sure it was an FBI jacker containment unit.

I knocked out the guard and quickly swept the rest of the facility—the staff were in a full-blown state of panic, trying to contain the demens who were working up to a riot. That should keep them occupied while we made a run for the gate. I jacked back into the controller mindware, searching for the gate release. We would need it open to have any hope of getting out before the backup help arrived. I found it, gave it a nudge to spring open the gate, and hurried back to Sasha's side.

Red splotches mottled his face, and his eyes were unfocused. "C'mon." I tugged him up to sitting and he didn't fight me. "We need to go."

Sasha worked his mouth, but nothing came out. Probably the juice had parched his throat. Then he croaked, "Traitor!" and shoved me away and fell off the gurney. I tried to catch him, but he thunked hard on the floor, which seemed to stun him, but also helped to wake him up. He batted at my hands trying to help him, so I stepped back and commanded the orderly to get him up.

"Molloy is the traitor, not me," I said slowly, but I could tell he didn't believe me. My fists curled up. "Look, I don't have time to explain everything. Julian is passed out upstairs. We need to go help him. Are you coming with me or not?"

Sasha clung to the edge of the gurney and blinked several times, like he was still fuzzed out from the thought grenade.

"Julian," he wheezed.

"Yes, Julian," I said, my fists unclenching. "He sent me to get the adrenaline for him and the rest of the mages so we can get everyone out." The orderly had only filled about ten doses of adrenaline, which would have to do, because that was all we had time for.

Finally Sasha nodded. As he lumbered toward the door, he said, "Ava? Is she—" He coughed and clutched the doorjamb.

"Ava's upstairs too." I handed him my dart gun. He looked surprised, but took it. "And Anna. There's a whole block of rooms where Kestrel's keeping the mages."

I held Harrier's gun in front of me, leading the way down the hall. The orderly trailed behind us, bumbling to hold on to all ten syringes. I urged Sasha to go faster up the stairs while I reached out to scan the rest of the building. There were a lot of sedated jackers in their cells, and I only had ten doses. Even stopping to unlock the doors would delay us in getting back to Julian and the mages, and I didn't know how much time we had.

My chest pulled tight. That meant leaving most of the inmates behind, including the changelings. *Again.*

I gripped the handle of the gun tighter and resolved that we would at least stop Kestrel. Without him in charge, maybe the others could escape. Or at least the experiments would stop. Sasha hobbled up the stairs, as if his legs weren't working right, and he was climbing on sheer force of will. The lingering effects of the thought grenade must have been more severe than I thought.

It was slow going, but we finally reached the second floor and the shielded rooms where the mages were kept. The orange scent of the gas tainted the air, but it wasn't too thick. I tucked the gun back in my pants and took most of the syringe doses out of the orderly's hands, leaving him with one. I jacked him to head straight for Julian.

Sasha braced his hands on his knees, gasping for breath, his face red.

"Are you okay?" I asked.

"Yes." He straightened and leaned a hand against the wall, then drew it back a moment later when the buzz of the shield rippled through it. A thud sounded from the end of the hall, followed by a clinking, skittering noise. The orderly had reached my cell only to be overcome by the gas.

I huffed out a breath. "Look," I said to Sasha. "The adrenaline should protect you from the effects of the gas, at least temporarily. Go get Julian out of that cell. I'll get the rest up and out of theirs. Then you need to do your scribing thing on Kestrel. We don't have much time. Reinforcements are on the way." I handed him another dose. "In case you need an extra one for Julian." *Or Kestrel,* I added in my head. I wasn't sure if Kestrel had to be awake for the scribing.

Sasha nodded and stumbled down the hall. I waved the passring across the scanner for the cell next to Anna's, took a deep breath of orange-tinged air, and shoved open the door. I figured I could dash in and out, but as soon as I stepped into the room, the gas burned my eyes. Holding my breath, I sprinted to the form lying on the cot and quickly shoved up the sleeve of his gown. As the injection was going in, I realized I didn't know him. Maybe I should have saved the doses for the mages, but it was too late now. He thrashed on the bed as he swam up out of unconsciousness. I tried to wrestle him up from the cot, but I was running out of air, so I sucked in a gas-filled breath and reached inside my mind to speed up my heart rate. The gas was already making me dizzy and my heart pounding harder only made it worse. My stomach heaved; I threw up on the cot. I grabbed the edge to keep upright, trying not to drop the handful of adrenaline doses or breathe in any more gas. I didn't have time to be sick. Wiping my mouth on an unsoiled edge of a blanket, I grabbed the boy's arm and hauled him up to sitting.

If it took this long to get every jacker awake, I was in serious trouble. I dragged him to standing and braced my shoulder under his. Fortunately, he was a skinny kid like me and didn't weigh too much. We hobbled to the door.

Once we were in the hall, I closed the door, trapping the gas inside the room. I took several gasping breaths and sprinted to the next cell. I scanned the passring and tore inside. As soon as I reached the cot, I recognized Hinckley. I found a bare spot on his arm and injected him. He thrashed around, and I took a step back. He was over six feet tall. There was no way I could wrestle him up off the cot, much less out the door.

As I stood there, trying not to breathe, the boy I had just

awoken stumbled to my side. Together we hoisted Hinckley up from the bunk and dragged him half-conscious out of the room. I gave four of the remaining doses to the boy, whose name I still didn't know, and kept two for myself. I unlocked the next four doors as I hurried down the hall to Ava's room.

Sasha had managed to revive Julian and the two of them were dragging Kestrel from my room so they could close the door. The gas in the hall had built up enough that a wisp of orange floated across the dart gun that Sasha had left lying on the floor.

Julian caught my eye and bit his lip. "Thanks for coming back for me, keeper."

He definitely had some explaining to do about handling me, but now was not the time. "I've jumped the front gate open and gotten the shield down," I said. "The whole place is on lockdown and there are reinforcements on the way. I don't think we have much time." My breath was unsteady with a strange wheezing sound rumbling in my chest. Julian didn't look much better, red-faced from the adrenaline and clenching his fists like he wanted to hit something. But he nodded.

I tilted my head toward the still-closed door to Ava's room. "Ava's in here, and Anna as well." His eyes widened. I handed a dose to him. "I'll need your help getting them out."

He took it and waited at the ready. I panted, sucking air in and out quickly, to get as much of the gas out of my system as possible before I plunged into Ava's gas-filled room. I shoved open the door and lurched inside, holding my breath, with Julian close behind. I nearly stepped on Anna, sprawled on the floor with orange mist curling over her. I hopped over her prone body and injected my final dose into Ava on the cot. I didn't wait until she woke up, just hooked my arms under her shoulders and dragged her across the floor. Julian was doing the same, pulling Anna from the room. Sasha immediately took Ava from my arms and cradled her on the floor. She wasn't moving—probably still recovering from the thought grenade, or possibly the dose of gas had put her under deep, both of which would be a problem. I pulled the door closed behind us, but we really needed to get everyone up and mobile. Julian was gently shaking Anna, who was already blinking awake.

I looked between Sasha and Ava and the inert form of Kestrel lying on the floor. "Did you do it?" I asked Sasha. "Did you scribe him?" I pointed at Kestrel. Sasha tore his gaze from Ava, unconscious in his arms, and the creases around his eyes made my heart sink. "Did you?" I demanded, leaning my face closer to his.

"I—" Sasha swallowed, his voice raspy. "I can't. His mind is still... jumbled. And so is mine." He meant the thought grenade. Both of them had been subjected to it.

"You have to try!"

"I did!" Sasha pulled Ava's head close to his chest, as if protecting her. "I told you, I can't do it."

I took a step back and stumbled into Kestrel's body. I righted myself and resisted the urge to kick him. "We can't just leave him here. There has to be a way." I turned to Julian. "We could revive him, give him one of the doses. That way Sasha can scribe him."

Julian darted a look to Sasha, but he shook his head.

"Even if we used a dose on him," Sasha said, his voice gaining strength. "I couldn't scribe him now. Julian, I can barely see straight. We'll have to do it later."

"Later?" My voice screeched, panic clawing my throat. "There may not *be* a later. We may get caught before we can get out of here." I pulled the gun from the back of my pants. I checked it again. It was the kind with bullets, the kind that killed.

Julian was on his feet, his voice cool. "What are you doing, keeper?"

I knew Sasha was telling the truth. He might not like me, might think I had betrayed him, but he had no reason not to scribe Kestrel. If Sasha could, he would eliminate any trace of the monster that had tormented him, me, Julian, and so many other people. If we didn't stop Kestrel, he would keep doing his experiments. He would never stop.

Never.

I pointed the gun at Kestrel. "We have to stop him." I wasn't sure who I was talking to now. My hand shook so badly that I stepped closer to Kestrel, afraid I might miss, even though he was motionless on the floor.

Kestrel was a monster. If I didn't kill him, he would keep doing horrible, terrible things. I should pull the trigger and stop him forever. But with him lying on the floor, a blank look on his face, my mind recoiled from that thought. If I shot him, it would be an execution. Plain and simple.

My hand trembled so violently, I thought it might make the

gun go off by itself. Maybe it would be fate that killed him, not me. Julian's hand stole over mine, gently pulling the gun down so that it was pointed at the floor.

"You're not a killer, Kira," he said softly. "Let us take care of this."

I peered up at his face, now close to mine. "We have to stop him, Julian." But my voice was choked. Because he was right. I couldn't kill him. Not like this. Not in cold blood.

"I know we do." Julian's voice was rough, but his hands were gentle as he took the gun from my hand. "But you shouldn't be the one to do it."

He leveled the gun at Kestrel. His hand was steady, but the muscles in his jaw flexed.

"Wait," a voice said from behind us. It was Anna. "Let's take him with us, Julian. He could be useful to us after Sasha is able to scribe him."

Julian didn't move an inch. "Are you sure, Anna?" The gun still pointed at Kestrel's head.

Anna scrambled to her feet. "I am sure that you're no more a killer than she is, Julian."

Julian still didn't move. Hinckley stumbled up to us with the boy I had revived and four other jackers: Myrtle, a girl who was barely a changeling, and two others who were older like Hinckley. They stared at Julian, his gun still trained on Kestrel, watching to see what would happen. Hinckley stepped over to Anna, taking a position to her right. He looked ready to spring into action with a word from her.

Anna turned her head and looked up at Hinckley's face, which was red from the effects of the adrenaline. "Do you have an extra dose of adrenaline?" He grimaced and shook his head.

"I have one." Sasha handed it up to her.

The idea of waking Kestrel up made my stomach heave again. There were enough of us, in various states of alertness, that maybe we could keep him under control. Myrtle could probably take him on her own, if she wasn't still recovering from the gas. But Kestrel ought to be reeling from the effects of the thought grenade too. It should be possible to control him.

Anna took the dose and scooped the dart gun off the floor. Kneeling down by Kestrel, she pressed the gun deep in his stomach with one hand and injected him with the adrenaline with the other. Only then did Julian lower the gun. He kept it in his hand, pointed at the floor. Emotions warred across his face. I don't think he liked the idea of waking up Kestrel any more than I did.

Kestrel grunted as the adrenaline coursed through his system. It took a moment, but he finally opened his eyes and tried to focus on Anna's face looming above him.

"I just saved your life, Kestrel," Anna said coolly. "But if you give me a reason to regret it, I'll happily put a bullet in you."

chapter TWENTY

Kestrel stumbled behind me as our group marched through the lobby and out the main entrance of the building. Julian kept pace with me, leading with the gun. Anna poked a dart gun into Kestrel's side and Myrtle kept a wrinkled hand on his shoulder. The two older jackers we had rescued followed right behind Kestrel. Sasha trailed them, carrying Ava, which was definitely slowing us down. Hinckley and the two younger jackers brought up the rear. Our minds were a multi-headed hydra, hyped up on adrenaline and reaching in all directions.

I made continuous sweeps of the buildings, afraid I had missed a lurking guard. The low morning sun lit up the west wing, where the reader staff had calmed the demens somewhat, but the lockdown had them all in a state of confusion. In the east wing, one armed jacker guarded the rear access tunnel and another kept the staff and demens under control. How many long-term jacker prisoners were trapped in the east wing, mixed in with the demens, either gassed or addled like Liam? Letting loose the entire wing of the demens, in hopes of freeing the jackers, had some serious appeal, but we needed to focus on getting ourselves out first.

A long minute stretched as we crept along the parking lot between the trio of buildings, a brigade of jackers with one prisoner. Kestrel kept his head down, but the redness in his face showed the adrenaline had found its mark. Anna and Myrtle had trapped him inside his own head with a mental grip in addition to the gun Anna had thrust into his side. If Sasha—who had been awake the longest after the thought grenade—had diminished jacking ability, and Ava was still knocked out from it, I hoped that meant that Kestrel was at reduced strength, even if he was awake and mobile. I was sure he was waiting for the right moment to run. He had to know that this wouldn't turn out well for him. I trusted Myrtle and Anna to keep Kestrel under control while I kept a lookout, sweeping the buildings and beyond.

As we neared the front gate, I reached through and checked the street. A few demens roamed the abandoned apartment buildings, but the street and surrounding buildings were clear of jackers as far as I could reach. Then a squeal of tires reached my ears, and two cars carrying four FBI agents slid into my range.

Jacker agents. They shoved me out of their heads the moment I brushed them.

"Julian!" I grabbed his arm, bringing our whole entourage to a stop. He had heard it too. "Four agents, all armed."

He cast a look over his shoulder. "Myrtle! We're going to have to jack our way out." The gate stood open, a narrow gap showing a sliver of the street outside the compound. Julian and Myrtle sprinted to the opening, and the whole group shuffled after them. The cars screeched to a stop, not thirty feet outside the gate.

I reached to the agents, trying to jack them or at least keep them distracted. The other inmates pressed on their minds as well. There were eleven of us, but Ava was unconscious and Sasha was in no shape to jack. Which meant Julian probably wasn't recovered enough to handle either. But he had the gun, and Myrtle was the strongest. With her, the agents were outnumbered, eight jackers to their four. It should be enough.

The agents couldn't even manage to leave their cars as they waged a mental battle with us. We continued to creep forward. A scuffle behind me drew my attention. Anna lay on the pavement and Kestrel was running back to the east wing.

"Julian!" I cried out.

Julian left Myrtle at the gate. Hinckley knelt by Anna and pulled a dart from her side. He threw it away with a growl of frustration. Kestrel must have grabbed the gun from her in the confusion of the agents arriving.

Julian thrust his gun into my hand. "Take Hinckley with you," he said. "And stop him, keeper. Do whatever you have to, but don't let him get away."

I ran, grabbing Hinckley's arm as I dashed past. Hinckley hesitated, like he didn't want to leave Anna's side, then heaved up from the ground and sprinted with me toward the east wing. Kestrel was already inside. I reached forward to jack into his head, and in his weakened state, I got in for a moment before he pushed me back out. Without Myrtle to keep him contained, he was strong—too strong. The adrenaline shot must have given him more strength than I thought, or he had recovered a lot faster from the thought grenade than Julian and Sasha. Then again, Kestrel hadn't been the subject of experiments for days on end.

I slammed my fist against the door to the east wing and rushed inside after Kestrel. A tall nurse came from nowhere and tackled me, pinning me to the floor. The jacker orderly controlled her mind. I wrestled with him mentally while struggling physically against the nurse's rough hands holding me down. A half second later, Hinckley shoved the nurse off me and pushed the jacker out of her mind. I scrambled up from the floor and searched for the two jackers in the building. One was still guarding the access tunnel, but the other was behind the glass partition that housed the demens, providing cover for Kestrel as he fled to the back of the ward.

Hinckley's hands danced in front of him. The demens on the other side of the glass rose up from their cots, all at once, stumbling and bumbling in a mass of confusion. The jacker orderly was swallowed by the chaos. I brushed through the demens minds, trying to find Kestrel, but the dizziness of their thoughts made me tip sideways. I braced against the wall and kept searching.

I had no idea how Hinckley could do it without going a little crazy himself.

I finally locked onto Kestrel, who was threading his way through the jumble of demens. Hinckley's dancing hands reached for him, but it wasn't as strong as a full jack. Turning heads and motivating people to amble around was different than jacking Kestrel to stop him from escaping out the back door. Kestrel had to know that the tunnel was gassed, so he must be going for a different exit.

I should have killed Kestrel when I had the chance.

I banged through the glass double doors and fought my way through the mass of demens, but I couldn't get a clean shot with all the dancing demens between us. I jacked into Kestrel's head, but he threw me out again. He stopped at the rear door and pointed something at me.

The dart gun.

I dashed behind a large patient in front of me. The dart stuck in the chest of another demens behind me, and he collapsed to the floor. Then the patient who was acting as my shield dropped facedown onto the cot next to us.

I ducked down, hiding out of Kestrel's line of sight. Then all the random motion of the demens around me ceased. I popped up, but I couldn't see Kestrel through the forest of stock-still figures. I pushed through two demens standing in the center aisle and elbowed another aside until I had a clear shot of Kestrel at the door. I aimed the gun at Kestrel, and just as I fired, he ducked through it. The crack of the shot pierced my ears, and the recoil of the gun jerked my arm back, but I could see that I had missed. Dust puffed from a bullet hole in the door. I ran after

Kestrel, reaching back to tell Hinckley to follow me, only to find him passed out, pumped full of juice from Kestrel's dart. And the jacker orderly was working his way through the demens toward Hinckley with a syringe. Hinckley was already unconscious, so whatever was in the syringe couldn't be good.

I stood frozen, uncertain.

I couldn't lose Kestrel. The mere thought of it made me want to scream for not being strong enough to kill him when he lay helpless at my feet. But if I didn't act fast, the orderly would inject Hinckley with whatever was in the syringe. And if I went after Kestrel by myself, when he had the dart gun and another jacker outside the access tunnel to help him, I'd just end up back in one of Kestrel's cells.

I growled as I spun back to Hinckley and jacked three of the demens to charge the orderly, choking down the sour taste that their minds surged up. The jacker orderly was so focused on Hinckley that he never saw the demens coming. They piled on top of him, and he wrestled with me in their minds, but that was enough distraction for one of the demens to grab the syringe and inject it into the orderly. His eyes flew wide, and his mind filled with horror. For his sake, I hoped it was only tranquilizer.

Thankfully, Hinckley still had the adrenaline pumping through his system, and it wasn't too difficult to jack him awake. We needed to get back to the gate and make sure Julian wasn't losing the fight there. Otherwise we'd all end up back in Kestrel's cells. Hinckley struggled up from the floor, and I guided him as we stumbled back out of the east wing.

The fight still raged at the front gate. Julian stood tensed at the edge with Anna lying at his feet. His fists were at the ready, prepared to punch his way out of the facility or possibly defend Anna from whoever might come through the gate. I reached out to the agents beyond. One had succumbed to the collective pressure of the mages' minds, turning on his partner and shooting him in the leg. The two agents that still had control of their minds had him pinned to the ground, while the injured one was passed out cold.

When we reached Julian, I could hardly say the words, they were so bitter in my mouth. "I lost him," I said. "I tried to... I had to get Hinckley out of there."

Julian nodded sharply, not looking my way, his attention on the gate and the agents beyond. Hinckley pushed me away to stand on his own and joined me in reaching for the remaining agents. Together, we were the tipping point of pressure on their minds, and they both collapsed under the collective mental strength of the mages.

Our motley crew—an unconscious Anna over Hinckley's shoulder, Sasha still carrying Ava, Julian and Myrtle leading the other four inmates—stumbled out the gate. We shoved all four agents out of the way and climbed in their cars.

Eleven mages, two cars.

It would have to do.

chapter TWENTY-ONE

We abandoned the agents' cars near the facility. Julian hailed a couple of autocabs, which had even less room than the FBI cars, but getting autocabs so close to Jackertown wasn't easy, and we didn't have time to hang around waiting for more. Decrepit brownstones blurred brown and gray past the window. My eyes didn't even try to track them.

I lost Kestrel. I lost my chance. I could have had revenge for the long list of horrors he had already committed. Simon's death. The experiments. The camp. And I could have prevented more. Now he would go right back to tormenting the changelings I had been forced to leave behind *again*.

I pressed my cheek against the cold flexiglass. He was a monster. Why wasn't I strong enough to stop him? My chest caved into the emptiness inside me. I couldn't pull the trigger when Kestrel was lying helpless at my feet, but I had no problem shooting when he was fleeing out the door. What difference did it make? Kestrel wouldn't have hesitated. If our positions had been reversed, he would have executed me without blinking. Maybe I had avoided becoming a monster like him by just a hair. But was that really more important than stopping Kestrel?

I had no answers. The emptiness grew and threatened to pull me in.

Anna shifted in the seat next to me, her arm falling against Julian in the command seat. Hinckley crammed in the back with Sasha, who still cradled Ava in his arms. I wanted to worry about her, but the emptiness inside me wouldn't allow it.

The glass grew warm with my cheek and the summer day. The overnight drizzle hadn't burned off, and stubborn drops of water clung to the outside of the flexiglass. As I stared, the drops slowly joined together and ribboned down the window.

Now that we had escaped Kestrel's facility, the reality of finding Raf hit me. I clung to the sliver of hope that he was still alive—that Molloy had lied to me and hadn't killed him after all—but the most likely outcome of a search for Raf would be finding his body. Or worse, seeing what the pravers had done to him before he died. Part of me wanted to take the autocab when the mages were done with it and set an autopath to a rocky beach a thousand miles away where I could sit and watch the waves beating on the shore. Go as far as the unos would take me and not look back. Pretend that I hadn't failed to kill the monster that had tormented countless jackers. Pretend that I hadn't failed to free the changelings. Pretend that I hadn't failed to keep Raf alive.

Anna twitched again, her muscular arm brushing mine in the

tight space. She was already rousing from the dart's sedative. She was so strong, and I was weak. Tired. Empty. If I had spent a long stretch of time in Kestrel's facility like her, I would probably be dead. I had been ready to give up after just one week. Someone like Anna would never give up. She would keep looking until she found Raf. She would bring the body back to his parents, saying she was sorry her love for their son had gotten him killed. Sorry she couldn't stay away from him long enough to keep him alive. Take the slap across her face that she deserved. My mind fled from that image, sinking into the black hole that was growing inside me, consuming me from the inside out.

I wasn't like Anna. I couldn't do it.

I was so mired in my thoughts that it surprised me when we pulled up to the mages' headquarters. I almost didn't get out, but I dragged myself from the front seat so Anna wouldn't have to climb over me. I followed the crew inside, stumbling over the threshold into the cavernous building. I had to find Raf, but I could barely think straight, much less figure out where to start. The couch beckoned, and I sank deep into it, drawing up my knees and locking my arms around them. A shudder threatened to shake me into pieces.

Sasha shuffled past me, taking Ava to the racks in the middle of their converted factory. Julian joined Anna at the kitchen table where she was talking to the others, including Hinckley, who stood at attention by her side. She was probably debriefing, already back in command as if she hadn't just woken up from a dart.

I should have been thinking of a way to find Raf, but instead I clamped my legs tighter to my chest, trying to keep all the pieces together. The mages bustled about, making their plans, whatever they were. I leaned my head against the back of the couch and closed my eyes. Minutes ticked by, and bit by bit, my body released the tension that was holding me together. Right as I thought sleep might take me, a weight pressed on the couch next to me, causing it to shift. I held still. Maybe whoever it was would go away. When they didn't, I drew in a breath and forced my eyes open.

"Are you all right, keeper?" Julian said it gently, as if speaking too loud might shatter the tight space I had drawn around me. He propped his arm on the back of the couch and scanned me like he expected to find a wound or maybe a dart sticking out.

"Yeah," I said, but it sounded like a lie. It *was* a lie. I slowly uncurled, and the cool air of the warehouse wafted away the warmth built up in my cocoon. Anna and the others were still discussing plans at the kitchen table and ignoring us. Julian had changed into all black clothes, looking more revolutionary now and less boardroom ready. Sasha and Ava were nowhere to be seen. "How's Ava?"

A brilliant smile flashed like lightning across Julian's face, then was gone just as fast. "She's resting in her bunk. Between the thought grenade and the gas, she was hard hit. She'll be fine, but it will be a while before she fully recovers."

"That's good. That she'll get better, I mean." I rubbed my forehead. My brain was still fogged, but I knew I needed help to find Raf—I had almost no chance on my own in Jackertown. If Molloy had traded Raf, that was where I would have to start. Would any of the mages be willing to help me search for a lost reader—especially one who was likely already dead? Was there something I could bargain with to get them to help? My brain couldn't sort it out. I wondered if the thought grenade did more than make me nauseous. Julian had taken the full brunt of the grenade, and he seemed fine.

"I need to find Raf," I said to Julian, "but I don't know where to start. It's like my head's stuffed with cotton."

"You're just tired." Julian peered at me. "I'll help you find him, keeper. You don't have to be alone in this. Not anymore."

Relief washed through me, and a bit of the fog lifted. It was very mesh of him to help.

I managed a small grateful smile. "Thanks." He smiled back, and that instinctual thing tugged at me again. It made me want to lean closer to him. Maybe something had gone wrong when he handled me, and a residual side effect was muddling my brain.

"What did you do to me?" I asked. "Back in my cell, when I linked into your mind? What did you do?"

Julian dropped his gaze and picked at lint on the couch. His face darkened and my eyebrows hiked up. Was he blushing?

"I didn't mean for that to happen," he said. "I'm sorry. I needed to talk to you and since I couldn't link into your head—"

"You wanted me to link into yours. Got it. But..." I still didn't understand. "One time I jack into your mind, and it's nothing but a horror sim. The next time, I fall in love with you. What is *that* all about?"

The disgust in my voice made Julian wince. "It's a reflex," he said, still not looking at me. "Like a defense mechanism. When someone tries to jack me, they get nothing but an overwhelming urge to run away. I don't know why it works that way, but it does. Like I said before, I don't jack like you do. My ability is more... instinctual. I can link thoughts, but not much more. I'm actually just a linker." A weak laugh escaped him, and he finally looked at me. "Normally, if I have to communicate without words, I can link in. If someone needs to link into my mind, I can try to control the effect that they experience. Reverse the response. But it takes a lot of effort. Usually I simply reflect the thoughts they want to hear, like I did with Harrier. With you..." He stared over the back of the couch at the distant machinery that was standing silent and unused. His voice was flat. "I needed to tell you the plan and we only had a short time. I thought if I triggered the mating instinct, you wouldn't blow my cover story to get Kestrel to let me into your room. I didn't think..." He turned back to me. "I swear I didn't know the effect would be so strong. You were only linked in, Kira. Normally, I would have to handle someone to create such a strong result."

"Normally?" I cocked my head to one side.

"Not normally with that particular instinct." He rubbed his temples with both hands. "With any instinct. I've never... I don't often have people linking into my mind. I underestimated the impact it would have. I'm sorry."

"Yeah, all right." Was the urge to forgive him left over from when he messed with my head? I didn't care for that idea *at all*. "Just don't ever do that again," I said, but the way he twitched made me feel bad for saying it. Maybe. Or perhaps it was that instinctual thing again.

"I won't be able to." He met my gaze. "Now that you know all my secrets, I'm sure you'll never come near my mind again."

"Secrets?" said Anna with a frown. While we were locked in our discussion, she had drifted over from the table. "I hope you mean your secret fondness for explosives and not something a little more..." She glanced at me. "Strategic."

Julian rose up from the couch to face her. Nearly eye to eye, I could see how identical they were. Both dark haired, although Anna's straight black hair hung neatly to her shoulders while Julian's was perpetually mussed, like he'd just gotten out of bed. The angles in their cheeks were both hidden by softness, but Julian's face seemed darker. Or perhaps he was blushing again.

"We're trying to plan our next step with Kestrel," Anna said. "Perhaps you'd like to join us?" Her tone said he was negligent in his duties, taking time to check on me. It rubbed me the wrong way, but I didn't say anything. I wanted Julian's help to find Raf, but it seemed like Anna was the one in charge. Could she order him not to?

"We can trust Kira," he said.

"So you keep saying." She peered down at me. "Still, things didn't exactly go according to plan, did they, Kira?"

Julian's jaw worked. "I told you—the plan failed because

Molloy betrayed us." He turned to me. "I figured Molloy set us up as soon as I woke up in Kestrel's cell. I would have come for you sooner, keeper, but the juice Kestrel used was dampening my handling ability."

"You would have come for *her* sooner?" Anna's voice hiked up, but she didn't seem offended that he came for me instead of her. More like she was shocked he would make such a bad strategic move.

All expression fled Julian's face. "Kestrel had her for less time. I thought she might be stronger, better able to withstand the effects of the grenade."

How could anyone think I was stronger than Anna? Maybe he was embarrassed to tell her how he had handled me.

Anna didn't seem convinced either, and her shock morphed into concern. "You also thought we could trust Molloy."

"I had no reason to doubt him," Julian said, sounding defensive now. "His every instinct, as far as I could tell, was protective of his brother Liam. Your disappearance wasn't a coincidence, Anna. I think Molloy arranged it, to bring Kira in. He was bent on having her on the team and forced her hand by holding her reader hostage." He turned to me again. "I would never have sent you in there if I thought it was a trap. You *do* know that, don't you, keeper?"

"Sure." I believed Julian, but Anna seemed to think his judgment had taken a vacation.

"Kira was a prisoner like we were," Julian continued. "And she helped us escape."

"She also lost Kestrel, the main target of the mission."

I was trying not to interfere, but I couldn't let that stand. "As I recall..." I rose up from the couch to stand next to Anna. She was a good three inches taller than me. "It was your job to guard Kestrel." Anna's eyes widened, like she couldn't quite believe my impertinence. Julian shot me a look like I wasn't helping. I gave him a *What?* shrug. It was the truth.

"He recovered more quickly than I expected," said Anna, the same intense eyes as Julian's boring down into mine. "You were the one with the gun. Twice. And yet Kestrel still lives. I'm thinking that you didn't want to kill him that badly after all."

"You let him live the first time," I countered.

She raised an eyebrow. "I thought he might be more useful to us alive."

"Well, if I was a better shot, Kestrel would be dead." I folded my arms. "I could have let that orderly inject Hinckley with whatever he had in his syringe so I could get a second shot. But I figured it was more important to save Hinckley than to go after Kestrel. What would you have done?"

Anna regarded me for a long moment, then nodded slowly. "I would have made the same choice." Her shoulders relaxed a little, and she turned to Julian, who was watching us with wide eyes. "However, that means we're no further ahead than we were before." Her voice lapsed into command mode. "Kestrel is still in control, and the changelings and other jackers are still being held in his facility. Except now we have inside knowledge of the facility's security systems. We should strike again, before they have a chance to regroup."

"It's too risky to attack now," Julian said.

"We need to act soon, before they can move the prisoners again," Anna said. "We should hit them hard while they're down. Now is the perfect time. They wouldn't expect it."

"Or the place could be crawling with Feds," he said.

She planted her fists on her hips. "I'm not going to leave them there, Julian."

"Of course not." Julian's back stiffened. "But some of our strongest mages are still recovering. Sasha's unable to scribe and he won't leave Ava's side while she's out. You know Sasha is key to any plan involving Kestrel." He put a hand on Anna's shoulder. "I know you want your vengeance, Anna—"

She smacked it away. "I want to complete the mission!"

"I know." Julian put his hands up but didn't seem to take any offense. In fact, he softened his tone even more. "But we have surveillance set up. If they start to move the prisoners, we can mobilize a rescue team and go after them. Much has happened since you were taken, Anna. The crews and clans are coming together—they're beginning to trust us. The mage cells have coordinated sentries at the outskirts of Jackertown in case Vellus decides to conduct another raid, and the clans are seeing the strength of working together. When we show them we've brought some of their fellow jackers home, they will see it even more. A rescue team is a perfect chance to bring people together, but we need time to recover and plan."

The fire left Anna's eyes during Julian's speech. Was he handling her? He said he could, even though she was a keeper, but he also said he never would—because she was his sister, I supposed. She pressed a fist to her lips, tapping lightly. It reminded me of Julian and how he templed his fingers and tapped his lips when he was thinking.

She dropped her hand. "Okay. We'll wait. But we'll start planning right away." She raised an eyebrow in my direction. "Are you up for another shot at Kestrel?"

"I have to find my boyfriend first." I glanced at Julian. "And I could use some help."

"Hinckley told me about your reader friend," Anna said. "That's an unfortunate business, but it's not our concern." Her voice turned formal. "While I do appreciate your help in getting out of Kestrel's facility, the hundreds of jackers still stuck in there are more important than one wayward reader."

I flexed my hands and tried to keep the bite out of my voice. "The only reason Raf's life is in danger is because Molloy wanted to bring the mages to Kestrel." I swept a hand out, gesturing at the mages clustered around the kitchen table. "Kestrel wanted all of you, all of *us*, for whatever his plans were, and he used Molloy to bring us in. Raf did nothing but get caught in the crossfire. I saved Hinckley because that was the right thing to do. Finding Raf is the right thing to do. I'm going after Molloy, and I'm going to keep looking until I find Raf. Are you going to help me or not?"

Anna's eyebrows had hiked up to the top of her forehead. "I don't think—"

"Anna," Julian stopped her with a low voice. "Molloy betrayed us—all of us. *He* is responsible for the failure of the mission. I want to pay him back for that. And," he glanced at me, "I made a promise."

"A promise?" Anna drew back, then looked me over like she was doing a threat assessment. Finally, she gave Julian an exasperated look. "I wish you would stop doing that."

"No," he said with a small smile. "You don't."

She rubbed her face with both hands and took a deep breath. "Fine! What do you need to find Molloy?" she asked Julian.

"Just some time," he said. "And possibly Sasha's help."

"Don't take too long." She jabbed a finger into his chest. "As soon as everyone is recovered, I want us ready to go."

He smiled, but she refused to smile back and ignored me completely, turning on her heel and stalking back to the kitchen table. Hinckley watched her return with crossed arms, his frown matching hers.

Julian leaned close and said softly, "She's not so bad once you get to know her."

"I'm just glad she's letting you help me," I said. "I don't even know where to start looking for Raf."

"There was never any doubt about me helping you, keeper," Julian said with a smile. "I've already been on the short comms. No one's seen anyone who meets your friend's description."

My shoulders sagged.

"That's better news than you might think."

"It's just... Molloy told me he killed him." The words choked me. "I saw Raf's body in his mind. If Molloy didn't kill him before, he's had more than enough time to do it by now."

"Just because Molloy's gotten what he wants," Julian said gently, "doesn't necessarily mean that your friend is dead."

"You mean Molloy might have traded him." I wanted to believe it, and saying it out loud made a tentative thrill of hope twirl up inside me.

"Maybe. Or Molloy could have set him loose in Jackertown," Julian said. "If he did, it's likely someone would have seen him. Jackertown's not that big of a community. Maybe Molloy went back to the family, asking for ransom, or sent a contractor to do it. If so, it's been long enough that the ransom would have been paid and your friend could be safely back home."

The twirl of hope burst into a gush of possibility. I hadn't thought of ransom. That happened—not as often as Vellus claimed or readers feared, but it did happen. Raf could be sitting at home, right now, worrying about me.

"Julian..." I couldn't breathe.

"I know," he said. "You need to go home. At once. And find out."

chapter TWENTY-TWO

The autocab rolled to a stop in front of the skinny suburban homes that surrounded my family's rental house. The early afternoon glare made me squint. I had already swept the neighborhood, but Julian was scanning the area like he thought jackers might jump out of the bushes.

"If Molloy's got wind that you've escaped," Julian said, "he might come here instead."

I wanted to program an autopath straight to Raf's front door, but that was exactly where Molloy would expect me to go. If Raf was alive, it would be tricky keeping him that way, especially if Molloy saw us coming. Going home first was safer.

"There are no jackers for at least a quarter mile," I said. "Except the ones in my house."

I strode ahead of Julian and reached into the house. My mom was shoving a tray of cookies in the oven. Worry about me was an endless loop in her mind, which wasn't a surprise—I had been missing for over a week. Xander was playing a violent sim on the living-room screen, but he responded to my featherlight brush.

Hey! he thought. *You're back!* He was about to call out to my mom, but thought better of it. Then I realized what had stopped him: my father was there. I stumbled to a stop on the grass and Julian bumped into me.

He stepped back. "What's wrong?"

"My dad," I said. "He's here." My dad hadn't reacted to my light touch, and I had quickly pulled back. A white-hot heat welled up in me. Was he still doing Vellus's dirty work?

"Maybe we should try your friend's house first," Julian said.

"No." I paused. "I'm sure my dad's been looking for us. If Raf is back, he'll know." Yet I couldn't get my legs to move toward the door. The press conference was long over. Had my dad come looking for me, like he promised? I couldn't imagine a world in which he hadn't. At least he was here, looking out for Mom and Xander. I had to give him credit for that.

Julian measured the door with his eyes, like it was rigged with explosives. "Well, this won't be the first trap I've followed you into."

I rolled my eyes. "Even if my dad's still working for Vellus, he's not going to haul you off to the Detention Center." At least, I couldn't imagine my dad succeeding in that, not against Julian. But he might try. "Just in case he's not super happy to see you, promise you won't do that handling thing."

"As long as he doesn't point a gun in my face, we should be fine."

I sighed, squared my shoulders, and marched toward the house. Xander must not have been able to contain himself, because my dad flung the door open before I got there.

"Kira!" He said my name like it was his first breath after nearly drowning. He rushed up to wrap me in a hug so strong it knocked the air out of me. "Kira, thank God, I've been so worried." The stubble on his face scraped my cheek as he pulled back, then he clasped my shoulders like he thought I might slip away if he didn't hold tight enough. "Where have you been? I've been looking all over Jackertown for you and Raf, back at the diner, everywhere." He paused for a breath and noticed Julian behind me. "What is *he* doing here?"

"He's helping me find Raf." I pulled out of my dad's grip.

He frowned and let his hands drop. "Helping you? Wait, wasn't Raf released from the prison? I thought that was the whole point of letting your shady friend here jack the prisoners out of the Detention Center."

Julian looked unimpressed by my dad's description and more than a little on edge.

"Raf was never in prison," I said, and the burst of hope I'd carried inside me from the mages' headquarters shriveled into a lump. "Molloy had him the whole time, holding him hostage. Are you sure Raf wasn't ransomed?"

"No, his parents are frantic. I'm sure they would have paid a ransom if they'd been contacted." He put a hand back on my shoulder and dropped his voice. "Why didn't you tell me Molloy was holding him hostage? I could have helped you, Kira!"

"I didn't tell you because you were too busy mindguarding for Vellus!" I stepped out of his reach and crossed my arms. "How can you work for someone like him?"

His hand hung in the air, then slowly dropped to his side. "I did what I had to."

"What exactly is *that*?"

When my dad hesitated, I linked into his head. *I need to know, Dad. Have you been mindguarding for Vellus all along? Did you ask him to do the raid on Jackertown?*

I had nothing to do with the raid. My dad stepped close to me, put his hand to the small of my back, and steered me a few steps away from Julian, who watched us go with a slightly amused expression. *But I have a feeling that Mr. Trullite did,* my dad thought. *He said if I didn't come out with you in an hour, he would send someone in to get us.*

Mr. Trullite asked Vellus to raid Jackertown to rescue me? The idea of Mr. Trullite and Vellus being buddies made my head go sideways. *Wait, in the interview, Vellus said he conducted the raid to get a kidnapped reader out of Jackertown. Was that Raf?*

Mr. Trullite didn't know Raf was with you, my dad thought. *He probably told Vellus that his granddaughter was in Jackertown and that Vellus could track my phone. Anyway, I'm pretty sure Vellus used it as a pretext for doing the raid. He rounded up a lot of jackers that night, more than just the ones that were released.*

How can you work for someone like that? I unlocked my arms and threw them out. *Why don't you just quit?*

My father's shoulders slumped. *It's not that simple, Kira.*

It is that simple!

It's not! My dad rubbed the back of his neck. *And I did quit... when I left Naval Intelligence. I was on Vellus's protection detail for a long time. I thought working for him was the right thing to do. I can't explain it. He made me believe we were doing good things. Maybe that's what politicians do. Talk people into doing things when they should know better.*

What kinds of things? My body tensed. Did my dad hurt people for Vellus?

It doesn't matter! But then his face pinched in and my insides shredded. What did my dad *do*? Maybe all jackers *were* dangerous, even the good ones like my dad. Maybe it was in our DNA, like Vellus said. The part of me that wanted to execute Kestrel on the floor—was that the monster inside me, just waiting to come out? Did I get that from my dad?

Did you... Did you kill people? I asked him. Because I needed to know.

My dad's mouth hung open for a second. I heard Julian on the grass behind me, moving closer. My dad noticed and switched to speaking out loud. "I'm not a killer, Kira." He cast a look over my shoulder to Julian. "Unless someone hurts you, then they had better watch out for me."

The horror that I might be *that*, that maybe I was a cold-blooded killer and my dad was too, drained out of me. My face heated up with the shame that I had actually believed my dad was a killer, even for a moment.

"Now that we've established that," my dad said with a gentle smile, "we can talk about what I do for Vellus later. Where have you've been for the last week, young lady? You've been driving us all insane with worry. *Again*." The last time I had disappeared for weeks on end, I had ended up in a showdown with the jacker FBI. This time wasn't much better.

Julian jumped it. "Your daughter has been breaking jackers out of jail. *Again*."

My dad might not be a killer, but the look on his face was downright murderous. "I don't recall asking *you*." He softened his voice when he turned to me. "What kind of trouble has he gotten you into—"

"Julian hasn't been getting me into trouble. Well, not exactly. But... well... I kind of broke into Kestrel's experimental facility." I sped up my words at the horrified look on my dad's face. "And broke out again. And got some people out too."

"What?" My dad's face turned a shade of purple I'd never seen before. "I didn't get you away from Vellus so you could run off and be a hero again! Kestrel is incredibly dangerous! How could you even think about—" The anger strangled his words.

"I didn't have a choice!" I said. "Molloy forced me, then he betrayed us to Kestrel and—" I really didn't want to tell my dad what happened inside Kestrel's facility. "Anyway, that's why I've been gone. Julian is not the enemy; he's here to help me find Raf. Will you help me too?"

My dad closed his eyes, and when he opened them again, they'd lost the murderous look. "Of course." He took a breath and let it out slowly. "I don't know where Raf is, but I'm sure Molloy doesn't have him. I saw Molloy in the holding pen at the Detention Center when I was mindguarding Vellus. It was his last press conference before he left town, a couple days after you went missing."

"How did Molloy end up in the Detention Center?" Maybe Kestrel had double-crossed Molloy. But why didn't Kestrel keep him at his facility? And what did that mean for Raf? There were too many possibilities and my mind spun trying to untangle them.

My dad was way ahead of me. "I don't know how Molloy got there, but if I can interrogate him, I can find out what he did with Raf. Vellus might agree to let me do that."

"Really?" I squeaked. Maybe my dad working for Vellus wasn't a bad thing after all. I frowned at that thought but stuffed it away. "So call Vellus!"

"I can't just call him up, Kira," my dad said patiently. "Our arrangement is... one-sided. I don't call him; he calls me. He spends most of his time at the capitol building in Springfield, and I only do work on occasion for him."

"Sounds like you need to pay him a visit in Springfield," said Julian.

My dad shot him a glare, then turned to me. "If I spoke to Vellus in person, he might agree to release Molloy into my custody."

Could my dad jack Vellus? Maybe, if he could get close to Vellus without him suspecting... whatever he was thinking, I was ready to try.

"Great!" I said. "Let's go."

"I said *I* would convince him," my dad said. "You're staying here and keeping out of trouble."

"Dad, I am *not* staying here while Raf is missing. And you're going to need help."

"I agree with your father, Kira." My mom's tremulous voice floated from the front door. Blotches of red marred her pretty face, like she had been crying while we were arguing, which made my heart twist. Xander lurked behind her. "I'm sure your father can handle Vellus. Please, just come inside, all of you. I don't like you standing on the lawn, attracting attention."

My dad nudged me. "Go hug your mother. She's been worried sick about you."

Guilt dragged down my shoulders, and I hustled across the lawn. I gave her a fierce hug and winked at Xander over her shoulder, pulling a big grin out of him.

"I'm okay, Mom, really." The permanent worry lines in her forehead had deepened since I saw her last. "But I have to find Raf. It's my fault he's in this mess."

My mom's slender hands cupped my cheeks. "He's in this because loves you, Kira. And he must love you a lot, otherwise he would have let you go when we left Gurnee." My lip trembled. She wasn't making this any easier. "I know what it's like, being a mindreader who loves a jacker. You're always afraid that someone will find out or that other jackers will hurt them. Raf wouldn't want you to do anything dangerous for him, sweetie. I'm sure he'd want your father to handle it." She stopped because she was fighting back tears.

I gently linked into her head. *Mom, Senator Vellus is a dangerous guy.*

Your father knows what he's doing...

Dad's just trying to protect me. He really does need my help. I was playing the mutant jacker card. My mom knew I could do more than my dad, even if she didn't understand it all. *It will be less dangerous if we're working together.* Which was true, but *less dangerous* was a pretty relative term.

Torment warred across her face, but she finally settled on having my dad keep an eye on me. Which wasn't what I was going for, but it would have to do. *Promise me you'll do what your father says. He's been around people like Vellus before.*

I promise.

Out loud, she said, "Xander, go get some of those cookies I made." She said it loud enough for Dad and Julian to hear from where they had held back on the lawn. "They'll need something to eat on the trip down to Springfield."

Xander dashed off. I mouthed the words *thank you* to my mom. As I brought a bag full of warm cookies back to my dad and Julian, my dad darted looks between me and my mom. Julian seemed to be fighting off a smile. We strode to the garage, and my dad swiped his passring to activate the door.

"What did you say to her?" my dad asked.

"That you'd be safer with me along."

Julian couldn't keep in his snort, which earned him a glare from both me and my dad. He shut it down quickly.

"That had better be it." My dad pointed a finger at me.

"I don't want you jacking your mother." My mouth dropped open. By the time my dad reached the driver's side of his hydro car, I had closed my mouth and settled for a huff at his accusation.

My dad put both hands on the roof of the car and stared at the floor. "I don't care what your mother says, I'm not taking you anywhere near Vellus. He's a brutal man, and he would be more than happy to lock you up if it suited his political purposes. You're staying here and your jackwork friend can find his way back to the city. I'm going to handle this on my own."

"By jacking Vellus?" I asked. "Because if you are, you're going to need help. Julian can easily handle any mindguards and get Vellus to release Molloy. It worked the last time."

"The last time, Vellus was convinced you jacked him and we both nearly ended up in prison!" My dad pushed off the car and paced the tight space between it and the wall.

"I wouldn't mind having another crack at Vellus." Julian captured my gaze. "Sasha would be very helpful as well."

If Sasha could scribe Vellus, that would solve a whole host of problems: we could get Molloy, save Raf, *and* rid the world of a heinous anti-jacker politician. "Dad, Julian has some powerful friends. We could make it work. You've got to at least let us try."

"Your friend and his jackwork pals aren't getting anywhere near Vellus!" my dad said. "Security at the capitol is tight. And I'm not planning on jacking Vellus at all. I'll get him to release Molloy with the one thing every politician doesn't want: bad publicity. Vellus's ambitions are pretty much limitless. He plans on being President someday. He won't want any skeletons coming out of the closet."

The idea of a President Vellus made my mouth run dry. Threatening to expose him seemed even more dangerous. "If you go in there alone, Vellus will just put you back in the Detention Center!"

"In which case, I'll get close to Molloy and find out what he knows."

"Dad!" I cried. "That's a horrible plan!"

"If I could make a suggestion?" Julian said calmly. "I would rather see Molloy sprung from the Detention Center than have you end up as his cell mate. But I agree that having Kira anywhere near Vellus is a bad idea."

I gave Julian an exasperated look that said *whose side are you on?*

Julian shrugged one shoulder. "I don't want to have to come rescue you again." He turned back to my dad. "Kira's right—I can handle any security Vellus has, even in the Capitol."

My dad braced one hand against the car, ran the other through his hair, and finally leveled a gaze straight at Julian. "Look, I don't know what kind of jacking you do, but unless you can jack through a shield like they had at Vellus's Detention Center, you're not getting in."

"A shield would present a problem." Julian's smirk said the solution might include blowing it up. I gave him a warning look. He ignored me and continued, "If security is as strong as you think, it would be difficult for all of us to get in. On your own, you may not even get through the front door, but with me handling the mindguard security and Kira doing any necessary jacking, you'll have a much better chance. Plus Kira makes an excellent scout and can give us the lay of the land before we proceed." Julian was giving me that *we make a good team* look again.

My dad drummed the top of the hydro car with his fingers, then frowned, like he was trying to piece together the puzzle that was Julian. "How do I know you're not planning a grand attempt on Vellus while we're there?"

"I'm here to help Kira find her friend," Julian said, "and I have my own reasons for wanting Mr. Molloy released. Regardless, I intend to make sure Kira stays a safe distance from the Senator. I don't want Vellus to get hold of her any more than you do."

My dad examined Julian, head to toe, as if seeing him for the first time. Julian stood with his feet planted wide and his arms crossed, looking slightly dangerous in his all-black clothes. Finally, my dad nodded. I thought it was bad when they didn't like each other; somehow my dad and Julian agreeing on something, particularly about me, was worse. Which made my brain hurt to think about, but it appeared that we were going to Springfield.

My dad slid into the front seat of the hydro car, and Julian smiled wide as he eased into the back. For a flash moment I wondered if Julian had handled my dad out of his concerns. As I climbed into the car, I threw a glare over the seatback, but

Julian was already busy on his phone, probably sending a scrit to Hinckley.

With any luck, we would soon need the mages' help with interrogating Molloy.

chapter TWENTY-THREE

Once we were outside the suburbs, my dad's hydro car flew down the arrow-straight road almost as fast as the bullet train from New Mexico. My dad didn't say a word and Julian was equally silent. The one-hour trip to Springfield ticked by in long minutes as cornfields stretched to the farmland ahead and scrolled past in endless mesmerizing waves.

Eventually, the crops gave way to the white marble buildings of Springfield. My dad switched the controls to manual, and we parked several blocks from the center of town. I automatically linked to the tourists and government workers filling the sidewalks. When we turned the corner to the capitol building, it struck me how pretentious it was. The original capitol had been rebuilt, expanded so that politicians wouldn't have to constantly listen to their political opponents' thoughts. The new capitol took up an entire city block and was adorned with a giant gold dome—it seemed a bit much for guys that worked for the people. Then again, the politicians inside had just passed a law declaring jackers second-class citizens in our own state. I guessed they only worked for *some* of the people.

We paused at the corner, a couple of hundred feet from the capitol building. Security guys in light gray jackets milled through the crowds on the giant stone steps leading inside, but they were only physical security. Their obvious uniforms were fear made visible—meant to reassure the public that mindjackers couldn't control the seats of power. But they were just a facade that covered the smaller number of mindguard security, all of whom were undercover, rooking as readers. One was stationed next to a hot dog stand, another haunted the street corner, a third pretended to watch a screen as he leaned against a light post. Several more rooked as mindreading security inside the building. So far none of them had detected my light touch.

The fact that the capitol was riddled with hidden jackers was an irony I didn't expect.

There's undercover jacker security on the street and more inside, I linked to my dad. *No one's noticed us yet, but if we get any closer, they will.*

They may not stop us until we're inside, my dad thought, *where it will be easier to contain us. Or they may shoot us in the street, depending how trigger-happy they are. How many are there inside?*

I skimmed the large lobby area as well as the disruptor field that protected the vast majority of the capitol building. *Half a dozen in the lobby, and two at a checkpoint by the shield.*

I think this is a good point to split up. Julian's voice rang in my dad's head. *Kira and I will go first, keep everyone calm, then you follow and make your move to get inside.*

My dad glared at him. *I don't like the idea of Kira in the middle of these guys. She can stay here. Or better yet, go back to the car and wait.*

Julian calmly met my father's stare. *That's a fine plan, if you'd like her to be alone and unprotected. She'll be safer with me.*

My dad gritted his teeth. *I don't see how a heavily mind-guarded government building is the safest place for her.*

See for yourself. Julian strolled toward the capitol steps, acting all casual and mesh with his hands in his pockets. The gray-jacket guys didn't even notice him. Two of the mindguards glanced his way, then went back to their undercover hot-dog cooking and light-post lounging. Julian stood in the dead center of the mini-plaza and waved at us.

Do they sense him? my dad asked.

No. Julian's the ultimate rook, Dad. They're not going to sense him because he's not a normal jacker.

He's not normal, that's for certain.

I half-grinned, but my dad's grumpy look killed it. *The mindguards will sense you for sure, Kira, even if you rook the rest.*

Julian will handle them. I'm just there in case we need to jack someone to get you in.

My dad made a sour face. *I think I can manage that on my own.*

Except once you're inside, we need to make sure you have a way out again.

Or I could send you back to the car, he thought.

You could try.

My dad sighed. *Don't be difficult, Kira. I'm just trying to keep you safe.*

And I'm trying to make sure this mission succeeds.

He frowned and looked me over the way he had Julian, as if he was seeing me for the first time. He reached inside his jacket and pulled out a palm-sized dart gun. My eyebrows flew up. Did he carry a weapon all the time now, or what?

Only if things go badly. He handed me the tiny gun. *And please don't do anything stupid.*

Thanks for the confidence. I tucked it into the back of my pants, draping my shirt over it. Only now my dad was going in unarmed to threaten Vellus with revealing his past.

Dad? What exactly did you do for Vellus?

He stared past me at the milling crowds. *Jacked people who stood in Vellus's way. Erased the memories of jackers and readers alike. Sent jackers to the camp who didn't belong there.* He pulled in a breath and looked back to me. *Not changelings. That was all Kestrel. But some of the people I sent to the camp... the only thing they did was cross Vellus. I thought it was the right thing at the time. It wasn't.*

The stone that had perpetually weighed in my stomach since my dad quit the Navy slowly crumbled into pieces. I had thought that losing his job was the price of me going public, but maybe it had actually helped him get out of a bad situation. Vellus used people, good people like my dad, twisting them into something else. No wonder my dad didn't want me anywhere near him.

Be careful, Dad.

Just stay out of trouble while I'm gone. This won't take long.

Julian was tapping his toes and checking his phone. I strode toward him while my dad pretended to inspect a tru-cast screen that scrolled capitol news. I smiled brightly and hooked my arm through Julian's, pulling him up the capitol steps. Julian handled the undercover mindguards out of their concern about me, and I jacked them to look away while my dad followed at the edge of the hundred-foot range of Julian's influence.

We stepped into the chilled lobby, overly cool for a summer day in downstate Illinois. The floor shone with white marble tiles inlaid with bits of colored stone. They formed a picture of a giant eagle with a curling red ribbon in its mouth. Julian and I rooked as a young couple visiting the capitol, blending in with the other readers scattered around the room: a family with three young boys on vacation, the elderly couple making a trek to see their congressman, a group of young political interns heading out for a late lunch. The only sounds in the great entryway were the echoey scraping of feet and shuffling of bodies.

The mindguards at the door watched us with little interest. I jacked them to look away while my dad crossed the ornate floor to the receptionist. He asked her several questions about Vellus, gently probing the information that floated behind her conscious thoughts without causing the mental anguish that would come if he drilled through her memories. Maybe my dad wasn't the strongest jacker in the world, but his years working for Naval Intelligence had netted him some skills.

I tugged Julian behind a large bronze statue in the middle of the lobby and peeked at the security checkpoint along the back wall. Two mindguards rooked as regular security guards stationed by the weapons detector, a giant silver arch that framed a doorway, beyond which stood a bank of elevators. The disruptor shield spanned the doorway and hugged the entire back wall.

My dad would have to go through the weapons detector as well as the shield. It was a good thing he had given me his gun. Thanks to Julian, the guards on *this* side of the shield wouldn't worry about letting an armed mindjacker into the capitol, but anyone on the *other* side of the shield would notice if the alarms went off. Not to mention security cameras had to be taking in every viewpoint of the lobby.

My dad headed for the checkpoint, and Julian overrode the mindguards' instinctual concerns. My dad flashed a badge to the guards, and his thoughts rang in their minds. *I'm from Naval Intelligence. I suggest you call Senator Vellus's office and tell him Patrick Moore is here to see him about an important matter.*

The taller, craggier mindguard didn't respond, but the shorter one tapped his ear and whispered into his earbud phone. My hands started to sweat. I took Julian's phone and jacked into the mindware to scrit a message, then held it up for him to see.

Do we need to move closer? If the guards freaked out, Julian might need to be closer to handle them both.

We're fine, he scrit back.

A long, tense moment stretched my nerves while the shorter mindguard waited for a response, but then he thought, *Your escort will be here in a moment.*

Within ten seconds, a burly security guard appeared on the far side of the weapons detector and the shield. He was the same oversized mindguard that Vellus had with him at Maria's interview! He reminded me of Harrier, arms rippling with muscles. Jackers with a penchant for weight lifting must be in high demand for government officials. I edged farther behind the cover of the statue, pulling on Julian's long-sleeved shirt to follow. My link to my dad's mind cut off with a painful break as he stepped through the shield.

I checked the time on Julian's phone. *2:30 pm.* Now for the hard part: waiting for my dad to come back out.

Your father's a good man, appeared on the phone, which startled me until I realized that Julian must have jacked in.

I nudged the mindware to scrit back, *Glad you noticed.*

For the record... Words scrolled across the phone. *I don't think he's responsible for the raid. Vellus would have found another excuse.*

I peered up at Julian. *You were listening in!* I scrit on the phone.

He grinned and shrugged. My mind skipped back over my conversation on the lawn with my dad. Was there anything

Julian shouldn't have heard? It was all personal, between me and my dad, but in a way I was glad Julian had heard it.

Having someone close to Vellus isn't entirely a bad thing, Julian scrit. *It could be useful in the future.*

What, like a double agent?

Julian's face lit up and his words scrolled across the phone. *You, keeper, would make a fine double agent. Your father could be a mindguard who would look the other way.* He was thinking about Sasha again. What would happen if the biggest anti-jacker politician had a sudden change of heart? Would the public realize he had been jacked or would they follow his lead?

Then I realized I was contemplating the very thing that my father had worked against his entire time in the Navy: jacker influence reaching into the highest levels of government. I frowned as that thought snarled in my head. I could help Anna and Julian finish their mission to capture Kestrel—he was evil and had to be stopped. And I still wanted to make good on my promise to get the changelings out of Kestrel's grasp. But Julian was after more than that, and I couldn't picture myself joining his revolution, much less see my dad signing up. I wasn't ready to answer the question that lingered on Julian's face, so I slid his phone into my pocket and ignored the disappointed downturn of his mouth. I avoided his gaze by examining the plaque on the statue in front of us.

The words on the plaque seeped into my brain as the minutes ticked by. The larger-than-life statue of a woman extended her arms to the visitors in the lobby. She represented the city of

Chicago welcoming people to the 1893 World's Fair. The statue must have been rescued from the demolition of the old capitol to grace the new one, but her spirit of welcoming had been left behind, at least for jackers in the world that Vellus envisioned.

Julian went rigid next to me. The craggy mindguard was coming straight for us, intent on delivering a message.

Miss Moore, Senator Vellus would like a word with you.

I took a step back, but the mindguard only clasped his hands behind his back, waiting patiently, as if I were a tourist who had lucked into a visit with the famous politician. Something must have gone wrong. My dad would never ask for me to come meet Vellus, so it must be Vellus himself. Had he seen me on the cameras? What did he want? It had to be some kind of trap. Julian seemed to be thinking the same thing, minutely shaking his head.

Why does the Senator want to see me? I linked to the mindguard.

I don't know, Miss. Didn't you request a visit?

No, she didn't request a visit. Julian's thoughts rang in the mindguard's mind.

A clattering of footsteps sounded at the entrance, then stopped. The three undercover mindguards from outside had rushed the building, only to enter Julian's range of influence and lose their desire to stop the dangerous jackers inside. Julian could handle these, but how many more could Vellus summon if I didn't do what he wanted?

The mindguard tapped the phone in his ear. Vellus's slick,

too-confident voice came through. *Tell Miss Moore that I'm willing to give her what she wants, but she'll have to come to my office to get it.*

The mindguard dutifully repeated Vellus's words. Was "what I wanted" Molloy's release or my dad's freedom? Regardless, the longer I waited, the worse the situation outside would get. It was quickly looking like I didn't have a choice.

Julian must have read my face. "Remember how your father told you not to do anything stupid?" he whispered. I jacked the mindguard to ignore us.

"Do you eavesdrop on *all* my conversations with my dad?"

"Keeper, you're not going to gain anything by going to see Vellus. We should leave now."

"My dad is still in there!"

"He was willing to take that risk and rather pointedly *didn't* want you taking it. Vellus is dangerous, and he apparently knows what you want. The problem is you don't know what Vellus wants."

"I know one way to find out."

"Your father wouldn't want you to try rescuing him," Julian said, as if that would sway me.

"My father wanted to send me back to the car," I said. "I don't know what's going on, but if my dad was free to go, he'd be here already."

Julian stepped back from me, ran his hands through his hair, and studied the guard. When Julian turned back to me, he reached both arms around me, like he was giving me a hug.

My arms went automatically around his neck, which welled up a surge of emotion that heated my cheeks. I almost pulled away, then I realized he was slipping out the gun tucked in the back of my pants. I stayed close while he fumbled to tuck the gun into the front of his pants and cover it.

Julian whispered, "If you're determined to go in, I'm going with you. We'll need to move fast." When he pulled back, my arms didn't untangle quick enough, which made my cheeks run even hotter. We finally managed to break apart and Julian ducked his head like he was embarrassed too.

The mindguard held his hand up to Julian. *I'm sorry, sir, but the Senator would only like Miss Moore to join him.*

Julian gave me a look that said *Will you please jack this guy?*

"No matter what I jack these guys to do," I whispered as we strode past the guard, who was now fascinated by the statue, "it's not going to hold once I'm past the shield."

"We'll go through together. Once I'm on the other side, I can handle things from there."

That might actually work. When we stepped through the shield, Julian's handling on this side could be cut off and all heck would break loose, but he should be able to handle anything on the other side. Coming back out, we could reverse the process. Maybe. Unless Vellus had already called in the National Guard. Julian was right—we needed to move fast.

The mindguard stationed by the shield blandly waved us toward the weapons detector. Julian nearly stepped on my shoes, he was following so close. Just as we were about to cross the threshold of the weapons detector, Vellus's bulky mindguard emerged from the elevators. I stopped and Julian bumped into me. The mindguard reached into his jacket and pulled out a gun. And not a dart gun. The kind with bullets that killed people.

My breath caught, and Julian moved behind me, no doubt taking out my dad's gun as well. About fifteen feet of air separated us from guard, but it was only three feet to the shield. As long as we were on this side, we couldn't jack him, but he could certainly shoot us. If we lunged across the shield, Julian might be able to handle him into lowering his weapon. Or we might both get shot.

Julian leaned into me, like he wanted to go for the lunging option, which only flashed up an image in my mind of Simon, lying bleeding in the desert with a bullet hole in him.

I turned to face Julian, sandwiching the gun between us. "Julian, don't! Getting shot won't help things."

He gripped the dart gun tighter. It was a fast-acting dart gun, but it wasn't that fast. He spoke through clenched teeth. "I don't like your odds going in there without me."

The mindguard watched us carefully, gun leveled at my back, but not moving any closer.

"If they wanted to kill me, I'd already be dead," I said. "He would have shot us as soon as he stepped out of the elevator."

"Shooting us *here* would cause some difficulties." Julian kept glaring at the guard. "It's what they'll do once you're in Vellus's office that I'm concerned about."

"If I don't come out in twenty minutes," I said, "you can come get me."

Julian peeled his gaze from the mindguard and peered down at me. I was suddenly aware of how close we were standing.

"Am I going to have to rescue you again?" Julian asked.

"Possibly," I said. "Just don't kiss me this time."

His shoulders relaxed, very slightly.

I turned and stepped through the weapons detector, my hair lifting up at the back of my neck as I passed through the shield.

chapter TWENTY-FOUR

Vellus's overmuscled mindguard backed toward the brass-trimmed elevators, keeping his eyes on Julian. Now that I had passed through the shield, I was tempted to brush the mindguard's brain to peer into his thoughts, but with his gun still trained on Julian, I didn't want to take any chances.

I slipped into the elevator, and the guard holstered his weapon once we were both inside. The elevator ride was short, then Mr. Muscle guided me to a room with red velvet carpet and paintings older than my great-grandma. A portrait of Vellus hung above his receptionist's desk, his chiseled features gleaming with holo-paint that made his face seem to move. The receptionist wrangled the mindware interface on her computer, and Mr. Muscle and I both linked into her mind and reflected her innocuous thoughts as if we were readers. Which made me look up the full height of the guard to his strong-jawed face. Did the receptionist not *know* he was a jacker?

Please have a seat, thought the receptionist without looking.

I'll let the Senator know you're here. I ignored the two ornately carved wooden chairs that lined the wall—I needed to be on my feet, ready for whatever Vellus had in store for me. I reached toward Vellus's office, but it was blocked by a disruptor shield.

Why was Vellus keeping me waiting? Maybe he wanted to make me nervous, although holding my dad captive and sending the armed guard seemed sufficient for that. Still, I didn't want to appear anxious, so I clasped my hands behind my back and pretended to size up Mr. Muscle like the side of beef he resembled. He could crush me physically, and probably mentally as well, if only he could get into my head. I smiled jauntily up at him, just to put him off balance. Amazingly, it worked. His face twitched, then he became fascinated by the paintings on the wall. For some reason I couldn't understand, I unnerved him.

The receptionist finally looked up from her work, and her nails tapped the desk as she rose.

Would you like to have a seat while you wait? she thought.

I turned to face her with a polite smile. *No thanks.*

Her sensible shoes whispered across the lush carpet, and she came to stand too close to me. Her wiry frame was short, probably no more than five foot, and she inspected me through her trufocus glasses, which adjusted as she leaned closer to peer at my face.

A smile snaked up her lips. "You've changed your hair." She cleared her throat, smoothing the roughness from not speaking aloud for so long. A chill creeped into my stomach as I realized she knew exactly who I was. "And I don't remember those tattoos from before," she continued. "Are they new?" The contradiction between her fake-polite spoken words and the fervently anti-jacker thoughts roiling beneath jarred me out of her head. Her glasses sparkled reflections from the plasma lights, but the menace in her eyes shone through. I could have taken her in a fist fight, or I could have jacked her, but instead I shrank away.

I'd never seen someone look at me like they wished I didn't exist.

"I watched all the tru-casts, you know." I pictured her glued to the screens, soaking up all the rhetoric that Vellus spewed. "You and those other snively jacker kids who acted frightened, as if they wouldn't like to kill us all in our sleep."

She was talking about the changelings I had rescued. The ones Kestrel had tortured with his experiments. The ones who were barefoot and hollow cheeked on the tru-casts, held at gun-point by jacker FBI agents. Her caricature of them was so awful, so ugly and wrong, that I couldn't even muster anger or outrage. It just left me speechless.

"That's right," she said. "Don't bother to deny it. I see right through that pretty little face of yours to what's inside. How many readers have you killed, Kira Moore? Or do you just con-trol them to do whatever nasty things you jackers do for fun? How many children have to grow up in fear of monsters like you lurking in our schools and our offices and our neighborhoods before people realize what you are and put a stop to it?"

I wanted to protest. I wanted to lash out at her. But words

completely failed me in the face of this volcano of hatred from this tiny person.

There was nothing I could say that would make any difference.

I didn't know I was leaning away from her until I bumped into Mr. Muscle. His face was expressionless. He certainly wasn't coming to the defense of jackers. I guessed he had already sold his soul if he was working for Vellus.

Just like my dad.

I took a couple steps back, my heart shrinking with that thought, when the door to Vellus's office swung open and banged against the wall. My dad stalked toward me, trailed by Vellus and another oversized mindguard. My dad looked ready to punch Vellus in the face, which halfway thrilled me. I wanted my dad to hit Vellus so badly it made my fists curl up. Whatever was up, I was ready to run or jack or possibly deck Vellus myself.

I reached for Vellus's mind, only to be swatted away by the mindguard closest to him and slammed back into my own head. He was so strong I couldn't even reach out to my dad. Vellus's personal mindguard was taller and not as bulked up as Mr. Muscle, but he was an incredibly strong jacker, almost like Myrtle. I searched my dad's reddened face for a clue about what had happened.

"So nice of you to join us, Kira." Vellus directed his words to me, but they stopped my dad in his tracks. "I didn't expect to see you again so soon." He sounded pleasantly surprised to see me, as if he weren't holding my dad hostage to get me up here. His secretary had retreated to her desk, but the heat of her smirk scorched me from across the room.

"I was planning on paying you a visit, sooner or later, and here you are, doing me the courtesy of coming to my office. It's nice to see you under less, shall we say, tense circumstances."

The room was feeling plenty tense to me. My dad reached my side, placing his body between me and Mr. Muscle.

"But I'm willing to let bygones be bygones." Vellus waved away the idea that I had jacked him in the tru-cast station. "As your father was explaining, it would appear that I have something you want, which is tremendously fortunate for me, as you have something I want as well."

"What do you want?"

Vellus grinned that sim-cast-ready smile. I didn't know what game we were playing, but it felt like I had already lost.

"I would like nothing more than to release Mr. Molloy to you, so that you can find your mindreader friend and return to the suburbs. I hear they serve a very fine pie at the Dutch Apple, although I've never tried it myself. I may have to remedy that sometime soon."

The idea of Vellus coming to the Dutch Apple sent a cold trickle down my back, and I was sure releasing Molloy came with a price tag. My dad tensed, edging a little closer. I wanted desperately to link into his mind, but Vellus's personal mind-guard and Mr. Muscle had lined me up between them, keeping me squarely in my own head. They didn't press or try to get inside, but it felt like being smothered in a mental blanket.

"What do you want from me?" I repeated.

"It's a small thing, actually, only a short bit of your time," Vellus said with a smile. "I want you to tell the truth. You like to do that, don't you?" His grin grew more evil with each tooth exposed. "I think we have more in common than it might appear, Kira. You wish to have your mindreading friend back, safe and sound, and you want to return home to your family and friends in the suburbs. I want to reassure mindreaders that their lives are going to be safe and secure too. I'm sure we can come to an agreement where we both get the things we want."

Anger still mottled my dad's face, but it was blank, with no clue as to what Vellus wanted, and minutes were ticking by while Vellus beat around the bush. I needed to talk our way out of this before Julian came charging up after us.

"What *exactly* will it take to get you to release Molloy?" I asked.

Vellus smirked. "I'd like you to do a tru-cast interview. Another one, although decidedly different from your first appearance on the national airwaves."

"An interview?" Maybe Vellus was demens after all.

"You can explain how dangerous jackers are and how much you regret all the harm and chaos caused by the mutant jackers living in our midst."

"I... I don't understand." People already thought jackers were dangerous, and haters like Vellus's secretary made up awful stories about jackers all by themselves. They didn't need my help. How would anything I said on a tru-cast make any difference?

"I want you to detail the grievous things that jackers in our own city have done," Vellus said. "Just tell the truth, Kira. That's all I want from the girl who is the face of the jackers."

Then it hit me: Vellus wanted me to talk about Jackertown. The crews and the contractors and the jackworkers. My thoughts flashed to Julian. And Ava and Myrtle and the changelings. Even Sasha and Hinckley. The looks on their faces when they saw me on a tru-cast with Vellus, talking about how the jackers in Jackertown were dangerous... and should be locked up in his Detention Center.

My mouth wouldn't work at first, then I finally blurted, "I can't do that!"

"Of course you can, Kira," he said calmly. "I'm not asking that much of you, and I'm giving you so much in return. A chance to get your friend back from a brute like Mr. Molloy. That would make a brilliant story, don't you think?" He trailed his hand across the air like a scrolling tru-cast headline. "Mindreader kidnapped by evil mindjacker! I would simply be the loyal public servant who helped you bring home your friend. So, you see, we truly *do* want the same things."

Blood pounded in my ears, and my dad's hand settled at the small of my back. Maybe he expected to find the gun there? His face didn't show disappointment, just high-voltage tension. He gave me an encouraging nod. He wanted me to tell Vellus yes. My chest hollowed out.

"No..." The words were a whisper to my dad, but Vellus took it as my answer.

He inclined his head to the side. "You haven't already settled in with those ragged types that rattle around Jackertown, have you?" His eyes took on a darker, sharper gleam. "Your friend in the lobby won't have much of a chance against the police, even with his jacking talents, if I'm forced to sound an alarm. You wouldn't want that, would you?"

I swallowed. "No," I said, louder this time.

Vellus sighed and looked like he was trying to be patient. "Kira, you may think that you and your little friends are stronger, more superior, but you're not. It's only a matter of time before readers find a way to keep jackers completely contained." He swept his hand back toward his shield-protected office. "With technology. With state-of-the art prisons to keep you safely quarantined. And with the knowledge that you are very, very different from them."

My face burned. "Different isn't a crime, you know."

"No," Vellus said. "Not yet. But I expect that will change, and soon. Society can't tolerate people like you in their midst, Kira. They fear you. And society has always destroyed what it fears. It's jackers or readers, Kira, and in the end, the readers will have to win."

I stared at Vellus. It was almost like he was warning me. Or perhaps toying with me. I couldn't quite keep the words in. "It doesn't have to be that way!"

He smiled indulgently. "Spoken like a true believer," he said. "It's a shame those ideals will only result in your friends getting hurt." He stepped a little closer and my dad's hand clutched the back of my shirt, like he would yank me out of harm's way if Vellus got too close.

Vellus peered down at me. "From everything I hear about you, Kira, you're not the kind of girl that likes to see people get hurt."

I leaned back into my dad's hand and shook my head.

"Good!" Vellus exclaimed. He stepped back and clasped his hands together. "I will make sure that Mr. Molloy is released to you as soon as you arrive at the Detention Center. I sincerely hope that you quickly find your mindreading friend safe and sound." He tipped his head in a genteel way. "This has been a most interesting discussion, Kira. I look forward to seeing more of you in the future." He turned to Mr. Muscle. "Please see our guests safely out of the building." Vellus pivoted on the heel of his expensive shoes and returned to his office.

My mouth hung open, watching him go. Had I really just agreed to Vellus's demand that I do a tru-cast for his anti-jacker campaign? My dad gently tugged on the back of my shirt, and I shuffled after him, following closely behind the bulky back of Mr. Muscle. It didn't matter what I said or what Vellus thought—as soon as we got Molloy and found Raf, I would just refuse to do it.

Once we were out of jacking range of Vellus's office, the mental blanket Mr. Muscle had wrapped around my head eased up. I quickly linked to my dad. *Will Vellus really release Molloy?*

Yes. My dad kept his eyes trained on the guard. *Molloy will be ready for release into my custody by the time we can get back to Vellus's Detention Center.*

Relief washed through me. *I hope you know I'm not going to do Vellus's tru-cast. I only agreed so that I could get us out of there.*

I know, my dad thought. *I know you can't. It's far too dangerous.*

I hadn't thought about how dangerous it would be, just how horribly *wrong* it was. But he was right—not only would Julian and his mages hate me, and rightly so, every jacker in the country would want me dead. Which wouldn't bother Vellus in the slightest. That might even be the whole point of it.

So, after we find Raf, I'll just tell Vellus I won't do it, I linked to my dad. *No matter how many muscle-bound mindguards Vellus has, he can't force me to do the tru-cast, right?*

He knows about you, Kira. My dad flicked a look to me. His thoughts were an anxious pit that pulled me in. *He knows about you breaking into Kestrel's facility.* My dad guided me into the elevator after our escort. *He's got a tape of you at Kestrel's facility, shooting a guard, and not just once. If you don't do what Vellus wants, he wouldn't need any more reason than that to lock you away. Did you see the new law? We don't have any rights anymore. The only thing keeping you free is that Vellus wants something from you.*

Suddenly the elevator felt like a cage, plummeting down and carrying me into a trap. Vellus meant it. He would force me to do the tru-cast or go to prison. And I knew what that meant: a one-way ticket back into Kestrel's cells.

Panic clamped on my throat, and I gripped my dad's arm. *What are we going to do?*

We get Molloy. We find Raf. Then we find a way to protect you from Vellus. He still wants me to work for him. Maybe I can convince him that the tru-cast is a bad idea. Or maybe Mr. Trullite can help. Worst case, we'll move again. Disappear and pray that Vellus can't find you.

My stomach looped in a knot that was strangling me. The guard walked us to the edge of the shield and the weapons detector. Julian stood on the other side, his hair messier than usual on one side, like he had spent the last ten minutes torturing it with his hands. I sprinted through the barrier, barely noticing the electric tingle of the shield, and grabbed hold of Julian's arm. I ignored his concerned look and towed him across the lobby with my dad close behind. There was no way I could explain what had happened, at least not yet. Right now we needed to leave the capitol before Vellus changed his mind about releasing Molloy. That was our only real chance of finding Raf.

I would explain later that one of the world's most powerful men expected me to join his anti-jacker campaign in return.

chapter TWENTY-FIVE

The autopath back to the city was even quieter than the ride down to Springfield.

I ignored Julian's stares and stayed out of my dad's head. The lines drawn tight across my dad's face told me he regretted going to the capitol. He wanted to save Raf, but if he had known what Vellus would ask, he wouldn't have gone. Not that it really mattered. Vellus said he was planning on "paying me a visit" sooner or later—I had only sped up the process by going to him first.

It didn't seem likely that Mr. Trullite could protect me, given his rescue attempt in Jackertown had only landed my dad in prison. No, I could already see how this would go. If there was any justice in the world, we would find Raf alive and unharmed. But however that worked out, I would have to run again. Just me this time. My dad wanted to take my family on the run, but I was done putting the people who loved me in danger. This time I would hide better, run farther, go somewhere that Vellus's influence wouldn't reach. It was either that or I would have to do what Vellus wanted: go on the tru-casts to spew hatred like Vellus's secretary. I wasn't sure if I could physically force myself to say the words. If I somehow managed it, I'd have every jacker in three states wanting my head. Only they wouldn't haul me into jail, like Vellus. They would kill my family too. No, that absolutely wouldn't work.

When this was all done, I would run and leave behind everyone that I loved. Including Raf.

I swallowed down that thought, and it sat like a lump of cold metal in my stomach. A haze threatened to descend on my mind like when I was locked in Kestrel's stark, white cell. If only I had killed Kestrel when I had the chance, maybe that tape wouldn't have landed in Vellus's hands. Or did Vellus already have it by then? It didn't matter now. I fought back the haze clouding my thoughts. I couldn't afford to sink into that dark place yet.

It was a relief when we finally arrived at Vellus's Detention Center. My dad eased the hydro car to a stop, and Sasha pushed off the brick alleyway wall to join us. He gave me a slow nod of acknowledgement. I nodded in return, grateful he was willing to help. I wished Julian had sent for Myrtle too—I didn't want to take any chances with Molloy getting away, but Julian seemed to think that the four of us would be sufficient.

My dad hopped out and hurried to the gate, his badge already out. I unfolded my body and slowly climbed out of the car, stretching out the kinks. Even my hands ached. I must have been clenching them the whole way. Julian was already out of the car, mindtalking to Sasha. My dad slipped from sight through the gate, making my heart lurch.

Julian left Sasha to stand next to me. He eyed the guard shack. "What's wrong, keeper?"

"Nothing. I'm just... worried. What if Molloy doesn't know where Raf is?" I paused. "Or what if he does and..." I couldn't say it. What if all this was for nothing? What if Raf was already dead?

Julian seemed to be struggling with what to say. I looked away, so he wouldn't have to answer. Less than a minute later, my dad came out with Molloy in mag-cuffs, holding a dart gun to his side and frog-marching Molloy across the street. When Molloy caught sight of us, or more accurately when he saw Julian, he stopped in the middle of the street. His face lost color. My dad shoved him from behind to get him moving again. Molloy took two steps but then whirled around, swinging one massive leg to catch my dad at the knees and knock him to the ground.

"Dad!"

I quickly jacked into Molloy's mind and wrestled with him as he lumbered down the street away from us. I couldn't slow him down, but a split second later, my dad was in his mind as well. Molloy put up quite a struggle for a second or two and then he stumbled to a stop.

He turned around, and in his mind, he saw us in a new light. We were his fellow jackers, his brothers-in-arms, who he owed a debt of loyalty beyond measure. We meant everything to him; his very life he owed to us.

Julian had reached him.

I shuddered a sigh of relief.

A picture of Raf, sprawled on a brown-carpeted floor, sprung up in Molloy's mind.

Oh no. My thoughts and Molloy's echoed each other, with the same expression of horror.

Julian focused on Molloy, his concentration intense. Molloy's thoughts kept tangling with mine. *Is Raf okay? We need to find him!*

The coupling of our thoughts was giving me vertigo, so I pulled out of Molloy's mind. He rushed past my dad who scrambled to scoop up his dropped dart gun from the pavement.

When Molloy reached me, he took my shoulders in his massive hands. "Kira!" he said, breathless. "We've got to get to Raf quickly, lass. He's probably dehydrated by now, or worse."

My hopes surged—Molloy thought Raf was alive! I nodded, overwhelmed by Molloy's fervent need to save my boyfriend, the one he was responsible for holding hostage in the first place. I shouldn't have been surprised—I'd had a taste of the intensity of what Julian could do. I had been completely convinced that I loved him: not simply believing it, or even feeling it in a swoony way, but urgently compelled to love him as if my existence depended on it.

And that had only been through a mind-link. Molloy was getting the full dose of Julian's ability.

He released me and turned to my dad. "We don't have any time to waste. Would this be your car, mate?"

My dad blinked. I couldn't imagine what he was thinking.

"I think we should take Mr. Molloy where he wants to go," said Julian. His voice was low and breathy. His eyes never left Molloy's face, even though Molloy seemed oblivious to anything other than hustling us into the hydro car and babbling directions to the autopath. He finally jacked into the mindware interface, cursing at it to hurry.

The ragged streets of downtown Chicago slipped by, and we veered past the south edge of Jackertown, still in the city, but getting closer to the suburbs. Julian sat next to Molloy in front, with my dad, Sasha, and me filling up the back seat. The stony expression on Julian's face never wavered. When he'd handled Molloy before, back at the mages' headquarters, he wasn't so intense about it. Maybe Molloy was more resistant now? Or was his self-preservation instinct harder to handle than the protective instinct for his brother?

Whatever it was, I vowed never to link into Julian's mind again.

Molloy babbled a nonstop stream of thoughts, like there was no longer a filter between his mind and his mouth. "There's not any food there, lass, and I'm not too keen on the water either." The rest of us sat in tense silence while he rambled. "Not that we needed as much. At least Raf didn't, not while I kept him there. It was my home, Liam's and mine actually, before Ma and Da were taken away and we were left on our own. We kept it though, even when the neighborhood was taken over by the demens. We were Molloy boys, and we could take care of ourselves. Proud of it, too! But then we realized there wasn't much in the way of pickings in the city. The suburbs on the other hand, aye, there's a fortune to be made there!"

Molloy paused to take a breath. I hoped I wouldn't have to hear his entire life story before we reached the house he had programmed into the autopath.

"Liam, though, he didn't last long in the greater New Metro," Molloy said. "He was barely out of shorts, still working his changeling abilities, when the Feds took him. He's been in that right monster's clutches ever since. Kestrel!" He spat out his name like it was something foul. "If I get the chance, I'll twist that demon's neck with my bare hands."

I wished Molloy had done exactly that. I wasn't sure if that made me a monster or not.

"Aye, but Liam!" Molloy shouted as if he had suddenly remembered his brother. "He's still in that cursed prison of Vellus's! Who will look out for the boy when I'm not there?"

That made me cringe. Liam would be defenseless in the Detention Center, but I couldn't let myself care about that. Julian edged closer to Molloy, resting his arm on the back of Molloy's seat.

"Of course, he's not going anywhere." Molloy's voice had lost its concern. "They'll lock him up in their medical facility, given he's not right of mind anymore. But Raf, the poor lad. He's been wasting away in some dank basement without proper nourishment for the better part of a week! We'd best be getting there first, before the boy passes on. That would be a terrible shame, such a weak creature, not able to defend himself from jackers at all."

Julian must be working him pretty hard to conjure those thoughts from the depths of Molloy's mind. He had turned Molloy's instinct to protect his helpless brother Liam to a strong, artificial imperative to protect Raf, who he now saw as one of "his own." Protecting *his own* had always been a powerful impulse in Molloy, which was probably why Julian chose it. Had it only been a week since Molloy left Raf? Was he really alive when Molloy left him? I couldn't imagine Molloy lying about that, not while Julian was handling him.

How long could Raf last, knocked out on the floor?

I scoured my brain, from that long-ago time when I took biology classes and dreamed of being a doctor. How long can a body live without water or food? Water had to be more important. And it must make a difference whether the person was awake or asleep, in the desert or locked in a damp basement. Maybe Raf was in the best possible state to survive: locked in a cool basement, unconscious.

Why had Molloy left him like that? Maybe he meant to come back after he was done betraying us, but didn't get the chance to trade Raf before he was picked up by Vellus's goons. The police wouldn't have caught him up in a random sweep—Molloy's house was nowhere near Jackertown. Maybe Kestrel had betrayed Molloy after all, only he called the police to take care of it. Maybe that had saved Raf's life.

My heart tripped as the car slowed in front of a run-down

one-story house. It was the two-hundred-year-old cracker-box style that happened to narrowly meet the range codes, but was too close to the city, so it sat in disrepair, taken over by the demens and their squatter's rights.

It was the perfect place to hide a body.

A ghostly chill made my hands shake. Maybe Molloy had never planned to come back at all. I pushed my way out of the car before it had come to a complete stop.

"Where?" I demanded of Molloy, but he was sprinting ahead of me.

"Hurry, lass," he said over his shoulder. "Before it's too late."

The front door looked like a good push would knock it down, but instead Molloy swiped a passring that barely fit on his pinkie. When he shoved the door open, it came off one hinge, which momentarily stalled him. I slipped between Molloy and the doorframe, simultaneously reaching out with my mind. I found Raf in the basement, deep in the unconscious state of someone who had been jacked that way.

But he was alive.

"How do we get to the basement?" I screeched. Dashing through the tiny, dust-filled living room, I searched for a door that would lead down below.

"Around the back." Molloy pushed past me, leading the way through a chipped and musty kitchen. A door at the back led outside, but instead of going through, he turned to another one opposite it. Molloy's giant frame barely fit in the tight hallway space between the doors, but he managed to pull the basement door open. I shoved past him and pounded down the steps. Molloy's thudding footfalls followed behind me, along with more that must have been Julian and my dad and Sasha.

Dust motes floated in the hazy light. The basement windows spotlighted an overturned recliner that bled stuffing onto the floor and a rotting blanket pooled next to it. In the middle of the room, Raf lay bent, like he had been struck and collapsed: his limbs were all at angles, and his curly dark hair obscured his face. It was the exact image that I had seen in Molloy's mind, all that time ago in Kestrel's office.

I leaped down the last stair step and sprinted across the carpeted floor. My foot twisted as it crunched a toy hydro car hidden in the gloom, making me stumble the last three feet before reaching his side.

Raf's chest rose and fell, once, very slowly.

chapter TWENTY-SIX

I sank to my knees on the carpet next to Raf, barely able to think with the emotion flooding my body. My hands shook as I brushed back the curls that had fallen across his eyes. His face wasn't peaceful, just blank, but there wasn't any pain etched on it either. Even in the murky light of the basement, I could see he was pale and his lips were cracked with dehydration. He had been unconscious for over a week, so I didn't know why I expected anything different. He must have been in this position all that time, and that couldn't be a good thing, all twisted up on the floor.

I gently took hold of his shoulders and straightened his body out so that he was lying flat on the floor. His chest rose and fell again, but there was absolutely no other sign of life. Footsteps swished on the carpet behind me, but I ignored them. I reached very slowly into Raf's mind. All conscious thoughts had been wiped clean, and Molloy had put him so far under that even his unconscious thoughts were still.

If I hadn't seen people in this state before, put them there myself, I might have panicked. But I knew I only had to wake him up. Slowly, gently, I sped up his heart and breathing just a tiny bit, to rouse him from the coma. I couldn't help touching him, running my fingertips along his chilled cheek to reassure myself that he was really here, alive, breathing. His body shifted ever so slightly, and his head moved, seeking my touch again. I cradled his cheek in my hand.

I could have jacked him harder, brought him around quicker, but I was afraid to go too fast after he had been unconscious so long. Raf's mind climbed out of the deep fog that held it. Someone hovered over me, probably my dad, but he hung back. Raf moaned, a weak sound that made my breath catch, and his eyelids fluttered but didn't open.

I leaned down close to his face, kissed his cheek, and whispered, "Raf, it's me. I'm here. Wake up."

He moved toward the sound of my voice and our cheeks brushed. I tucked my hands under his heavy, near-unconscious body and pulled him slightly off the floor in a fierce hug. My lips were still near his ear. "Please, Raf, wake up."

He stirred in my arms and I reluctantly released him. When I pulled back, his eyes finally opened, deep brown and gorgeous and staring up at me. His mind was a swirl of confusion. He tried to swallow, his throat no doubt parched.

My grin was a mile wide. "It's okay," I said, answering his unspoken thoughts. "It's all right now, I've found you, everything's going to be okay now." I was babbling and I didn't care. I ran my fingertips along his cheek again, but this time he frowned and pulled back.

My hand froze.

Raf pulled in a ragged breath, as if his lungs were catching up with the rest of his slowly waking body, then he grimaced and struggled to inch away from me. His eyes widened as he realized how weak he was.

What... what happened to me? Who are you?

His thoughts turned my insides into a solid chunk of ice.

My dad handed me a paper cup of water over my shoulder. I fumbled for it, then held it out to Raf, but he just eyed it.

It's okay. It's only water. You need it. My hand shook as I set the cup in front of him. He watched me carefully, then his eyes landed on the tangled lines of the tattoo on my wrist. Confusion still gripped his mind, but thirst drove him to reach for the cup. When he saw the same tattoo on his own wrist, he jerked back, dropping the cup and holding his wrist away from his body, like it no longer belonged to him.

What have you done to me? He was awash in the blind terror of someone who has woken up in a basement with no memory and no strength to do anything about it. My mouth worked but there were no words. Raf didn't know me. Didn't remember me. Was *afraid* of me.

The ice core inside me cracked and shattered into million pieces.

What did Molloy do?

I shut my eyes and dove into Raf's mind, searching. There

was no memory of running through Jackertown together. No memory of our last phone call. No recognition that I had finally come for him. I pushed deeper. Did he remember the diner? *No.* Did he remember all the times he kissed me, the times he touched me and told me he loved me? *No.* Nothing but giant blank spots where his memories of me had been. I tunneled deeper, before we were a mindreader and mindjacker, when we were just kids. There had to be something, somewhere. Some trace of me. What about the times we had played soccer together? What about junior high, when we passed notes in the hall? What about the time he stole my scribepad, only to return it with a lock code I spent a week guessing? *No.* I kept scouring, going farther into the folds of his mind where his earliest memories were locked away forever.

It was gone, all of it. There was one tiny memory left, of when Raf and I met that first day in kindergarten. As far as Raf was concerned, that was the last time he had ever talked to me.

Molloy had stolen Raf's memories of me. He had stolen *me.*

A giant hole punched through my chest, whistling the vacuum as it left an empty space where my heart should be. Air sucked out of my body and it grew still.

I pulled out of Raf's mind and blinked the tears until they ran down my face in a steady stream. He was afraid of *me,* even though Molloy was the one who had taken a mental scalpel to his memories, slicing and cutting me out of his life.

I sprang to my feet and whirled around. Julian and Sasha had Molloy parked on the bottom step of the stairwell. Their gazes flitted back and forth between Raf and me. They might not understand, but Molloy knew exactly what he had done. I rushed at Molloy, but my dad's hands caught me by the waist, gentle but firm.

I struggled against his grip. "Give them back!" I yelled at Molloy, still a dozen feet away. "Give back his memories, you monster!"

Molloy just shook his head and wrung his hands. He looked up from the floor. "I can't, lassie." His face was a picture of mourning, as if he actually cared. Julian stared hard at Molloy, shifting closer and placing a hand on Molloy's shoulder. Molloy started to cry, large tears dripping off his chin. "I wish I could; there's too much. Too many memories, too much time. I don't know what possessed me, lass, but I took them all, with no way to remember them for putting back. I never thought I would have need of it, I... I..." Molloy looked like he couldn't imagine why he would do such a thing.

But I knew. He had done it to hurt me in the worst way possible. He had shredded full of holes the thing I treasured most in the world. The thing that I would rush into a burning building to save. The thing that made Raf the only person to see me for who I really was: the pure goodness of his heart. Molloy stole it. Destroyed it.

"Julian." My voice was a whimper. "Please. Please make him put it back."

Julian's face had already turned two shades darker. His stare would bore a hole into Molloy's head if it were any stronger.

Molloy concentrated on Raf behind me, trying. Tears were a steady stream dripping off his face. Then he just sobbed, his internal agony reduced to mumbled words. "That's all. All I have. All I can do. The one or two, I've put them back. Bits. Pieces. I don't know how, I can't do it, I can't, I can't..." He collapsed against the railing of the stairwell. Julian gasped and braced himself against the wall. He slowly looked up at me, his face a torment of words he wasn't saying.

But I already knew. Molloy couldn't resist Julian. If he could fix it, he would have. It was truly gone, all the memories of me. Gone except for the fragments Molloy could remember from a week ago or whenever he tore apart my boyfriend's mind.

Molloy's sobs were the only sound in the room.

I wanted to scream, but the anger was trapped inside me, boiling red and raw. Molloy couldn't steal Raf from me; I wouldn't allow it. I would give Raf back all of his memories, everything that Molloy had taken from him. From us.

I stumbled back to Raf and knelt near him, plunging into his mind. He cringed away from me, so I closed my eyes. I couldn't replace memories that I hadn't taken in the first place, but maybe I could recreate them, play them like a sim. Rebuild from scratch the life we had, growing up together. I squeezed my eyes tighter, concentrating, trying to remember. The time I kissed him on the couch in the mages' headquarters was vivid in my mind, so I replayed it, recreating every touch, every emotion. But those memories were mine, not Raf's. What would it have felt like, from Raf's perspective? But that quickly got tangled up in my own memories.

An ocean of grief washed over me, threatening to drag me down under the waves.

I fought through the undertow of fear that it wouldn't work. I replayed the time in the car when he held my hand and told me everything would be okay. I sped ahead to when he kissed me in my bedroom after teasing me about throwing away the stuffed animals he had won. He had loved me then. It was real. I *knew* it. I had *felt* it. I had linked into his mind and his every small thought and feeling was open to me. What were his exact thoughts? If only I could remember his exact thoughts! I could replay them again, and he would remember how much he loved me.

Hands landed on my shoulders, and I snapped open my eyes. Raf lay writhing on the floor, the pain of my intrusions torturing his face. I gasped and yanked out of his mind.

What have I done?

My lungs fought for breath and my arms reached for Raf, but the hands on my shoulders were like iron, holding me in place. Keeping me from him. My father's voice wafted over me, but his words were a million miles away.

"Don't, Kira," he said. "You can't do any more. I'm sorry."

The pain drained from Raf's face, but when he opened his eyes, they were wild with fear, and he tried to move his weakened body away from me. Every urge in me cried out to make him come back to me. But whatever thoughts I forced into Raf's mind, they wouldn't be *his* memories, they would be *mine*.

What Molloy had stolen couldn't be fixed.

The hole in my chest tore wider. I shook off my father's hands and struggled up from the floor. It took every ounce of will that I had to turn away from Raf. Molloy leaned against the wall, his large body heaving with sobs. I didn't dare move closer. My legs were shaking so badly, I didn't think they would hold me up.

I threw the full force of my rage at Molloy, diving deep into his mind, searching for the place that controlled his heart rate and the stuttered breathing that went with his sobs. He pushed back against my invasion of his mind. Julian's handling of him to fix Raf didn't go so far as to allow me to kill him without resistance. In a short moment, he had flung me out again, but it didn't matter. I had already decided that was too good a fate for him.

Instead, I met Sasha's stare, hoping he would understand what I wanted. Hoping he would be willing to do it, no matter what he thought of me. He gave me an appraising look, then turned to Julian.

He pushed off the wall and nodded to Sasha. "Please put Mr. Molloy out of his misery."

Sasha's face fell blank as he laid a hand on the back of Molloy's head. Molloy flinched, then his eyes turned glassy, his head slowly slumping forward. Sasha was erasing everything that made Molloy who he was. It would be more thorough than the butchery that Molloy had done on Raf's memories. More complete, rewriting him permanently into another person.

Molloy would be *erased*, and every part of me felt he deserved every bit of it.

I was *glad* he would be gone.

If that made me a monster, I didn't care. I was glad there was something worse than being dead, just so Molloy could experience it.

A shudder rippled through my body. My dad slowly turned me toward him and away from the emptiness of Molloy's face. He wrapped me in his arms, locking them around me.

Short gasps were all I could pull in. All the hate I had for Molloy disappeared into the hollow space in my chest. Loving me was the worst mistake Raf had ever made.

The only tiny consolation was that now he would never make that mistake again.

chapter TWENTY-SEVEN

It had been a week, and no word from Vellus.

I shuffled in the back door of the Dutch Apple and past Mrs. Weissmann in her office, tallying up receipts. She didn't even look up, her thoughts barely registering that I was late for my shift, then she returned to her work. My feet dragged me through the kitchen as I linked into the minds of the staff, intent on their lunchtime-rush prep. There were a few stray thoughts about their normal lives, but mostly they focused on chopping onions or frying burgers.

I stopped at the employee closet to get my apron and stared at my reflection. My hair was black again, the color it had been before I found myself in Jackertown, on the run from government officials and dangerous jackers. Mrs. Weissmann had let me come back to work even though I'd dropped off the face of the earth for a couple of weeks. My dad wanted me to keep working at the Dutch Apple, for the moment. If Vellus thought I had returned to my normal life in Libertyville, he wouldn't be so suspicious that we were planning on making a run for it.

My dad said Vellus would call on me to do my public tru-cast announcement when he decided the political time was right. And before he came calling, we needed to be long gone. My dad was making plans for where we could go. Maybe Texas. He thought it would be easier to get lost in the sprawling suburban wilderness that was Austin-Houston. Mr. Trullite would get us new names again and shepherd us through a series of safe houses—places we could stay without a trail of unos or autocabs or camera surveillance being left behind. Beyond that, Mr. Trullite had used up all his favors with the Senator and wouldn't be able to forestall him.

Of course I had no intention of letting my family go on the run to protect me. I would leave on my own, and soon. I had it all worked out: I would sneak out in the middle of the night, leaving a note on my bed so they wouldn't think Vellus had kidnapped me. It would tell them not to look for me, because that would only make it easier for Vellus to find me, and I would scrit them from a throwaway phone when I could. I was going to do all of those things before my dad finished making his plans. Before Vellus came calling. Soon.

I just hadn't managed to make myself leave yet.

If I stuck around long enough, I could get caught in Vellus's trap and go on his tru-cast to tell the world how dangerous jackers were. How there were jackers out there that would ruin your life, steal it from you, if they could. It would be the truth, after all. Only then jackers everywhere would be after me and my family, not to mention that I would hate myself for the rest of my life. A jacker like Molloy got what he deserved, in rough Jackertown-style justice, but countless innocent jackers would suffer if I gave Vellus the political cover he was craving.

No, I was leaving. Soon. I would have left already, except I wanted to make sure Raf got home okay. I even spied on him a few times just to see that he had recovered from the trauma. I stopped when I couldn't take the thoughts from his family anymore. The tattoo on my wrist still shone bright red, only now instead of interweaving lines, all I saw were the holes. And the two halves that reached for each other, but never really touched.

I didn't want to leave, but I couldn't think of anything else to do. In fact, my brain seemed like it had completely shut down since we found Raf. Or rather since I had lost Raf.

I slid my apron over my head, tying it in back, then tapped the Dutch Apple nameplate until *Lucy* came up. Through the swing door, the mental volume of the diner notched higher, the readers' simultaneous conversations bouncing thought waves all over the room. I let it wash over me, like the miniature waves of Lake Michigan. I stood in the threshold and waited for someone to notice me.

No one did.

I had to buy another apron from Mrs. Weissmann, because I'd ruined the first one in the city. The fabric of it was crisp and new against my neck, but I was the same old me in the same disguise. Just a different day. As if nothing had happened. As if I hadn't lost my best and only true friend in the world.

I sucked in a breath and let it out slow. I couldn't think about Raf without crying and that wouldn't be mesh here in the diner. People might wonder why my thoughts didn't match my face.

Table seven is waiting to order, Tracey thought as she sailed by, flying two plates of fried chicken, one in each hand.

I'm on it. I willed my feet to move away from the swinging door before I caused a traffic jam or a waitress collision.

The couple at table seven couldn't have been cuter, holding hands with their Second Skin gloves and gazing into each other's eyes. Their thoughts were almost linked, in spite of not touching, because they were so in tune with each other. The hole that sat in my chest full time whistled like a ghostly wind blowing across an open grave. It literally hurt to watch them, but I gritted my teeth and linked to them, *Can I take your order?*

Burgers? Yes, burgers! Wait no, what's the special? I think it's corned beef? No, the special is the pie, that's what this place is famous for. We can't have pie for lunch, that's silly. I think we should be silly! Pie for lunch!

Their thoughts tumbled over each other, like playful puppies. I almost couldn't bear it.

I recommend the Dutch Apple, I thought. *Everyone loves it.*

Apple? I think I like peaches better. Peaches aren't in season yet. You don't think? No, no! They're no good unless they're from Michigan anyway, and those aren't in season yet. What about cherry? Wisconsin has great cherries and they have to be in season by now.

I was tempted to jack them both into having the lemon cream pie and loving every bite. I resisted.

Cherry! thought the boy. He was slightly older than Raf. His hair was dark like Raf's, but without the curls at the tips. His eyes turned up to me, dark chocolate-brown pools filled with happiness, just like Raf's when he looked at me. The wind whistled a little stronger across the grave in my chest. *We'd love to have cherry pie, for both of us!* thought Raf.

I blinked. No, not Raf. Just some boy, a reader, who was in love with someone else.

Of course, I answered. *I'll get that right away.*

I turned away from the table and nearly ran into Tracey gliding past. As I recovered, the thought waves in the room sharpened and shifted as a tru-cast came on the corner screen. I had figured Mrs. Weissmann would have tossed out the screen by now, but apparently no. Angry red words inched across the bottom. Senator Vellus with his gleaming white teeth dazzled the young tru-cast reporter who was interviewing him.

There was a breach in a high-security containment facility downtown last week, Vellus thought. *I was just now informed of it, but I wanted to assure the people of Chicago New Metro that the Chicago Jacker Police Detail have every officer looking for these escaped prisoners.*

The vast amount of lying that Vellus seemed capable of still stunned me. The reporter's doe eyes went wider. *Do you think there's a danger to reader-citizens in the suburban New Metro areas?* she asked. *Is it possible that these dangerous jackers will leave the city?*

Well, I don't want to alarm anyone, Vellus thought. *But that's certainly possible.*

The acrid taste of fear rippled through the Dutch Apple. Of course Vellus was trying to alarm everyone. That was the whole point of disclosing this supposed breakout of dangerous jackers. Unless there was some other radical group breaking in and out of Kestrel's facility, I was pretty sure he was referring to me and Julian and the other mages.

Can you tell us about this Jacker Police Detail? the tru-cast reporter asked. *Are they specially trained in dealing with jackers?*

Yes, they are. Vellus beamed, apparently excited to talk about his new toy. *They have all the latest anti-jacker technology at their disposal and with the new laws that our representatives in Springfield have had the foresight to pass, they have even more flexibility to apprehend these criminals.*

It's a good thing the Vellus Detention Center is up and running, thought the tru-caster. *I assume that's where the jackers will be housed, when they are apprehended?*

I looked away from the screen. The news transfixed every patron of the Dutch Apple. The bitter tastes of fear and anger flavored their minds, along with the sour-milk taste of outright hate. But that wasn't what made my stomach twist in knots. The time when Vellus would ask me to join him in his anti-jacker campaign seemed to be rushing at me.

I stuffed that fear down while I stumbled to the pie rotisserie and tugged out the cherry pie. I carved two slices, dished them, and was carrying them back to table seven when the quiet bell on the door chimed, and Raf walked through the door into the diner.

I stopped in my tracks and stared at him, which was possibly the dumbest thing I could do. He stared back, frozen in place, torn between turning around and coming all the way into the diner. His thoughts of shock and anger drew the collective mental attention of the diner patrons away from Vellus's anti-jacker rambling.

Right to the jacker in their midst.

A pie plate crashed on the floor next to my foot, and the sound jarred me out of my fog. I turned and dashed into the kitchen, still holding the second pie plate. I set it down on the counter and wove my way through the staff, trying not to cause any more breakage on my way out. The staff parted before me, then turned toward the kitchen door.

"Kira!"

I lurched to a stop. Raf had followed me into the kitchen. I slowly turned to face him.

"That's your name, isn't it?" His voice was cold and split the air. The staff froze, their faces shocked at the spoken language that filled the kitchen. Tracey had followed Raf and stood stunned in the swing doorway.

I didn't answer. The entire diner now knew I was a jacker. How I could fix this? Could I jack Raf to walk back out? I would have to jack everyone else too, tamper with their memories, erase the last minute of time from their lives.

The hair raised on the back of my head. I could do it if I had to.

When I didn't say anything, Raf mumbled, "I remember some things." What did he remember? My heart nearly exploded with hope. Maybe a remnant that Molloy had implanted had driven him here. Maybe it wasn't just chance.

Louder, he said, "But my parents explained everything to me." His words sliced the hope into shreds. "They explained how you've been controlling me all along. Making me love you." He grimaced. "What kind of monster are you, that you would mess with someone that way?"

I wanted to tell him it was a lie. The truth was that he *had* loved me. But those words would only hurt him. And me. Because they were no longer true.

"I keep remembering these things..." He pressed the heel of his hand to his head. "These snippets that I don't understand! I can't help it if I end up places where you happen to be. I don't want to..." He searched for the words. "...stumble across you in my life." He pointed a finger, like he wanted to stab me with it. "I don't want you controlling me anymore!"

My lips trembled, but I pinched them tight and spun around, nearly mowing down tiny Mrs. Weissmann in her tied-up tight gray bun.

"You!" Mrs. Weissmann said, making me nearly jump out of my skin. For a split second, I thought she was yelling at me, but she shook her tiny fist at Raf. "Get outen my kitchen!"

Raf glared at her, then stomped his way out of the diner. The bell crashed when the door flew open and made a tiny ding when it slowly closed. The kitchen staff stared at Mrs. Weissmann and me. My mouth worked, but I came up with nothing to say.

She turned her back on me and stalked to her office.

The kitchen eased back into its normal motions. Silence fell as everyone returned to mindtalking. I didn't bother linking into their heads—the look on Tracey's face, still standing by the swing door, told me what they were thinking. Unless I was going to erase all of their memories, I could never come back to the diner. And there was no point in erasing their memories, unless I tracked down Raf and erased his too.

Which I didn't even consider.

I forced my legs to walk down the hall to Mrs. Weissmann's office. Raf not only forgot he loved me—he believed the lies that his parents told him. I shouldn't have expected any less. It was just my spectacular bad luck that he ended up in the diner and outted me to Mrs. Weissmann's patrons. I should have left sooner—that way Mrs. Weissmann wouldn't have to pay the price for employing a jacker.

I stood in her doorway. "I'm sorry, Mrs. Weissmann."

"Sorry?" she said. "What do you have to be sorry for? That boy should be sorry! Coming into my kitchen and causing a scene! He's a strubblich bum, nothing more." She coughed to clear the roughness from her throat. It was the first time I had heard her speak out loud. Her Pennsylvania Dutch accent was even stronger verbally than it was mentally.

"I'm sorry I lied to you," I said even quieter. "I'm sorry..." I gestured to the kitchen down the hall. "I'm sorry that people will think badly of you for hiring a jacker."

"Sorry, sorry, sorry." She waved her hand at me as if fanning away my words. "Enough of dis sorry. One does what one has to, Kira. You wait tables. I pay you. There's no need for sorry."

She had called me *Kira*. I smiled through the pain that was tearing the hole in my heart wider. It was the first time she had used my name. The first time I had known for sure that she knew who I was. When did she know? Did it matter? It didn't seem to matter to her. Mrs. Weissmann would keep me on, let me earn money for my family because she knew we needed it. Even if I was a jacker. Even if everyone knew it. A peculiar shame burned my cheeks, like I didn't deserve her kindness.

I slowly untied my apron. Even though Mrs. Weissmann meant well, I was done with other people paying the price for who I was. I pulled the apron over my head and bunched it up until I found the nameplate among the folds of fabric. I tapped it several times, scrolling through the names. Not finding the one I wanted, I jacked into the mindware interface and scrit a new name.

Kira.

I handed the wadded up apron and nameplate to her.

"Thank you, Mrs. Weissmann," I said. "For being a good friend."

She frowned, but took the apron from me. "It's not right." Her voice was soft. "What this criker Vellus is doing."

I nodded.

It wasn't right, and it would get worse. Because, ultimately, Vellus was right. Jackers and readers couldn't coexist. They couldn't love one another. They would hate and fight and with someone like Vellus leading the way, the dangers of being a jacker—or a jacker sympathizer—would only get more extreme. It wouldn't only be dangerous for good-hearted people like Mrs. Weissmann who intentionally hired me to work in her diner. It would be dangerous for anyone I rooked into thinking I was a reader.

I walked out the back door of the Dutch Apple and pulled out my phone to hail an autocab. A few minutes later, it whispered up to the dumpsters behind the diner. I fed it every last uno that I had from tips, climbed in, and set an autopath for the lake. I didn't look back as the Dutch Apple got swallowed up in the endless, winding suburban streets.

The bright afternoon sun glared the windows, making it difficult to see the thin stretch of beach. Weeds and blown trash snarled the sand, which rose and fell in mounds tufted with grass. This was where Raf and I would have come, if we could. If the world hadn't gone demens.

If things were different.

Different? Raf's voice rang in my memories. *Different how?* He had wanted to know why I wouldn't kiss him, that long ago day in the chem lab, when I still thought I would be a zero my whole life. When I thought not reading minds like everyone else was the worst thing that could happen to me. I should have kissed him and not cared what other people thought.

Instead, I said, *If I was different*. It was the only truth I could tell him then. If *I* was different, things would have been different between us. But all my wishful thinking hadn't changed the world one bit, and now I was the only one who remembered that moment—Raf's version was lost forever.

I pressed my hand to the autocab window, peering through my fingers at the weak waves lapping the shore. The beach was just as unreachable as it had ever been.

People like Vellus and Kestrel and that diner full of readers would never let me pretend I was someone I wasn't. No matter where I ran, no matter how well I hid, I would always be in danger of being found out. I could leave my family behind, but anyone else—any friends I dared to make, any employer I tricked into hiring me—they would always be in danger of getting caught in the cross fire when my past caught up to me. There would always be the threat of dangerous jackers or ruthless reader politicians dropping in and ruining their lives. Running away would only delay the inevitable.

There was only one place I could go where that wouldn't be true.

One place where I would have no danger of running into Raf ever again. Where I wouldn't be alone and I wouldn't have to hide. Vellus was right: the future would be a fight. It would be readers versus jackers, and with Vellus's anti-jacker crusade, Kestrel's experimental torture chambers, and more and better anti-jacker technology, jackers would lose.

Unless they decided to fight to win.

I jacked into the mindware interface of the autocab and set a different autopath.

The autocab flew past businessmen hurrying between sky-scrapers on their way to the next appointment in their normal lives. The demens wandered out in the open, the spring air fresh with the potential of warm days to come. The towers of the city shrank as the autocab wound away from downtown. It slowed as it neared the end of the autopath. The sunshine had drawn out the changelings, and they perched on the steps of Myrtle's brownstone, watching me go by.

I sent my dad a scrit to let him know I was okay, then left the phone in the autocab, so it would be carried far from Jackertown. The door of the mages' converted factory was brand-new, black with a purplish sheen, like Mr. Trullite's limo. It looked strange against the crumbling brick of the factory and made a dull thud-ding sound when I pounded on it. Julian pulled it open, dressed in jeans and a black t-shirt that was scuffed with dirt. He looked like he'd been repairing machinery, grease on his hands and dark marks on his arms.

Or maybe he had been assembling weapons.

His eyebrows flew up. For once, words seemed to fail him as the shock of me showing up on his doorstep took hold. But he didn't look unhappy to see me. Finally, he said, "Keeper!"

"My name is Kira."

free souls
Susan Kaye Quinn

The **Mindjack Trilogy**
continues with **free Souls**

When your mind is a weapon, freedom comes at a price.

our months have passed since Kira left home to join Julian's Jacker Freedom Alliance, but the hole in her heart still whistles empty where her boyfriend Raf used to be. She fills it with weapons training, JFA patrols, and an obsessive hunt for FBI agent Kestrel, ignoring Julian's worries about her safety and repeated attempts to recruit her for his revolutionary chat-casts. When anti-jacker politician Vellus surrounds Jackertown with the National Guard, Kira discovers there's more to Julian's concerns than she knew, but she's forced to take on a mission that neither want and that might be her last: assassinating Senator Vellus before he can snuff out Julian's revolution and the jackers she's come to love.

more from SUSAN KAYE QUINN

Susan writes speculative fiction all up and down the age spectrum. She's always dreaming up something new, so subscribe to her mailing list (http://bit.ly/SubscribeToSusansNewsletter) to be the first to know what's up! (Oh, and new subscribers get a free short story, too!)

Faery Swap
(middle grade)

Mindjack Trilogy
(young adult science fiction)

The Dharian Affairs
(steampunk romance)

Debt Collector
(adult future-noir)

Acknowledgements

irst and foremost, thanks to the many people who read *Open Minds* while I was writing *Closed Hearts*. Your enthusiasm, reviews, and general cheering-on made the process of writing this book a joy as well as a labor of love.

My amazing cover designer, D. Robert Pease, made me look good again by creating a beautiful face for the story inside—thank you, Dale, for lending out your genius. Many thanks go to Anne of Victory Editing for catching my typos, correcting my hideous comma abuse, and compensating for my complete inability to hypenate. Any mistakes that remain are due to things I messed up after she fixed them. (Un grand merci pour ton amitié to Julien Morgan for allowing me to borrow his name for a certain revolutionary character. I hope you like him.)

Critique partners are invaluable to any writer, and I'm lucky to have had brilliant ones to help me fill in the holes and bolster the structure of *Closed Hearts*. Much appreciation goes to Rebecca Carlson, Adam Heine, and Sherrie Petersen for braving that early draft: I hope you'll be pleasantly surprised with the final version. Thanks go to Rebecca Carlson (again—seriously, what would I do without you?), Rick Daley, Laura Pauling, Dianne Salerni, and Magan Vernon for their insightful critiques of a more reasonably polished version of the story. Finally, a grateful cyber-hug to Carol Riggs and Sheryl Hart for being typo-sleuths for the final version of the story.

A special thanks goes to my son Adam Quinn, a writer in his own right, for being my teen beta reader this round. I'm grateful to my entire family for letting me hijack our dinner discussions with talk of mindreading and mindjacking. To my sons Sam and Ryan: thank you for your many helpful suggestions for Books Two and Three, and even if I don't actually use the squad of hyperactive mindjacked squirrels in the story, please know they'll be there in spirit.

A final thanks to my husband: for making everything possible and at the same time making it worthwhile.

About the Author

Susan Kaye Quinn grew up in California, where she wrote snippets of stories and passed them to her friends during class. Her teachers pretended not to notice and only confiscated her notes a couple times. She pursued a bunch of engineering degrees (Aerospace, Mechanical, and Environmental) and worked a lot of geeky jobs, including turns at GE Aircraft Engines, NASA, and NCAR. Now that she writes novels, her business card says "Author and Rocket Scientist" and she doesn't have to sneak her notes anymore.

Which is too bad.

All that engineering comes in handy when dreaming up paranormal powers in future worlds or mixing science with fantasy to conjure slightly plausible inventions. For her stories, of course. Just ignore that stuff in her basement.

Susan writes from the Chicago suburbs with her three boys, two cats, and one husband. Which, it turns out, is exactly as much as she can handle.